THE ROAD HOME

LANGLEY PARK SERIES

KRISTA SANDOR

CANDY CASTLE BOOKS

COPYRIGHT

A NOTE TO THE READER

This book is intended for mature readers. It contains descriptions of adult relationships, sexually graphic situations, and adult language. If such things offend you, this book is not for you.

DEDICATION

For David

1

Jenna Lewis sat cloaked in the dim light of the hotel bar sipping on a velvety cabernet. The low hum of the business crowd was sprinkled with a few tourist types, their conversations a reassuring stream of sound.

This was her comfort, being surrounded while remaining unseen. Jenna closed her eyes and bent her neck from side to side, trying to loosen the kinks and knots she always felt on this day. She was about to open her eyes, but she couldn't breathe. Her senses on high alert, she recognized the song playing in the background underneath the buzz of conversation.

The Police.

Every Breath You Take.

Those first five notes had haunted her for years.

Jenna's body tensed, and she splayed her hands on the granite surface of the bar. Forcing herself to take a deep breath, she tried to calm the panic welling inside her. She hated how these episodes could still catch her off-guard. She opened her eyes to find the bartender, a slight man, watching her with concern.

"Is everything okay, miss?"

"I'm all right. Must be the altitude," she said, masking the lie with a sip of wine.

"Denver is the Mile High City. Just remember to drink plenty of water," he said with practiced expertise.

It's just this day. This damned day.

Jenna took a deep breath and glanced at her phone. Two missed calls from a Kansas City number and one unplayed voicemail message met her gaze.

She turned the phone over and steadied her breath. She rarely had panic attacks anymore. A steady diet of yoga and running had helped reduce these moments when she found herself paralyzed with fear.

You're all right. You're not a little girl.

She focused on the mantra, but her eyes betrayed her, and she stared at the phone as if her glare alone could make the calls disappear.

Today was Mother's Day.

This year, she went out of her way to steer clear of witnessing any family celebrations. A little past nine o'clock in the evening, Jenna had hoped the hotel's bar would be free of families and children. Blessedly, she was right.

Last year, she made the mistake of visiting the Denver Botanic Gardens on Mother's Day. She'd been seeking peace and solitude but instead found throngs of mothers and grandmothers taking in the scenery and enjoying each other's company.

She'd known almost immediately she'd made a horrible mistake by going there. Her heart ached as she watched the displays of love and affection all around her. She turned to leave and escape back to the confines of her cozy bungalow, but before she reached the exit, she spied an empty bench. Like a glutton for punishment, she sat and watched, keeping an eye out for pairs of mothers and daughters.

She'd stayed on that bench watching the garden patrons for the better part of an hour when her gaze was drawn toward two women strolling together, arms linked.

As if under a spell, Jenna stood. She followed the pair away from the exit and into the heart of the gardens.

Jenna took in the ease with which the women spoke to each other, remarking on this flower and that tree. She wanted to link her arm with the older woman and feel her warmth, smell her scent, and know her kindness.

Unable to stop herself, she pictured what her life might have been like had this stranger been her mother. Thoughts of bedtime stories and trips to museums flooded her mind.

She was so lost in her fantasy that she walked right into the younger woman when the pair stopped to remark on an ash tree.

"I'm so very sorry. I guess I got lost in my thoughts," Jenna said, embarrassed not only by her folly but for the childish dreams she had running through her head.

"This is an easy place to do that. My daughter and I come here every year for Mother's Day. It was our favorite place to go together when she was a child," the older woman said as her daughter's lips curved into a smile filled with affection. "I certainly hope you've called *your* mother today."

"I lost my mother when I was a teenager," Jenna replied, caught off guard by the comment.

"I'm sorry. I can't imagine what that must be like," the younger woman said, tightening her grip on her mother's arm.

Jenna's hands twitched. "I'm so sorry I bumped into you. I hope you both enjoy this lovely day."

She walked away from the women without waiting for them to respond, desperate to escape the bond of mother and daughter that had bewitched her only moments ago.

JENNA TOOK another sip of her wine as the panic attack subsided, but she needed a distraction. She retrieved her laptop from her bag then looked at the latest reading scores from her school in Denver. It was almost the end of the school year as well as the end of Jenna's time implementing the Gwyer Reading Program in a high-risk elementary school.

Jenna worked for a pair of professors from her Iowa alma mater,

Gwyer College. These educational researchers had created a reading curriculum targeting struggling students in high-risk schools. Jenna would spend two years at the same school working with students, gathering data, and training teachers. After that time, she was sent on to the next location. Over the last ten years, she'd lived in Louisville, St. Paul, Chicago, and Omaha, and was now getting ready to end her stint in Denver.

Jenna loved her work. She loved giving children the gift of reading—a gift no one could ever take away. Jenna believed the ability to read could open a child's eyes to the bigger world that existed beyond the confines of hardship, pain, or poverty.

She couldn't remember how many schools she'd attended as a child, but what she did remember was the kindness of her teachers. How many times had she dreamed of a life where she didn't have to go home after the school dismissal bell rang?

Too many to count.

As a teacher now herself, Jenna wondered if her teachers had shown her extra kindness because they sensed her pain, just as she was able to sense the most vulnerable among the children she taught.

At thirty-two years old, Jenna's school days were well behind her, but the dark echoes of her childhood lived in her heart, a part of her just like her blood and bones.

Jenna had learned, like many children raised in chaos, how to smile and say the right things. And how to lie and do it convincingly.

As a child, she learned the lies helped her survive. But by the time she knew lying was wrong, the lies had become such a part of her, such a part of her identity, she found it hard to piece out where the lie ended and the truth began.

Many nights she'd sit at her desk and write out all the lies she could remember telling. She'd write and write and write; then she'd sob because no matter how pretty a picture her lies painted, underneath that thin veneer the canvas was slashed, ugly, and beyond repair.

Then there was the fear. The fear of others knowing the truth, of seeing the damaged girl seep through the veil of her deception. She fought that with distance, with proclamations of having too much work to socialize, and never allowing anyone to know the real Jenna.

She knew when she left a town she left no imprint. There were no friends waving goodbye, no boyfriend she'd promised to call when she made it to the next city. She was like a nomad, there one minute, gone the next.

Many of Jenna's Gwyer colleagues didn't last long in the reading intervention program. Moving every two years made it hard to settle down or start a family. Luckily, the prestige of the Gwyer Reading Program opened doors to any teacher wanting a long-term teaching position. Several of her colleagues found themselves in a town they grew to love with people who embraced them and decided to stay on, leaving the Gwyer program to plant roots and start a life.

THE BAR WAS QUIETING down as Jenna read through the latest reading scores when a warm hand settled on her bare shoulder. Turning on her stool, she smiled at the attractive man dressed in uniform, a pilot's hat perched atop his head.

"I've been thinking of this neck. Miss me?" the pilot said, the gentle rolling of his Kentucky accent smooth as a single malt whiskey.

Captain Nick Kincade flew airplanes for UPS. Jenna had met him nearly a decade ago when she was setting up the Gwyer Reading Program in a Louisville public school. They had a one-night stand that turned into an arrangement of sorts. When he was in town, he'd text Jenna, and they'd meet. No flowers on Valentine's Day or cards on birthdays. Sex and comfortable conversation had been their norm for the last several years.

Nick flew all over the country, and Jenna wasn't naïve enough to think that she was the only girl waiting for him to breeze into town. He had that all-American blond hair, blue-eyed charm and an easy way about him that made women sit up a little straighter when he entered a room. But that's not what Jenna liked most about Nick Kincade. What made him most attractive to her was that, while he was a kind man, Nick had no interest in monogamy and no intention of settling down.

"I was wondering what happened to you," Jenna said, taking the pilot's hat off his head and placing it on her own.

"Storms got us coming out of Houston. Delayed us about an hour."

"No packages for me?" Jenna asked with a teasing smile.

"If I told you once, I've told you a million times. I am not your personal delivery pilot. But that does sound like the first line of a very, very bad porno."

Jenna laughed, shaking her head. Then she looked up at his handsome face.

Nick made it easy to forget.

"All done with that?" he asked, nodding toward her drink.

"All done."

Without another word, Nick picked up her laptop and slipped it into the side pocket of her overnight case. He slung the bag over his shoulder and led Jenna from the bar into the hotel elevator. As soon as the doors shut, he dropped the bag and had Jenna against the wall, kissing her neck. Her hands wrapped around his biceps as she craned her head giving him more room to nip and suck.

When the elevator doors opened on their floor, Jenna gave Nick a teasing smile. "Long flight?"

"You have no idea."

Nick found the room, opened the door, and placed the 'Do Not Disturb' sign securely on the doorknob. Whisking her inside and dropping their bags, Nick's hands made quick work of her pencil skirt and blouse. They kept the lights off as Jenna turned her head toward the window and gazed out at the twinkling lights of downtown Denver. It could be any city, she thought, watching the red and white smears of light from the passing cars below.

She heard Nick shrugging out of his uniform and the unmistakable sound of a condom wrapper being torn open as he positioned himself behind her. Jenna had been on the pill since she was eighteen, but she never trusted anyone enough not to use a condom.

While she liked Nick, even after all their years of meeting like this, it had always been just sex, never making love.

They hadn't even kissed. Jenna's lips had never met Nick's, and it was an unspoken rule that he'd always take her from behind, negating the need for eye contact or even the smallest hint of intimacy. They were well suited in the sense that neither of them had anything else to give besides a few fleeting moments of pleasure.

Bracing herself on a chest of drawers, Nick thrust inside her.

"This good?" he asked, his voice thick, one hand gripping her hip while the other massaged her breast.

Letting her head fall back on his chest, she closed her eyes and let herself get lost, at least for a little while, in the rhythm of their bodies.

JENNA BLINKED as the bright Colorado sun streamed through the window. She rolled over and felt the space once occupied by Nick. It was cold to her touch. She pushed up on her elbows and saw Nick standing in front of the mirror, hair still wet from a shower, buttoning up a crisp dress shirt, his flight bag parked at the ready next to the door.

Jenna gave him a sleepy smile.

"What's next for you?" Nick asked, reaching for his tie as he watched her through the reflection in the mirror.

Jenna reclined back on the pillows and looked up at the ceiling. "My work in Denver is pretty much done. I've got all the data, and the teachers are doing a great job implementing the program. Just a few more days, and then I'm off to Albuquerque for the next two years."

"Albuquerque, huh? You know UPS flies there, too."

Jenna smiled. "They do, do they?"

Her phone buzzed, and she glanced at it, noticing the same Kansas City number that had left a message. The message she'd been ignoring since Friday.

Jenna let the call go to voicemail and sat up, looking at her phone. She scrolled to find the message from Friday, pressed play, and listened.

"This call is for Jenna Lewis. My name is Carol Lucas. I'm a social worker at the Rose Brooks Women's Shelter in Kansas City. I'm calling regarding your mother, Judith."

Jenna's pulse quickened. She hadn't seen or spoken to her mother in more than a decade. A wave of uneasiness washed over her and settled in the pit of her stomach.

"I'm sorry to have to tell you this over voicemail, but it's quite urgent. Your mother was threatening to hurt herself. Threatening to kill herself."

Jenna took in a sharp breath.

"Your mother was brought to Midwest Medical and Psychiatric Center in Langley Park. She left your name and this number with us at the shelter when she checked in."

The woman finished the message again giving her name, contact number, and the name of a social worker at the psychiatric center that Jenna could call for more information. And then the recording ended.

Jenna's hand shook, and she dropped the phone to the floor. Her hand went to her thigh, digging her thumbnail into the soft flesh, trying to stop the flood of emotions threatening to come tumbling out.

Nick rushed over to her. Going down on one knee, he picked up her phone and looked at it. He searched her ashen face. "Jenna, what is it? Who was on the phone?"

Caught between two worlds, Jenna stared at Nick. "It's my mother. She's in a psychiatric facility near Kansas City. I have to go there. I have to go home."

"Jenna, you told me you didn't have any family. You said your mother was dead, that she passed away when you were a teenager."

The lies. Her lies.

The fictitious life she'd created to cover up the ugliness of her true reality was starting to unravel like the frayed edge of an old, worn sweater. With one little tug, she'd be exposed to everything her mind had tried so hard to forget.

2

Jenna pulled into a parking space at Midwest Hospital and Psychiatric Center, the nine-hour drive having gone by in a blur of gas stations and roadside rest stops. She'd set her phone's navigation app to take her directly to the hospital, but she hadn't thought anything through past getting to Langley Park.

It was late, nearly eight in the evening—too late to go inside. She couldn't help the utter rush of relief that flooded her system knowing she didn't have to face her mother quite yet.

Jenna sat in her car and listened as the first haunting notes of Beethoven's "Moonlight Sonata" played on the radio. She rubbed her tired eyes, feeling the music all around her as the weight of her situation sunk in.

She'd driven straight through Kansas. The state she'd sworn never to set foot in again.

"What am I doing here? I owe her nothing," she whispered.

No matter how many times she recounted the memories of her childhood, there was still a part of her that hoped her mother would want her, would choose her, would protect her. Jenna shook her head, removing her hands from her bleary eyes and pushed the lost hopes of a little girl out of her mind.

She didn't need saving anymore. She had a career and financial security. She had saved herself.

She tried to tell herself this was just another place on a map. But Langley Park was more than that.

Jenna had spent a few months of her sophomore year at a high school a few miles away in the quaintly named town of Village East. She wasn't at Village East High very long, but she did have one good memory of her time there.

It had been many years since Jenna set foot in Langley Park, but from what she remembered, the town had certainly changed.

Langley Park was still a small municipality with a population of only four thousand or so, located just a stone's throw from Kansas City. Most people new to the area didn't even realize they'd entered the town until they stumbled upon its tree-lined streets and beautifully maintained homes built in the 1930s.

Back when Jenna was in high school, Langley Park was populated with older residents and sported a sleepy town center. But today, as she sped through town on her way to the hospital, she noticed a transformation had occurred. The former home to mainly octogenarians was now a hip, bustling area filled with boutiques, bookshops, restaurants, small art galleries, and juice bars. The actual park in Langley Park had been filled with children climbing on giant play structures in the last rays of the late day sun.

Staring up at the hospital, Jenna listened as Beethoven's haunting piece ended and "Clair De Lune" began to play. The last few days had passed in a whirlwind of activity, and she'd barely had a moment to reflect on how quickly her life had changed.

She'd left Nick early Monday morning, hastily gathering her things and leaving without any further explanation. Nick was concerned, wrapping his arms around her, trying to get her to talk, but she couldn't. Their relationship wasn't built on heart-to-heart confessions. The fact that Nick hadn't tried to call or text let her know he too understood the parameters of their arrangement, even if in that earlier moment, he'd seemed to have forgotten.

This was supposed to be Jenna's last week at her school in Denver.

After explaining to the school's principal and the Iowa researchers that she needed to attend to a family emergency in Kansas City, all parties were understanding.

When the principal pressed her for more information, she lied and said an elderly aunt had fallen and needed help after hip surgery.

Lying made it easier. It always did when it came to her mother.

She didn't officially report to her new school in Albuquerque until early September. During the summer, she spent her time working from home analyzing reading data, learning any new tweaks the researchers had made to the curriculum, and consulting on textbooks for educational publishing companies. Compared to the school year, Jenna's summers were quiet and solitary, only interacting with colleagues through email.

She had planned on leaving Denver and going directly to Albuquerque. Her work provided a generous stipend for living expenses, and Jenna always rented fully furnished houses or apartments. The sum total of her possessions fit in the back of her SUV.

It was almost half past eight now, and Jenna decided to call Eric Lucero, the social worker at Midwest Psychiatric Center assigned to her mother. She needed to leave a message and let him know she'd made it into town. Although, from their last conversation, she learned she wouldn't be able to see her mother for at least a few more days.

She'd spoken with Eric on Monday morning, just two days ago. The soft-spoken social worker had explained that, to the best of his understanding, her mother had been participating in a group counseling session at the women's shelter when she told the group she was planning on killing herself. Then she showed them a razor blade she had wrapped in tissue. The counselor was able to stop her, but the therapists at the shelter decided her mother required more in-depth psychiatric services than they were able to provide.

"I don't want to make any presumptions about your mother's behavior, but as someone who's been in this business almost thirty-five years, it sounds to me like a cry for help," Eric explained during their first conversation.

"What happens from here?"

"Your mother is going to be with us for about five weeks. She was able to tell us she's had issues with alcohol and drug abuse in the past, and we're working to get her body physically stable. After that, we can start working on the issues that brought her here."

Jenna told him she would leave immediately, but Eric had cautioned her against it.

"Take a few days to get your affairs in order. Your mother won't be able to have visitors for at least a couple more days. Get here safely, and we'll go from there. Do you have any questions?"

She swallowed hard. "Just one question. Am I the only person you've contacted regarding my mother?"

"Yes, just you. Are there other family members you'd like to involve in the process?"

Jenna's body flooded with relief. "No, there's no one else."

STILL SITTING in the safety of her car, Jenna turned off the radio and dialed Eric's number. She wasn't surprised when she got his voicemail and left a message letting him know she'd made it to Langley Park. As she pressed the end call button, she let out a shaky breath.

For someone who had become regimented in her work and life, someone who was always in control and always had a plan for what came next, Jenna had arrived in Langley Park completely unprepared. She had no place to stay and no idea how long she'd be there.

She decided to drive into Langley Park's town center. She had seen a few restaurants when she passed by on her way to the hospital and decided to stop at the first place she found and order a glass of wine and a bite to eat. It was time to get back on track, make a plan, and figure things out.

A restaurant called Park Tavern came into view as she drove into the heart of the town center. Parking on the street, she grabbed her purse and laptop and walked toward the entrance hoping they'd have decent WiFi.

"You're not a little girl," she said, repeating her mantra. "Go inside and get organized."

She entered the restaurant and took a seat at the bar. The tavern wasn't very busy, just a few couples having drinks and a group of men in their early twenties laughing and doing shots at a table in the back corner.

Taking a closer look at her new surroundings, Jenna noticed that the old-fashioned bar was made of gleaming dark Cherrywood. Bottles of spirits were stacked in tidy rows set in front of a mirrored wall. Lit from behind, the bottles gave off an almost luminescent effect as the warm light made the spirits glow in shades of brown and gold. The establishment had a comforting warmth, and Jenna relaxed as she settled in, taking out her laptop.

"What'll we be having tonight?"

She looked up to see a hulk of a man with a friendly smile and a mop of curly, auburn hair. He wore a gray shirt with the sleeves rolled up to his elbows revealing some very nice ink.

Jenna gave the man a tired smile as she glanced at the menu. "I'll have the veggie sliders and a glass of red wine."

Nodding, the bartender turned toward a cash register and put in her order. He looked over a few bottles of red, selected one, and poured a small amount for her to sample. "You look like you've had a long day. Try this cabernet. It's from Washington state, and it's one of my favorites."

Jenna took a sip. "Mmm, this is mmm," she moaned, instantly flushing pink with embarrassment. "I'm sorry. I sound like an idiot. This is just..."

"Just what you needed?" he asked, pouring more wine into the glass.

Jenna took another sip.

"My name's Sam Sinclair. I know most everyone in town. Are you new here?"

"I'm Jenna," she replied, wringing her hands.

Sam eyed her hands. "I think there's a story here, Jenna."

The door to Park Tavern opened, and Jenna looked over to see a large group coming in, taking Sam and his questioning eyes away.

"Saved by the bell," he said, giving her a playful wink before heading toward the group.

She spent the next hour finishing her sliders and a second glass of cabernet while looking online at nearby hotels and some not very appealing vacation-rental-by-owner options when a waitress came over holding a mixed drink with a look of exasperation etched on her face.

"The guys in the back wanted to send this over to you," she said, rolling her eyes.

Not wanting to give anyone the wrong impression, Jenna glanced toward the men, then she turned to the waitress. "Listen, would you mind telling them no thanks?"

The waitress nodded, a resigned expression on her face as she looked at the table of rowdy men. Business had picked up, and the restaurant was now buzzing with patrons. Jenna could tell this was the last thing the server wanted to be doing, but she smiled tightly and headed back to the table, drink in hand.

About ten minutes later, the waitress named Addison—Jenna now knew her name thanks to her name tag—walked back over. "They want me to send you a drink every five minutes until you accept. Those guys are total Mission Springs d-bags."

Jenna had to laugh. It was the first time she'd laughed in days. As a teenager, she remembered passing through the nearby Mission Springs neighborhood, marveling at the sprawling estates.

"Can you tell them I'm trying to work?" Not exactly the truth but close enough.

Addison nodded, then headed back to return the drink.

Moments later, Jenna heard a roar of laughter and turned toward the rowdy group. One of the men was pouring her returned drink on the floor as Addison stood by, frozen with panic.

Jenna shook her head, rose to her feet, and headed toward the addled waitress. She placed her hand protectively on Addison's arm.

"All right boys, you've had your fun. Let's let Addison get back to work without any more of your shenanigans."

"I told you she'd be feisty." The table erupted with hoots and laughter.

A frat boy type with eyes that seemed a bit too close together barked out, "Not into guys? I could change that." He grabbed his crotch for emphasis.

"I've got this," Jenna said to a bewildered looking Addison who scurried through a door leading back into the kitchen.

After Addison's departure, Jenna set her gaze on frat boy. "No, I'm not into guys. I prefer men, and unfortunately, I don't see any at this table."

Jenna was still watching frat boy as his friends slapped him on the back and hurled crude insults his way. All the while, frat boy's gaze remained trained on Jenna; only he wasn't laughing. "Have a nice night," she added over her shoulder, walking toward the restrooms. She needed to calm down.

Feeling better after splashing cool water on her face, Jenna exited the ladies room and was surprised to see her frat boy, jaw clenched, standing right outside the restroom door. His body filled up the narrow hallway, and he blocked her way back to the bar.

He was drunk. Jenna could smell him from a mile away, and he was also bigger than she had expected.

"You need a man to teach you a lesson. Pull that stick out of your tight ass." His words were clipped as if holding back a river of fury as he moved toward her.

Jenna's arms went up instinctively, and he grabbed her right wrist. She could smell the cigarette stench on his breath as he pulled her in closer.

"You need to stop," she said, trying to keep her voice firm.

Her mind raced as she looked down at his hand wrapped around her forearm. Oddly enough, his grip on her arm reminded her of Aaron Sanchez, a fifth-grade student she'd worked with back in Denver.

Aaron wouldn't participate in class, and his teacher said she was concerned he'd never learn to read. Working with Aaron during their first session, Jenna found him as despondent as his teacher had reported.

At the beginning of their second session, Jenna had an idea. She asked Aaron to describe his favorite activity. She was fascinated to hear him talk animatedly about helping teach Jujitsu and martial arts at the local community center.

By the end of that tutoring session, Aaron had agreed to start working with her as long as she allowed him to teach her how to execute a cross-grab wrist lock. After only a few months, Aaron was reading at grade level, and Jenna had learned a cool martial arts move.

"I don't want to hurt you," Jenna said, trying to turn away from her assailant.

Frat boy gave her a sadistic smile. But before he could move an inch closer, she pushed into him and, like Aaron had taught her, placed the thumb of her free hand on the hand that was grabbing her arm. Then she reached her fingers around frat boy's wrist and twisted into him, placing him into what looked like a very painful wrist lock.

"Fuck! Jesus! Fuck." The words flew out of frat boy's mouth as his face contorted with pain.

Holy cow. It worked.

Jenna looked up and saw patrons turning their heads in her direction as Sam rushed toward them. She released her grip as Sam grabbed onto frat boy's shoulder.

"That's it, Hadley. It's time for you and your band of miscreants to leave."

"Jesus, Sam! That bitch nearly broke my fucking wrist."

"Hadley, you moron, I can see down this hall from the bar. I saw you go for her."

Jenna was light headed. Had the whole exchange lasted only moments? It seemed like hours.

Sam turned to her. "Do you want me to call the police?"

"No, I'm fine," she said, still amazed the move worked.

Hadley broke free from Sam's grasp and stormed past them. He joined his friends, who, sensing the night had gone awry, were throwing money on the table and heading for the door.

"Sam, what's going on?"

Jenna looked on as a concerned brunette walked up to them and put a hand on Sam's forearm.

"Hadley. Something is not right with that kid."

Jenna watched as the door closed, breathing a sigh of relief. She was thankful Hadley and his friends had left without further incident.

"Thanks for your help, Sam. I don't think I hurt him too badly."

"Just his pride," Sam answered, frowning and shaking his head. Then his expression changed, and he looked at her, a bit of wonder in his green eyes. "Are you some blonde, ninja black belt?"

"No, I'm a teacher. One of my students taught me how to do that. I just never thought it would really work."

"Hadley wasn't expecting it. Are you sure you're okay?"

Jenna nodded, then stole another glance at the woman still standing by Sam's side. There was something familiar about her.

"Where are my manners?" Sam said, his gaze darting back and forth between Jenna and the petite brunette. "Zoe Stein, this is Jenna. She's new in town."

"Of course, it's Jenna," the woman replied.

3

Jenna couldn't believe her eyes. "Zoe Stein?"

"The one and only."

"You look so..."

"Put together? Adult-ish in appearance?" Zoe asked with a sly grin. But then her expression became more serious. "Are you really all right? That thing with Hadley looked pretty intense."

"I'm fine. Hopefully, he'll think twice before trying to put his hands on a woman without permission."

Jenna and Zoe glanced over at Sam who had become very quiet. He was standing stock-still as if he couldn't believe what was going on right in front of him.

"Earth to Sam," Zoe said, snapping her fingers to break his trance. "Remember that year I spent in Iowa at Gwyer College?"

Sam nodded.

"To make a little extra cash, I waited tables at this hole in the wall Mexican joint near Gwyer. Jenna saved my ass more than once trying to help me keep that waitressing job," she said with a laugh, but Jenna detected something not so jovial in her eyes.

"Somebody let her carry other people's food? On plates?" Sam asked, directing the question to Jenna but eyeing Zoe doubtfully.

"Hey! Waitressing just wasn't in my skill set."

"As I recall, you and the giant serving tray were not on friendly terms," Jenna added.

The women laughed, and Sam shook his head. "Times haven't changed. How many plates have you dropped at my place?"

Zoe gave him a swat on the arm, and then she turned to hug Jenna. "Jesus, Jenna Lewis! How are you? What are you doing in Langley Park?"

Jenna was surprised by Zoe's warm reception. Despite her waitressing debacles, everyone had loved Zoe at the restaurant. Truth be told, Jenna didn't even expect Zoe to remember her, let alone greet her so enthusiastically.

Sam looked toward the crowded bar. "Duty calls. Grab a booth," he said, then he turned to Jenna. "I'll send a server over with your laptop and some drinks."

"On the house?" Zoe asked, batting her eyelashes.

Sam threw her an exasperated look, but the hint of a smile pulled at the corner of his mouth.

Jenna and Zoe found a U-shaped booth and moved toward the center to talk.

Zoe settled back in the seat. "It's so great to see you. I've wondered how you were doing all these years."

Jenna never contemplated that anyone from her past wondered about her. She always kept to herself and assumed that others had forgotten her.

Her college days weren't spent partying or dating. She was either studying, working as an education research assistant, or spending nights and weekends waiting tables at Santiago's Mexican Cantina.

She'd never been the outgoing type, but there was something about Zoe she found comforting. They would often chat while doing prep work in the restaurant. Zoe seemed to have a way about her that made people feel instantly at ease.

"How are you? Do you work nearby?" Jenna asked, deflecting the conversation away from herself.

"I'm really good. I'm doing some producing and reporting for

KPR, that's Kansas Public Radio for you newbies to the area. I've got a place about an hour away in Lawrence by the station. But with so many friends and my family here in Langley Park, I seem to spend more time here than I do there. My mom and dad live close by, and they don't mind me crashing."

The women stopped talking as a waiter approached the table and handed Jenna her laptop, then he set a glass of red wine and a bottle of beer on the table.

"As you can tell, I've changed a little. My pink hair and punk rock days are solidly behind me," Zoe said as she touched her wavy, brown bob.

"Zoe, you always looked great. Are you and Sam…" Jenna trailed off letting Zoe fill the space.

"Oh, no! We're just good friends. I used to come here quite a bit when I was living nearby with my brother," she said.

Zoe took a long sip of her beer and narrowed her eyes. "Change of subject. I need to know how you ended up on my doorstep. I thought you were from somewhere out in farm country?"

"You're right. I graduated from high school in a little town almost due south of here close to the Kansas-Oklahoma border. You've got a great memory. That's probably a good thing for what you do."

Zoe laughed. "That's what I love about my job. I've always enjoyed getting to know people. I love learning their stories, their complexities. That's what's so great about getting to work at KPR. I get to help put together stories that make a difference."

Zoe stopped talking and again narrowed her eyes. "You are very good at deflecting questions, Jenna Lewis! Enough about me. Did you become a teacher? That's what you wanted to do, right?"

Jenna filled Zoe in on her job and all the cities she'd lived in during the last ten years. Talking about her work was the one topic of conversation that always came easily.

"Is it ever lonely?"

Jenna paused before answering. It wasn't the first time someone had asked her this, and she had her canned reply at the ready. "Not at all, I get to work with great kids and train equally amazing teachers. I'm happy, really happy."

Zoe nodded. "Is Kansas City your next stop? God knows the public schools could use some support. School funding out here is a real shit show."

And here's where Jenna didn't know how to go on. What was she doing here? It was such a simple question.

She thought about the lie she told her principal about helping an elderly aunt after hip surgery. It was a believable enough tale to tell, but something inside her was holding back from regurgitating another falsehood. Maybe it was the long drive or the shock of being back in Kansas. Maybe it was her surreal encounter with Hadley or reconnecting with Zoe Stein.

Jenna felt like Alice falling down the rabbit hole, trapped in a world that didn't make sense. For the last fourteen years, she'd been in control, in charge of her trajectory; but now, in Langley Park, there were so many unknown variables. Her carefully modulated life, crafted to protect her heart, had vanished with a single voicemail.

It had been relatively easy to keep her guard up when she controlled every aspect of her life. Easy to get lost in her work and ignore the weight of all the untruths. In essence, by keeping herself walled off from any emotional connection, she had created a life where there was zero risk of being hurt. But she paid the price for keeping those walls so strongly fortified. It had been many, many years since she had love in her life.

But now, sitting next to Zoe, she didn't see someone who wanted to break her heart into a million pieces. All she could see was compassion and genuine concern.

Under the table, Jenna positioned her thumbnail and pressed it into the flesh of her thigh, feeling that familiar jolt of pain. "I'm here because my mother was admitted to Midwest. She threatened suicide during a therapy session, and now she's at the psychiatric center for the next couple of weeks, maybe longer."

Stunned by her admission, Jenna released her thumb and placed her hands on the table. She took a slow breath as the pain in her leg dissipated.

"I'm so sorry, Jenna. I didn't even know you had family here."

"No family, just her. I didn't even know she was in Langley Park until a few days ago. I haven't seen or heard from her in many years."

"This has got to be so hard on you."

"I don't know why I'm burdening you with all this," Jenna said, the sensation of speaking the truth making her almost queasy, like the feeling you get looking into one of those funhouse mirrors.

"You aren't putting any burden on me. You're a friend. I'm here for you, whatever you need. What can I do to help?"

Jenna let out a nervous laugh. She needed to change the subject to something less charged and more pragmatic. "Help me pick a hotel. Is the Country Club Plaza still a nice area? I only visited once when we lived in Village East."

Zoe sat up ramrod straight in her seat. "Wait a second. When the hell did you live in Village East? I went to Village East High School. All the Langley Park kids go there."

"I went to Village East High but just for the first semester of my sophomore year. I wasn't there long."

"Jenna, that's crazy! So, if you were a sophomore, I'd have been in eighth grade. Still middle school," she frowned. "Did you keep in touch with anyone from Village East High? I'm sure we have some friends in common."

"No," Jenna shook her head, taking another sip of wine. "I went to a bunch of schools growing up, so I never had much time to make any lasting friendships." She couldn't help the memory from Langley Park that flashed through her mind, but she wasn't about to share it. She'd never even spoken about it to anyone. That memory was a treasure she'd kept locked in her heart since she was fifteen years old.

Zoe nodded and pulled out her phone. She tapped it on the table, her gaze directed at the ceiling as if she was contemplating something. "We need a place for you to stay."

Jenna watched as Zoe started texting.

The two, or was it three, glasses of wine Sam had sent over were starting to make her head feel a little fuzzy. "I was looking online, but I'm not even sure what I'm looking for. I was hoping to be close to the hospital, but I don't think there are any hotels in Langley Park. I even checked a house rental site, but it didn't come up with anything in the area."

"Jenna, I've got it all worked out," Zoe said, clapping her hands and cutting off her tipsy banter. "You're not going to need a hotel."

4

"Stop telling me no and let me show you the place," Zoe said, ushering Jenna out of Park Tavern and into the muggy May evening.

Jenna had almost forgotten the unforgiving Midwest humidity. Two years in Denver's dry climate had spoiled her.

"Zoe, I don't even know your brother. I can't imagine imposing on him like this."

"Listen, the walk will do us both good after all that wine and my many, many beers. You're not driving anywhere, sister. Might as well enjoy the scenery."

Zoe was right. Langley Park's town center was picturesque. If you had to close your eyes and imagine a charming town square, this was it. By this time, all the families had gone home, but the strings of white lights hanging above the square were still softly illuminating a large fountain. The sound of water mingling with the crickets provided a soothing background soundtrack.

The town center's design was elegant in its simplicity. It ran four blocks east to west and three blocks north to south with the Langley Park Botanic Gardens on the far east side separating the town center from Lake Boley. The Midwest Medical and Psychiatric Center was situated on the other side of the lake.

The neighborhood homes, consisting of several blocks, encased the town center on its north, west, and south sides. Langley Park was an urban planner's delight. Walkable and bicycle friendly, it was no wonder the well-to-do were flocking to the area and paying top dollar for the quaint bungalows and charming Tudor, American Foursquare, and Federal style homes.

Making their way toward the neighborhood, Zoe led Jenna past a small bookstore on Bellflower Street then north on Baneberry Drive.

"I've forgotten so much," Jenna said, a bit of nostalgia in her voice as she remembered all the streets in Langley Park were named after plant life native to the region. "This was always such a sweet town. It almost makes you forget you're only a few miles away from Kansas City."

"Yep, it's like you've died and ended up in Mayberry. Except we're not in North Carolina, and there's nobody named Goober around here that I know of."

The women laughed and then settled into a comfortable silence.

It was a lovely place. The lawns were all meticulously maintained, and Jenna's heart swelled seeing children's bicycles stacked next to front doors, waiting for their riders to awaken.

Many residences had motion sensor lights that came to life as they walked past, allowing Jenna to admire the painstakingly cared for homes.

After they had walked about five blocks due north from the town center, they stopped at a red brick Tudor style home. A large oak tree stood tall, sleepily casting branches over the home's high gables.

"This is it," Zoe whispered.

The house was dark with only an outdoor light illuminating the front door while a few landscape lights twinkled along the perimeter. Jenna and Zoe walked up the driveway and headed toward a small structure.

The structure turned out to be a two-story, freestanding garage nestled in the back corner of the property. Built in the same Tudor style as the main house, it sported a gable in its center and below that a trio of windows.

They went to the side of the garage, and Zoe started digging inside her purse. This was all starting to become very real.

"I bet there's a key hidden under one of the pots," Zoe said, gesturing to the many ceramic planters lined up along the side of the garage. She dug through her large tote bag. "I've got my own key I can give you somewhere in this mess."

"Zoe, you don't have to do this for me. I'd be fine in a hotel."

"Bingo," Zoe said, holding up a silver key in triumph. Then her face became serious. "Jesus, Jenna, it's not like I'm letting an ax murderer crash in my brother's garage. You're a freaking teacher who goes state to state helping poor kids learn to read, right? I might as well be showing this place to Mother Teresa."

"If you put it that way," Jenna answered, conceding defeat.

Zoe opened the door and flipped on a light switch, revealing a small mudroom and a narrow staircase. Zoe led her up the stairs and flipped on another light when she got to the top.

Jenna had to blink her eyes a few times to get used to the bright lights. The apartment was a large rectangle mirroring the size of the garage below. It was beautifully decorated in whites, blues, and grays. Tasteful pottery and framed art added to the room's coziness.

As Jenna walked further inside, it was as if she'd stumbled into a Crate and Barrel catalog. To her right, there was a full kitchen with gleaming stainless steel appliances. The cabinetry was white with brushed nickel pulls. An island with a creamy granite counter separated the kitchen from the rest of the apartment. A round table with four chairs and gray upholstered cushions sat further in the room.

Jenna immediately noticed a desk in the far corner. It was crafted in a way that fit all the angles of the space perfectly, giving plenty of room to work and an unobstructed view of the backyard and the main house. Across from the desk, there was a cozy gray couch with throw pillows and a large flat screen television.

Zoe walked out from what looked like the bedroom and turned on the light. "What do you think? Not too bad, huh?"

"This is really nice. Are you sure no one uses it? Your brother doesn't need this space?"

"Let me show you the bedroom," Zoe said, her voice sounding a bit heavy-hearted.

Jenna walked into the small bedroom where she was met with the same blue, white, and gray color scheme. It made her feel like she was at a seaside cottage.

"The closet and washer and dryer are through there." Zoe pointed toward a small hallway leading out of the bedroom. "And then the bathroom is right past that. It was the door that was right across from the kitchen. What do you think? Will this work?" Zoe flopped onto the bed.

"It's gorgeous. Is this where you lived when you stayed with your brother? I almost feel like I'm at the beach."

Zoe's face darkened. "That's what they were going for."

"What do you mean, they?"

Zoe sighed and flopped back on the bed. "This carriage house apartment was supposed to be for my brother's mother-in-law."

"What happened?"

"She passed away suddenly. Heart attack. It was really hard on Sara."

"Sara? That's your brother's wife?"

"Sara *was* Ben's wife."

"Zoe, are you sure it's okay if I stay here?"

"She died years ago. It would do the place good to have someone breathe some life into it. Plus, this is the perfect set-up for you. You're not even sure how long you're going to be in Langley Park. You could stay a week or a month. There's no hurry. You'll have a kitchen to cook in—no living on takeout, and there's plenty of room for you to work. I know you have a lot on your plate. Having a safe place to crash close to the hospital is one less thing to worry about, don't you think?"

"And your brother? You're sure he's all right with this?"

Zoe yawned. "Don't worry about my brother. He's out of town with Kate, but I sent him a text."

Jenna nodded, hoping this Kate wouldn't mind her living in her boyfriend's garage. She had to admit that this was an ideal living situation. With the hospital only a few miles away, she could divide her time easily between working here in the carriage house and making trips to see her mother.

"All right, Zoe. I'd love to stay here. This is so generous of you and your brother. I'm going to insist on paying though."

"You can work that out with Ben. We better head back to Park Tavern. You need to get your car, and I need to let Sam know we haven't been abducted by aliens." Zoe held up her phone as a long stream of texts from Sam lit up the screen.

By the time they made it back to Park Tavern, Sam was the sole inhabitant, quietly stocking craft brews in the coolers below the bar. "Did everything go okay? I was about to send out a search party."

Zoe hoisted herself onto the bar and swung her legs back and forth. "It took a little arm twisting, but Jenna's gonna stay in Ben's carriage house."

Sam smiled, leaning his elbows on the bar next to Zoe. "I think the carriage house will be good for you, Jenna. Just watch out for Kate."

"I'm pretty sure I'm either going to be working or at the hospital. Hopefully, they won't even know I'm there. I mean, I never even met my neighbors back in Denver. I'm pretty good at keeping to myself."

Sam gave Jenna a kind, sad smile, but after a few awkward seconds, Zoe hopped off the bar and wrapped her in a warm hug. "Don't be a stranger. You've got us."

"Thank you. I can't even begin to tell you how much I appreciate all this."

"And remember, I have your cell number. I have your email. And I know where you live," Zoe said, her teasing tone back in place.

BY NOW, it was nearly one in the morning. Jenna had driven the few blocks to Zoe's brother's house and sat parked in the driveway, her gaze trained on the carriage house. This was going to be her home for the foreseeable future. As she turned off the engine, fatigue washed over her body. She opened the back hatch of her SUV and grabbed the small suitcase containing her toiletries. She could unload the rest in the morning.

Bag in hand, Jenna walked over to the side door. The night air hummed with the songs of cicadas, the familiar sound triggering memories she'd spent years trying to forget.

She closed the door behind her, then trudged up the steps and into the bedroom, setting her bag on the small nightstand next to the bed. Flicking on a lamp, she crawled onto the bed and arranged the pillows so she could sit upright against the headboard. Looking down at her thighs, she lifted the fabric of her skirt, exposing the crescent shaped indentations caused by her thumbnail. Red and inflamed, the marks seemed to be glaring up at her. Observing her legs more closely, she saw the faint lines of past scars, now barely visible, but still engrained in her mind.

Jenna extended her legs and traced her fingers over each indentation. She leaned her head back against the soft pillows and closed her eyes. Fingers still massaging her thigh, one lone tear escaped down her cheek as childhood memories flooded her mind.

"You made him go!"

Her mother was screaming again. Her Alabama accent was still thick though she hadn't lived in the South since before Jenna was born.

"Why did you do that? Why Jenna Jo? Do you hate me that much? Why would you even think about callin' the police?"

"You weren't here, and Travis came in the house. He started yelling at me, saying crazy things like I'd taken money from him. Mom, I didn't. I wouldn't. Then he tried to grab me. I ran to your room and locked the door. You weren't here. I didn't know what else to do." Jenna choked out a sob as she tried to reason with her mother.

Judith lit a cigarette, and the smoke swirled, obscuring Jenna's view of the red and blue flashing lights of the police car parked outside. Judith had arrived home from a shopping trip just as the police were pulling in.

"You don't know what you're talkin' about." Her mother's tone was full of irritation.

"Mom, I was scared."

"You better shape up, JJ. You know, there's nobody that wants you. I'm it. I don't know what kind of hellhole they'd put you in if the state took you away. I guess you wouldn't be my problem anymore. Maybe we *should* talk to that nice police officer." A syrupy smile appeared on her face as she took a long drag on her cigarette.

"I'm sorry. I promise. I'll never do anything like this again. Please don't let them take me away," Jenna sobbed.

Then there was a knock on the door, and a police officer walked inside the house. "Ma'am, are you sure this was just a misunderstanding?"

"Ask my Jenna Jo. She'll tell you." Judith stubbed out her cigarette and walked over to the officer. She was a beautiful woman and knew it. Jenna watched through her tears as her mother fixed a placating smile on her face.

Jenna felt the eyes of the officer and her mother fall upon her like a one-two punch. "I'm sorry, sir. I was just playing a prank."

"There you go, officer. My JJ has a wild imagination. And of course, I'm not pressin' charges. Nothin' happened."

The officer looked to Jenna and then back to her mother. "Ma'am, we've asked Mr. Mayer to spend the night somewhere else—at least for tonight. He's agreed to that."

Jenna was relieved, but that respite disappeared when she saw her mother's hand go to her chest in mock surprise. "Officer, can I go speak to Travis, real quick?"

The officer nodded as Judith hurried out the door toward Travis' truck. He crossed his arms and trained his gaze on Jenna. "You shouldn't be playing these silly games, young lady. Don't be upsetting that pretty mother of yours. You only call the police for a real emergency. Do you understand?"

"Yes, sir," she said, her eyes trained on her shoelaces as she listened to the officer's heavy footsteps fade away as he left the house.

It would be useless to try and talk to him. Between Judith's lovely petite frame and deceptively sweet southern accent, Jenna had watched her mother charm men to get what she wanted.

She stood there in silence for what seemed like hours before Judith returned. Jenna watched as Travis' truck drove down the street with the police cruiser trailing behind. Moments later, Judith retrieved her purse and rummaged through it.

"What's going on? Are you leaving?"

Judith gave her daughter a withering look of disgust as she pulled a lipstick out and applied it to her pursed lips. Finishing her application, she dropped the lipstick back into her purse and met Jenna's pleading gaze with a pointed glare.

"Mom, you're not leaving, are you?"

"Who the hell do you think you are? I don't answer to you. You're not my mother. I'm yours. And I'd say you're pretty damn lucky to still be livin' in this house." Judith tossed a pack of cigarettes into her purse then glanced out the window. "If you have to know, Travis *is* comin' back to get me. You think I'd want to be anywhere near you after the stunt you pulled?"

Travis' truck roared into the driveway.

Jenna's lip quivered as her mother grabbed her lighter, threw it into her purse, and walked out the door. Judith didn't even look back. She never did.

Jenna ran to her room and slammed the door. She slumped down onto the floor and rested her back against the wall. No one could help her. She was stuck, trapped. Her mother would always choose Travis.

She kicked the side of her dresser. Items which were once settled neatly on the tabletop rained down on the floor next to her. She glanced over and saw a pair of nail scissors along with a pencil and a few rubber bands.

Jenna reached for the scissors, small and silver, and drew red lines on her upper thigh with the point. She scraped the tender flesh with the sharp tip, watching the skin redden and become inflamed with each pointed stroke.

As if in a trance, she pinched the skin of her thigh, opened the mouth of the scissors, and cut into the smooth flesh. Something morbidly satisfying happened. Like the flicking of a switch, the pain caused by those scissors turned off every awful emotion and erased all thoughts of her mother and Travis. The pain became her only focus as she gazed down in childish wonder at the delicate crescent shape, blood trickling out and smearing down the side of her leg.

5

Jenna woke in a daze still wearing her clothes from the day before. She'd fallen into a fitful sleep, her dreams a scattering of childhood memories threaded with images of a farmhouse.

For a moment, she thought the last few days had been a dream. She rubbed her bleary eyes then watched as shades of pale blue and gray came into focus.

She was in the carriage house apartment Zoe had taken her to last night. This was all real.

Needing to busy herself, she got to work unloading a few things from her car and setting up her laptop on the cozy corner desk. She turned on her computer and realized she needed to ask Zoe's brother for the WiFi password and wrote herself a quick note.

A spark of apprehension prickled in her chest. She didn't even know the person whose carriage house she was currently residing in. Jenna pushed the thought aside and scribbled out a to-do list.

Get coffee.

Get coffee.

Get coffee.

She glanced around the carriage house. After she satisfied her caffeine fix, she would need to purchase groceries. She added a few items to her list, and then the hint of a smile pulled at her lips. She sketched out two wheels held together with a frame. She added handlebars and a seat. Her smile bloomed as she ran her finger across her crude drawing of a bicycle.

A close third behind running and yoga, mountain biking was a surefire way to clear her mind when the echoes of her past came haunting.

As a child, her bike had been her means of escape. As a woman, riding reminded her she was strong, independent, and in control. For Jenna, the harder the trail, the better. She loved navigating bumps and rocks, her mind fully engaged in the sole pursuit of propelling forward.

She never brought her mountain bike with her when it was time to move on to a new city. It was a tradition of sorts that started after she was sent to her first school implementing the Gwyer Reading Program in Louisville, Kentucky.

Just twenty-two years old, she was excited to be working in the field she loved and was making good money doing it. She'd never had a nice bike as a child, so her first grown-up purchase was a Specialized S-Works Stumpjumper mountain bike. It was silver and white and one of the most beautiful things she'd ever seen.

As Jenna's two years in Louisville were coming to a close, she couldn't stop thinking about Jordan, a fifth-grade girl she had taught to read.

Jordan lived alone with her mother. A mother who never answered any of Jenna's calls or responded to notes from the school. Jordan was soft-spoken and often wore the same dress day in and day out. Jenna couldn't help feeling a kinship with the girl and wanted to leave her something to bring her happiness.

On their last day working together, Jenna had explained she would be moving to a new city to help children learn to read and asked if Jordan wouldn't mind taking her bike. The girl listened wide-eyed as Jenna explained she didn't have room in her car to take it with her.

And that's how it started. City by city, she would purchase a new mountain bike knowing she was going to leave it in the care of one of her students. Even in her haste to leave Denver, she was able to gift her bike to a worthy recipient.

Now she was in Langley Park which was technically a new city. While she wasn't planning on staying long, she reasoned that under the circumstances, she needed a new bike now more than ever.

Jenna left the carriage house and walked down the driveway. She glanced at the main house, trying to get a look inside. She wanted to get a feel for the occupants, but the blinds in every window had been lowered and pulled shut.

Her first stop was the coffee shop she'd remembered seeing last night. As she made her way into town, she watched the families bustling about and assumed that there must be a school nearby. In the light of day, she easily found The Drip Coffee Shop.

"Good morning! What can I get you?" came the cheerful greeting of the young woman standing behind the counter.

"Your strongest coffee and a blueberry muffin, please."

The girl went to work assembling the order as Jenna surveyed the shop. It was small with a few tables inside and a few more out on the sidewalk. A group of older gentlemen were sitting together talking and laughing. Two mothers sat chatting with sleeping infants in strollers. Zoe was right. Langley Park did have a Mayberry kind of feel.

"Here you go. One blueberry muffin and a large brew."

Jenna settled in at an outdoor table and watched Langley Park come to life as she ate her breakfast. There was a yoga studio next door to the coffee shop that piqued her interest. She popped the last bite of blueberry muffin into her mouth and grabbed her coffee. It wouldn't hurt to check if the yoga shop had its class schedule posted on the door. But before she could even look, the door swung open and a slew of women came walking out.

Jenna stood out of the way to allow the yoga patrons to exit the studio when an attractive, older woman stopped walking and looked her over. Oddly enough, the woman seemed vaguely familiar. Trying not to look uncomfortable, Jenna smiled.

"You must be Jenna. I'm Kathy Stein, Zoe and Ben's mom."

"Oh, hello," Jenna replied, caught off guard. Word got out fast in this town.

"I didn't mean to surprise you, honey. Zoe texted me. I want to get this right," she said, digging her phone out of her yoga bag. "Just a heads up. My friend Jenna Lewis from Gwyer is going to be staying in Ben's carriage house. If you see a tall, blonde, Barbie-looking chick, that's her. No need to call the police."

Jenna laughed. "I'm very pleased to meet you, Kathy."

They shook hands, and Kathy tossed her phone back into her bag. "Zoe is insisting I start texting. I still don't see what's so awful about actually speaking to people, but I'm trying to get with the times."

It was uncanny how much Zoe resembled her mother. Even their mannerisms were similar. And they both seemed to share this innate ability to befriend anyone at a moment's notice.

"What brings you to town?" she asked casually.

Jenna sipped her coffee, wondering if Zoe had already told her mother why she was here, and now Kathy was just being polite.

"My mother was admitted to Midwest Hospital last week," Jenna said, trying to gauge Kathy's response.

"I'm so sorry to hear that. It's an excellent hospital. I'm sure she's in good hands."

Jenna stood there a moment, not quite sure what to say or do next. Maybe Zoe hadn't mentioned anything about her mother's situation.

Kathy started to ask how long she was planning on staying in Langley Park when Jenna interrupted her, unable to hold back her words. "My mother's been admitted to the psychiatric center."

Kathy's expression became serious. "I know we just met, but would you mind if I gave you a little advice?"

"Not at all," Jenna said, still stunned she'd shared the truth.

"I don't know your mother's situation, but I can tell you one thing for sure," she began, her blue eyes meeting Jenna's. "It's not your job to save her. Remember that. You can support her, but she has to do the work."

Jenna nodded and swallowed past the lump in her throat. Those were the very words she needed to hear.

She took another sip of coffee to compose herself and, not knowing how to thank a virtual stranger for giving her the advice she desperately needed, changed the subject. "Could you tell me if there's a grocery store close by?"

"Yes, yes," Kathy answered, sensing the shift. "It's just a block down off Bellflower and Mulberry. Pete's Organic Market."

As they said their goodbyes, Jenna turned to head toward the market when Kathy touched her arm. "Take care, dear."

Jenna felt a calm come over her that she hadn't known in days and marveled at how Zoe and her mother, with just a kind word or gentle touch, could make you feel like everything was going to be all right.

BACK IN THE CARRIAGE HOUSE, Jenna unpacked the items she purchased at the organic market. It seemed too permanent to use the cabinets, so she placed the fruit as well as a box of cereal on the counter. She didn't need much. She wasn't planning on staying in Langley Park any longer than necessary.

Just as she put a carton of milk in the refrigerator, her cell phone buzzed with an incoming call.

"Hello, I'm calling for Jenna Lewis."

She recognized the social worker's voice. "Hi, Eric, it's Jenna."

"I'm glad I was able to reach you. Is this a good time?"

"Of course." She wondered if this was how Eric began all his calls to patients' families. She tried to keep her voice impassive. When it came to anything relating to her mother, Jenna needed to keep her guard up.

"Jenna, I was hoping that you could come in today. Would around eleven work?"

She looked at her watch. It was 9:30.

"Sure," she answered, trying to keep her voice steady.

The call ended, and she released a shaky breath. Her respite in Langley Park had just ended.

She walked into the bathroom and turned on the shower. Grabbing her shampoo, she caught her reflection in the mirror above the small pedestal sink. She stared at herself and saw her mother's golden hair and her mother's brown eyes.

In appearance, she was her mother's daughter. It didn't matter how many lies she told or how many years they were apart. They would always be connected. The physical proof was reflected right in front of her. She gazed intently at the mirror as it fogged up from the heat generated by the shower. Her face blurred and disappeared into the haze.

JENNA ENTERED the Midwest Psychiatric Center. She had to admit, the facility seemed quite inviting. It was open and airy with the sounds of a gentle water feature tinkling peacefully. It had a Zen-like, expensive feel to it. She wasn't sure how her mother would feel about the Zen part, but the expensive part sounded about right.

Eric greeted her with a kind smile, then walked her back to his office and gestured toward a pair of chairs. Jenna sat, keeping her expression pleasant but neutral.

"Thank you for coming in today, Jenna. I know it means a lot to your mother to have you here."

Most people would find comfort in that statement, but Jenna knew better. She nodded, a tight smile stretched across her lips. Eric leaned forward and picked up a folder, but before he could say anything, Jenna asked, "How's my mother doing? Are you all under her thumb?"

It was a combative way to start the meeting, but Judith had a way of playing the victim and twisting the situation. As the icy words left her lips, Jenna immediately regretted them, remembering her mother had been staying at a women's shelter.

Was her mother trying to escape Travis? Was she still even with him? Fourteen years apart was a long time. Things may have changed.

The tension in her shoulders softened just a fraction as her mind wrapped around the possibility her mother could have been abused. If she was still with Travis, Judith may have gone to the Rose Brooks shelter to escape the kind of pain Jenna knew all too well.

Eric smiled, clearly used to antagonistic family members, and placed the folder back on the table. "Let's talk about that. Your mother shared with me that she wants to be completely open with you. I'll do my best to answer any questions you have."

Jenna bit down on her lip and tried to decide where to begin. "I haven't seen or spoken with my mother since I was eighteen years old. I'm assuming she was given my contact information from the trust attorney."

"Actually, we've never spoken about how she got your contact information or anything regarding a trust."

This surprised her. Growing up, Jenna had listened to her mother's countless rants about her *self-righteous* family and her *measly* trust fund. Judith would go on for hours detailing how her family had wronged her and then discarded her, leaving her only a fraction of what she was owed.

Her mother's primary complaint had been that, until her thirty-second birthday, she was only granted a set amount of money each month—an allowance of sorts.

Thinking back on Judith's extravagant spending, Jenna surmised the allowance itself must have been pretty substantial. Then she realized her mother was now well over thirty-two.

"My mother's family is from Alabama," Jenna began, trying to disconnect herself from the words. "I've never met them. Since she was twenty-one, my mother's been receiving payments from a trust. There's also a trust set up in my name as well. I only learned about it when I turned twenty-one. I knew that the same law firm handled both of our trusts because I recognized the letterhead from documents I had seen during my childhood." She paused. "I didn't know how to contact my mother after I left home. She moved around quite a bit. So, several years ago, I started leaving my contact information with the trust lawyers and asked them to pass it on to her."

Eric nodded and jotted a few things on a notepad. "If I hear you right, you're wondering why Judith reached out to you after all this time?"

Jenna folded her arms. She knew he'd read it as a protective gesture, but she didn't care. "Has my mother shared anything about our past with you?"

Eric leaned forward, setting the pad aside. "From what your mother has told me, I think she feels a lot of regret about the past."

Jenna sat quietly, not knowing how to respond to this information.

After a few long beats of silence, Eric sat back in his chair and folded his hands in his lap. "Jenna, I think you're here because you still care for your mother and are concerned for her well-being."

Her arms still crossed, Jenna dropped her gaze to the floor. "I don't know why I'm here." She felt the weight of the situation closing in on her and forced herself to meet Eric's gaze.

"How about we talk about your mother's treatment plan and go from there." His tone was soft as if he were trying to coax a frightened animal out of a cage.

She nodded, glad to have something more concrete to focus on.

For the next twenty minutes, Eric explained Judith had told him she was battling alcohol addiction. After undergoing a psychiatric evaluation, the doctors had also diagnosed her with bipolar disorder. The alcohol abuse wasn't surprising to Jenna, but the bipolar disorder came as quite a shock until Eric shared that individuals suffering from the disorder were often manipulative, unpredictable, and childlike.

He went on to say those with the illness could exhibit severe impulsivity and long-term patterns of unstable relationships often with a frantic need to avoid abandonment.

"And the suicide attempt, could that be part of it?"

He gave Jenna a consoling smile. "Certainly, substance abuse, risk of suicide, and depression are all commonly associated with bipolar disorder."

"Can she get better?" Jenna asked, knowing the shake in her voice betrayed her stony expression.

"In most cases, yes. Behavioral therapy combined with medication has helped many people with this illness live normal, productive lives."

And then Jenna felt it. The tiny glimmer of hope she'd always harbored in her heart twitched. Though she had tried for years, she could never suppress that small part of her still yearning for her mother's love.

"What now?" she asked. Her limbs were begging to run, begging to leave this place, if only for a moment.

Eric motioned to the door. "Now, we'll go see your mother."

6

Jenna had to take a second to make sure her heart was still beating.

Trailing behind Eric, she focused on counting her footsteps. It was a pointless exercise, but she needed something to distract herself from what lay beyond the set of double doors. Eric swiped a keycard, and the doors opened. She followed, still silently counting, then joined him at the nurses' station.

"Is Judith available?" Eric asked, directing the question to the nurse sitting in front of a computer.

Jenna's pulse raced. The moment was surreal. This was happening. Would she even recognize her mother? What would she say?

"She has a session with Dr. Walker at one o'clock," the nurse said, looking at the screen. "It looks like she's got time for a quick visit."

Jenna's hammering pulse slowed.

A short visit. She could get through a quick visit.

"Judith's in room 206," Eric said as they continued down a hallway.

She hoped she looked composed on the outside because, on the inside, she was vibrating. Every instinct told her to run. What was she going to accomplish here? She had no plan to stay in contact with her mother after this ordeal was over.

Now, too late, she realized she hadn't thought this all the way through. Her face flushed and a bead of perspiration slid between her breasts.

Eric gave Jenna a comforting smile. "There are no expectations for this visit, Jenna. I can imagine this brings up many emotions for you."

She caught herself wringing her hands. "I'm just not sure what to say, or where to start."

"I could guide the conversation. Would that help?"

She nodded, giving Eric a tight smile, then forced her fidgeting hands to hang at her sides.

Before she knew it, Eric knocked on door 206.

"Come on in."

Jenna froze. That was her mother's voice. The lilt of her southern accent floated through the air like poisoned gas.

Eric opened the door. "Hi, Judith, I have your daughter with me."

The room wasn't what Jenna had expected. It was more like a studio apartment with a tidy bedroom and small adjacent bath. Judith sat on a small couch in a compact living area reading a book. A book. Jenna had never seen her mother so much as touch a book, let alone read one.

Pushing aside the bizarre image of Judith reading, Jenna couldn't help noticing how small her mother looked. Was she always that tiny? She seemed almost childlike sitting on the couch with her legs curled beneath her.

As they entered the room, Judith rose to her feet and came padding over with a bright smile. "JJ, sweet girl, I knew you'd come."

JJ.

She hadn't been called that in years. The sound of her mother calling her by her nickname was as comforting as nails on a chalkboard.

Judith looked her over. "Isn't she so pretty, Eric? I told you, she was always a beauty."

A statement that couldn't be farther from the truth.

One of Judith's greatest talents was ridiculing her daughter's appearance. She vividly remembered sweating bullets in a department store fitting room as her mother yelled for her to suck in her gut, pulling violently on the zipper of a pair of jeans two sizes too small. That was the last time Judith Lewis had taken her daughter shopping.

Jenna looked at this wisp of a woman and willed herself to smile. Judith reached toward her, and she wasn't sure what was happening until she realized her mother was trying to hug her.

Bending down, Jenna breathed in her mother's familiar scent. Slightly musky with a hint of spice, the smell of perfume mingled with tobacco smoke evoked a torrent of emotions. It made her feel shaky and off-balance. She bit the inside of her cheek, trying to block the wave of anxiety that threatened to paralyze her.

Only able to endure her mother's touch for a few seconds, she pulled away, drawing herself up to her five-foot-eight-inch frame.

Eric motioned to the sitting area. "Let's sit down and chat. Judith, you've got a session with Dr. Walker coming up at one, but I thought we'd have just enough time to talk a little bit about your treatment and how you hope Jenna will be involved."

Jenna took the chair, leaving the small couch to Eric and Judith. She needed some distance from her mother. She couldn't even remember the last time her mother had touched her with kindness.

"Jenna, I know your mother is very glad you're here. When I told her you were coming in today, she was very pleased."

"Yes, Eric, I am pleased as punch. And sweetheart, look at those lovely shoes." Judith eyed her daughter's boots approvingly.

Jenna looked down at her Prada boots. She couldn't believe that after fourteen years of no contact, Judith was commenting on her footwear. Jenna couldn't stomach any more of this charade. All the nervousness drained from her body as a simmering anger took its place.

"Mom, are you still with Travis?"

"Why would you even ask me that, JJ?" Judith's smile faltered just a fraction.

"Yes or no? You know it's important."

Judith glanced at Eric with a wounded expression. The poor abandoned mother and her insolent daughter.

"Judith," Eric began, "you told me you wanted to be completely open with your daughter."

Judith nodded and took a dramatic breath. "I'm done with him. He's no good for me."

Words Jenna had heard before.

The room was quiet for three long beats before Eric broke in. "It's very common when people have been apart for some time for it to feel awkward. But I think we can all agree that Judith is on the road to living a sober, healthier life. And Jenna, we are very pleased you are here to be a part of that. There is healing that needs to happen in your relationship, and I feel our work here will be beneficial to you both. I think we can all agree on that."

Jenna glanced at Eric, and then she met her mother's gaze. She was trying to read Judith. Could her mother be ready to turn over a new leaf?

"I agree. I want you to get better, Mom. I'll do what I can to be a part of that."

Judith patted her daughter's knee. "JJ! Thank you, baby. Thank you so much. I know with your support I'm gonna make it."

Jenna smiled tightly, unnerved by her mother's enthusiasm.

"Okay," Eric said. "Let's talk about our first step. Our family group therapy session is on Mondays from one to two in the afternoon. We'll start there. Jenna, does that sound like something you can commit to?"

Waves of competing thoughts crashed through her mind as she weighed Eric's proposal. She wanted to believe Judith honestly did want to change, while she also worried her mother was going to abandon her for Travis yet again.

"Yes, I can agree to that," Jenna said, attempting to sound resolute.

A knock at the door interrupted them.

"Judith, I'm here to take you to see Dr. Walker."

"Hi Sally," Judith called out. "This is my gorgeous daughter, JJ."

"How nice for you, Judith. She's just as pretty as you are."

Jenna still couldn't understand what her mother was doing. Was all this affection for show, or was Judith genuinely trying to make amends?

As they said their goodbyes, Judith grabbed her hand. "Thank you for comin', JJ. I know this must be hard on you."

Jenna gazed down at their clasped hands. Her mother's delicate, manicured hands intertwined with her plain, long fingers seemed completely foreign.

Nodding her head and trying her best to smile, Jenna gave her mother's hand a quick squeeze. She searched her mother's face but couldn't read her eyes. Judith wanted something from her, but Jenna couldn't tell what.

As Judith turned to leave, Jenna realized that watching her mother walk away had been the only part of this interaction that felt natural.

HEART PUMPING, limbs moving, Jenna ran.

After seeing her mother, this was the only way to process what had just happened. After getting back to the carriage house, she changed clothes, laced up, and took off for the trail.

Jenna ran down Prairie Rose, the street that bordered the north side of the town center. A path appeared, and she veered off the road and found herself at the Lake Boley trailhead. The trail looped around the lake and was at least a good three miles. Jenna had lost count of how many times she'd gone around, but it didn't matter. She would run for as long as it took. Comforted by the sounds of the trail beneath her feet, she kept going over her mother's face, trying to discern what was in her eyes, but was at a loss.

Fourteen years apart had hindered her ability to read Judith Lewis.

Slowing down, Jenna walked toward the town center. She was

parched. She looked at her phone and checked the timer. She'd been running for nearly two hours.

She headed toward Pete's Organic Market to grab a coconut water when she came upon a row of bikes parked in front of a shop called The Pedal on Honeysuckle Way. A bike shop. Jenna stopped, forgetting her thirst, and peered in through the large display window.

A yoga studio, an organic market, running trails, and now a bike shop. She had barely even explored Langley Park and already found herself falling in love with the place, then shooed the thought away.

Langley Park wasn't her home. It never would be.

"You look like you just fell in love."

Jenna was startled, then she smiled as Zoe walked toward her.

"I think I may have. It's a Yeti Beti," she replied, pointing at a bright red mountain bike hanging inside.

"Yeti, what? I'm pretty sure I'm missing something here."

"It's the name of the bike. I saw a few of them on the trails back in Denver."

"Shiny bikes are your thing, duly noted," Zoe said, giving Jenna an amused look. "I was about to text you, but I'm glad I ran into you. I'm much harder to turn down in person."

"Should I be worried?"

"No, I'm a very considerate friend. I always wait until alcohol has been consumed before I drop any real bombs."

Jenna smiled. Zoe had just called her a friend.

"Come to Park Tavern tonight and have dinner and drinks with Sam and me. My brother's back in town and will probably swing by. You'll get to meet your landlord."

She gave Zoe an apprehensive look. Despite her friend's many reassurances, Jenna was not so sure Zoe's brother would be okay with some random stranger living above his garage.

"Go home and shower, then meet me at Park Tavern around seven," Zoe said, pretending to fan off Jenna's post-workout scent.

"I don't think saying no is an option."

Zoe cocked her head to the side. "I'll tell you one thing, Jenna Lewis, you're a fast learner. Seven o'clock."

. . .

A FEW HOURS LATER, Jenna found herself showered, dressed, and sitting at a table near the bar with Zoe and Sam at Park Tavern. She enjoyed their company. It was a welcomed distraction from the worries that surrounded her mother.

Sam opened a bottle of her favorite cabernet and had been chatting with them when a harried server passed by the table. "I'm still technically on the clock. I better get back to work. Enjoy the wine, and I'll catch up with you after things slow down." Sam started to back away, he reached over and took a huge bite of Zoe's BLT.

Sam wasn't just a bartender at Park Tavern. He and his brother, Gabe, owned the establishment. However, his brother rarely made an appearance, acting more like a silent partner.

"Hey, Big Red! You forgot this," Zoe said, mock outrage in her voice.

She proceeded to throw a french fry at Sam's head which he caught deftly in his mouth, giving her a cheeky grin.

"Sweet Jesus! He makes me crazy."

Jenna laughed politely. There had to be something more than just friendship going on between Zoe and Sam, but she wasn't in Langley Park to stir that pot.

She checked her watch. It was getting close to nine. She wasn't sure if Zoe's brother was going to show or not. She was hoping to meet him here, thinking Park Tavern was a more neutral location. It would be quite awkward if their first meeting occurred at the house.

Hello there, no need to call the police. I'm just the stranger living above your garage.

Zoe's phone buzzed with an incoming text. "Ben's on his way. He just got held up at my mom and dad's place dropping Kate off."

"Why would he be dropping off Kate at your parents' house?"

"They just got back into town, and Kate's doing a sleepover with them."

Jenna's face registered total confusion.

"Ben and Kate go away every year on Mother's Day. This year

she's six, and Ben told her when she turned six, they'd do Disney. He still likes Kate to do a Mother's Day-ish thing with my mom, so it's more like a Grandmother's Day. Kate gets to spend tonight at my parents' place, and then she plays hooky from school tomorrow."

"Wait? Kate's six?"

"Yep, six going on sixteen."

"Kate is Ben's daughter?"

"Yeah, I thought I told you Ben had a daughter?"

Zoe had told her about a Kate, but Jenna misconstrued the information.

"I thought Kate was your brother's girlfriend."

"Hell no!" Zoe laughed. But then her tone became serious. "My brother doesn't date. He doesn't do much besides work and spend time with..." She didn't finish the sentence, but her face lit up. "Well, speak of the devil!"

Jenna turned around to greet Zoe's brother, and her breath caught in her throat.

Zoe began to make introductions, "Jenna, this is—"

"Ben Fisher?" Jenna said, cutting her off, not sure if she could believe her eyes. "Ben Fisher's your *brother*?"

7

"**B**en, do you remember Jenna? She was at Village East High for a bit. You would have been a senior when she was a sophomore."

Ben only allowed himself a brief glance at Jenna before meeting his sister's gaze. Of course, he remembered Jenna Lewis. Village East High School didn't get many new students. When there was a new face in the crowd people noticed, and Jenna was no exception.

Taller than most high school girls, her golden blonde hair had hung well past her shoulders. She'd often tilt her head forward and use her hair as a shield, closing her off from the outside. They'd had one class together. He couldn't remember which one because his attention had been completely focused on her.

Ben had spent what must have been hours watching her twirl her hair around her finger, wishing it were his hands in her glossy locks. She invaded his mind, and he couldn't stop wondering why her brown eyes always looked so sad.

"Were you guys friends?" Zoe asked.

Ben couldn't answer. Where was he supposed to start?

"Your brother and I evaded the police one evening," Jenna said, filling in the gap.

Zoe's eyes popped open like a surprised cartoon character. "This guy? Mr. Honors Classes, Mr. Tennis Team Captain, Mr. Every-Parent's-Wet-Dream Child? He evaded the police! How the hell do I not know this story?"

A waitress came by and set a beer on the table next to Ben, giving him a moment to collect his thoughts. He turned toward Jenna, still dumbstruck that she was here. As their eyes met, something familiar and heartbreaking ripped through his chest, but he masked his emotions with a stony expression.

"It wasn't like we robbed a bank or anything like that," Jenna added with a nervous laugh.

"For Pete's freaking sake," Zoe sighed. "Somebody needs to elaborate on this!"

"Do you want to tell it, Ben? I can't remember the name of that park or where we..."

He smiled tightly. "It was right before Thanksgiving break, and some idiot got his hands on a keg. Word got out to meet at that park off Rockcress Street. You know it, Zoe. It's the one set back a bit near the creek with the giant play structure and climbing wall."

"Yes, yes! You know I know it. Now please, get to the evading."

"Well, there was a big group of us standing by that giant climbing wall drinking crap beer when three or four police cars pulled in."

"Jeez, Jenna! At least in college, you didn't strike me as the evading the law type. Who were you there with?"

"I can't remember his name. It may have been Adam or Able?"

"I know! It had to be Able Duran. By the way, he's living in Hong Kong with his boyfriend! He designs the interiors for Starbucks or H&M or something fabulous like that. Wait? Able asked you out?"

"No, not really. He was my partner for a biology assignment. We were meeting over at that sub shop near the high school to hash some things out early so we wouldn't have to worry about doing any work over the Thanksgiving break. A couple of kids came in and told Able about some keg party at a park. One thing led to another, and I found myself riding in a stranger's car heading over."

"I see," Zoe said. "So, there you are, Miss New Girl, headed to your first Village party at a children's playground. Wow, we sure know how to live it up."

A beat of silence passed.

"Come on, big brother. What happened?" Zoe asked, leaning in.

Ben released a breath. "Zoe, you know the drill. The cops came, and kids started running."

"What made you run with Jenna? Did you guys even know each other?"

DID WE KNOW EACH OTHER?

Ben didn't know how to answer.

His mind went back to that November night. He was standing with his friends, talking and laughing when Jenna walked up to the group with Able Duran. She was wringing her hands, and, even in the dimly lit park, he could make out her forced smile.

Moments later, police cars pulled onto the grass, and bright lights cut through the night, sharply illuminating the group. He should have started running with his friends, but he hesitated and looked back at Jenna. She was just standing there, her head turning back and forth, like a lost child.

Some protective instinct took over, and he ran to her. "Jenna, we've got to go."

Those were the first words he had ever spoken to her.

Jenna snapped out of her confused panic and nodded as she looked up at him with those dark, haunting brown eyes. Even amid all the chaos, he nearly drowned in the depths of them.

He led her toward the creek and helped her down the steep embankment. The creek separated the park from the main road, and, at this time of year, it was quite shallow with large rocks providing a dry path across. Ben was just about to step onto the first flat rock when he heard footsteps and a police radio chattered above them.

He stopped and pulled Jenna into him, pressing her into the high side of the embankment behind a tree growing sideways out of the earth. He rounded his body around her, and the tip of his nose brushed against hers. It was cold as they listened, barely breathing, their eyes locked on each other in the darkness.

Another officer caught up with the one pursuing them.

"Don't worry about a few stragglers. We caught a group of geniuses trying to run off with a pony keg."

"Ah, to be young and stupid," replied the other officer.

Ben stood there, holding onto Jenna and listened as the officers walked back to the park.

"Are you all right?" he whispered, feeling her shallow breaths against his lips.

"I don't know where we are. I don't know how to get home from here. I came with Able, but he wasn't the one driving."

Jenna was rambling, shaken up by the events. He could hear the panic in her voice.

He smiled down at her, then took her hands into his. They were so cold and so small compared to his large, warm hands, but they fit perfectly as if they were made for each other.

He tilted his head toward the gas pumps across the intersection. "Let's head over to that gas station. We can grab something to eat, and then we'll walk back to my car—it's parked a few blocks away from the park. My guess is, that in about an hour or so, the cops will be gone, and we can get back to my car without anyone seeing us. Then I can take you home."

Jenna looked relieved and nodded.

Ben led her up the creek bank. He was still holding her hand when a jolt of heat radiated through his palm and traveled all the way to his heart. Jenna had shifted her fingers and laced them tightly with his.

"Do you have a curfew? You can call your parents. There's a pay phone at the gas station," he asked, forcing himself to focus on the situation.

"No, there's nobody I need to call," she answered.

They made it up the embankment and were standing under a lamppost. After a few steps, Jenna stopped. "I could really use a Kit Kat right about now."

"A Kit Kat, huh?" He asked, his mouth quirking into a lopsided smile.

Then Jenna smiled at him and time stopped.

His breath caught in his throat as he watched the warmth return to her eyes like adding cream to a cup of coffee. The darkness that haunted her disappeared. The November breeze blew golden wisps of hair across her face, and, at that moment, he would have sworn she was an angel.

Even after all these years, the image of a teenage Jenna had never faded from his memory.

He wanted to kiss her. He wanted it more than he had wanted anything in his entire life. He wanted to put his arms around her and never let go. He wanted to talk to her about everything and nothing. He wanted to tell her how he spent hours thinking about her and sketching her beautiful face. But against every impulse, he released her hand.

"I think I could handle a Kit Kat right about now, too," was all he could gather the courage to say.

Ben picked at the edge of his beer bottle's label. He couldn't believe that Jenna, his high school Jenna, was Zoe's friend and was now living in his carriage house.

Jenna didn't come back to school after Thanksgiving break. He looked for her all over campus and even drove past her empty house dozens of times. It was torture. Jenna Lewis had vanished without a trace.

"Hey, Space Cadet! For the second time, why did you run with Jenna?" Zoe asked, pulling Ben from the past.

He took a sip of beer and swallowed back his memories. "Jenna and I just ran in the same direction to get away from the police. It's not much of a story."

JENNA'S HEART sank at Ben's abrupt explanation. She told herself their night had happened a long time ago. Of course, he didn't remember the details. It was just one crazy high school night for Ben, and he probably had many more just like it. She was surprised at how much this hurt because she remembered every little detail about the beautiful boy who had held her hand and bought her a Kit Kat.

Zoe clapped her hands. "This is great! You guys already know each other. I told you this was going to work out just fine, Jenna."

Ben's posture was rigid as he sipped his beer. He gave his sister a placating smile, but Jenna couldn't help noticing the smile didn't reach his eyes, not even close.

The night passed quickly. Zoe was funny and engaging, but Ben barely said a word. Jenna was concerned he was angry about the carriage house arrangement. His demeanor toward her was cool at best, and he'd hardly even glanced at her after sharing his brief rendition of their night running from the police.

Jenna reached for her purse. She needed to put some distance between herself and Ben Fisher. "I better be getting back. I've got a video conference tomorrow morning I need to prepare for."

"Stuff for work?" Zoe asked, her gaze wandering to where Sam was talking to a couple seated at the bar.

"Yes, I just need to touch base with some teachers. Nothing earth-shattering."

"You're a teacher?"

Jenna was startled to see the question was from Ben.

"For all intents and purposes, yes," she began, keeping her tone professional. "I work for a pair of educational researchers from Gwyer College. I'm part of a small group of teachers who travel from school to school implementing a reading program targeting inner city schools nationwide."

Ben seemed to take this in.

"You walked, right? Do you want me to give you a ride home?" Zoe chimed in, ignoring her brother.

"I can walk her back," Ben said.

Jenna tried not to look shocked. The man had barely acknowledged her existence the entire evening.

"Great! I'll stay and wait for Sam. Let's talk tomorrow. Maybe grab a coffee?" Zoe said, giving Jenna a hug.

Jenna nodded to Zoe, but her mind was spinning.

What just happened? Did Ben just offer to escort her back to the carriage house?

He must have because he gestured for her to walk in front of him. But as they neared the door, she slowed her step as a large group clambered in.

Jenna reared back, bumping into Ben and took in a sharp breath as one of the men entering the tavern looked her up and down, his gaze lingering on her breasts.

Aidan Hadley.

The jerk who tried to corner her outside the bathroom.

"Fucking cunt," Hadley hissed as he stepped toward her.

She wasn't about to make a scene, but Ben reached out and grabbed Hadley by his shirt collar and pulled him back.

"I don't know who you think you are, but you're going to apologize."

"Jesus. Can't anybody around here take a joke?" Hadley said, slurring and rocking back-and-forth.

Sam came up and stood next to Ben. Both men, well over six feet tall, had at least a good four inches on Hadley.

"This jerk's going to apologize to Jenna," Ben said, tightening his grip on Hadley as he exchanged a look with Sam.

"And then you're getting the hell out of my bar," Sam added sharply.

Shrugging off Ben's grip, Hadley took a step back. "Look at her for fuck's sake. She's asking for it."

Jenna was wearing a pale green wrap dress and flats. She taught children in this outfit.

She eyed Hadley more carefully. It was evident from his bloodshot eyes and unbalanced stance that he'd definitely been drinking and was probably on drugs.

"It's not worth it. Look at him. I'm not sure how he's even able to stand," Jenna said.

Sam glanced over at Hadley and shook his head in disgust.

"Are you good?" Ben asked Sam as he placed his hand protectively on Jenna's back.

Sam nodded. "I think Hadley and his asshat friends have permanently worn out their welcome at Park Tavern."

Jenna gave Sam an apologetic smile then left the restaurant. Ben was right behind her.

"Let's go," he said curtly.

After a block, Jenna stopped walking. Her cheeks burned with embarrassment. "I don't know what's wrong with that guy. That was my second run-in with him in two days."

"You're doing a pretty shitty job of making friends here."

Jenna's jaw dropped.

"It's late. We should go," he said and started up the street.

She didn't move. "I almost broke his wrist yesterday."

This brought Ben to a halt.

"It was self-defense. He cornered me when I was coming out of the bathroom and tried to get handsy. I did this cross-grab-wrist-lock maneuver a student taught me, and it worked. Stopped him right in his tracks."

"Handsy?" Ben asked.

"Yes, handsy. It's a word."

She was talking to fill the silence. Talking wasn't usually her default setting when she was nervous, but something about Ben made her feel fidgety and off-center.

Built like an Olympic swimmer, Ben took her breath away with his dark curls and piercing blue eyes. She'd found him attractive in high school, but seeing him now gave her that tingly anticipation feeling you get right before a roller coaster takes the first plunge.

Jenna crossed her arms, a useless attempt to dampen her response to him. She continued walking and vowed not to say another ridiculous thing. It was apparent from the cold reception he'd given her tonight he thought of her as some crazy girl from high school who just happened to blow into town and start brawling at the local tavern. This was the absolute opposite of the simple, quiet life she had left just days ago.

Ben broke the silence. "Zoe said in her text that your mom's at Midwest."

Both Ben's sister and his mother knew why Judith was at Midwest Medical and Psychiatric Center. There was a good chance he already knew of her mother's situation.

"Yes, she's in the psychiatric center completing a program for mental health issues and substance abuse."

There, she'd said it. Those were the facts. Telling the truth almost felt normal. She hadn't realized how exhausting inventing lies and excuses had been until she didn't have to do it anymore.

The way she saw it, this time in Langley Park was going to be a respite from the web of lies she had created to protect herself from the past. She would be in Albuquerque soon enough, and then she'd resurrect the lies and excuses just as she did in every new town.

Ben didn't react to her words. They were only inches apart, and the night was quiet all around them. She knew he had heard her.

"I'm not sure how long I'm going to be here. I guess at least two or three weeks, maybe longer. The garage apartment is great, but I don't want to inconvenience you."

Jenna paused, waiting for Ben to answer, but there was no response.

"Of course, I'm going to pay you. I was looking online to get an idea of what would be reasonable and—"

"It's a carriage house. And I'm not charging you rent."

"I'd feel better if we came to some arrangement," she said, her tone becoming firm. Then added more delicately, "I could also really use your WiFi password."

Ben barked out a laugh. "WiFi, huh?"

An awkward silence descended as the sound of an engine turning over resonated through the night air.

"Please, Ben. You've got to let me do something to repay you."

They arrived at the house and walked up the path toward the front door. The porch was cozy and framed by a hedge on each side. A small light cast a warm glow, making it seem like they were the only two people in the world.

"We're not going to discuss compensation anymore. You're my sister's friend, and you need a place to stay. End of discussion," Ben said without an ounce of humor as he unlocked the door. "Come in. I have the WiFi password written down in the kitchen."

The house was dark, lit only by a few dim lamps as they made their way back to the kitchen. To her left, Jenna noticed a formal dining room and to her right, a study with a large desk, piled high with sheets of construction drawings and rolls of tracing paper. Both rooms were beautifully decorated in the same blues, whites, and grays as the carriage house.

Ben flicked on a light switch as they entered the kitchen. Jenna found herself surrounded by whitewashed cabinets and stainless steel appliances. The kitchen was gorgeous, the kind of space you would see in a fancy design magazine with a cozy den decorated in the same tones situated opposite the kitchen area.

"You have a beautiful home, and this kitchen is amazing," Jenna said, her voice touched with a bit of wonder.

"You sound surprised about that," Ben replied.

"I just didn't expect it to look so..."

"So, what?" Ben asked, a bit of amusement in his eyes.

"Put together, I guess."

"I designed it."

"Is that what you do? You're a kitchen designer?"

That garnered a laugh. "Sort of. I'm an architect."

"You did have all those sketches on your notebook covers," she said, then bit her tongue. She had to stop bringing up the past. Ben barely remembered her, and here she was talking about him as if they had been close friends.

Jenna never stayed at a school long enough to make friends. But that didn't stop her from remembering others, and she had spent her fair share of time daydreaming about Ben Fisher.

Ben went to the counter, grabbed a pen, and started writing on a sticky note. He handed her the paper. It contained a long string of numbers and letters.

"Here's the WiFi password and my phone number, just in case anything comes up with the carriage house."

Jenna took the piece of paper, careful not to let her fingers brush his. Then her gaze was drawn over his shoulder to a large pile of children's workbooks.

"You've got quite a few of those," she said, professional curiosity taking over as she gestured to the stack.

Ben glanced back at the reading workbooks and crossed his arms. "They're for my daughter, Kate. I'm not sure how much Zoe's told you about her?"

"I know she's six. First grade?"

Ben nodded and walked over to the stack of workbooks.

"She's having a hard time with reading. She gets frustrated easily. Most nights, it's a fight to get her to read anything. We've gone through a string of tutors. My daughter can be...strong-willed."

Jenna examined the books. From what she saw, there was no consistency from workbook to workbook. Struggling readers needed a consistent learning plan built on the skills they had already mastered, and Kate's tutoring looked to be disjointed at best.

Her educator's mind flipped on, and she went into teacher mode. "Do you have any family members with dyslexia or a learning disability?"

"No," Ben answered, his voice softening.

"Any significant life changes or health issues?"

It was a common question. Jenna had asked hundreds, maybe thousands of parents this very question over the course of her career. Often, children having difficulty learning to read had other external factors impacting their learning: a big move, divorce, death. Ben's wife had passed away, but she didn't know the circumstances. However, she knew she'd overstepped when his jaw tightened.

"Kate lost her mother when she was three, and she was treated for carbon monoxide exposure, but the doctors said there was no evidence of any damage. That was also when she was three."

Jenna nodded. She took two workbooks off the stack and went to sit at the kitchen table. Ben followed, taking the seat across from her.

"I hate to tell you this, but I don't think these are going to help your daughter. The skills in these books aren't taught coherently and jumping from book to book adds more confusion to the mix. I'm sure Kate's teacher is doing her best, but I'm guessing there are twenty, maybe twenty-five students in her class. It's easy for kids like Kate to fall through the cracks."

Ben flashed an accusatory look of disbelief. "You get all that from a pile of reading workbooks?"

"It's what I do. This is exactly what I do. I teach children how to read." Then an idea sparked. "Ben, I'm going to be here for the next few weeks. I could work with your daughter."

She tried to read him. The anger that had erupted only seconds ago was gone, but it was replaced with the mask of indifference he had worn most of the night.

"You and Zoe have shown me so much kindness. You won't take any money for rent. I hope you'll take me up on this."

Ben didn't meet her gaze as silence filled the room.

Unsure of what to say, Jenna picked up her purse and tucked the paper with Ben's phone number and WiFi password into a side pocket. She stood and walked toward a pair of French doors that led from the kitchen out to the backyard. Ben's back was to her now, and she watched his sculpted shoulders rise and fall with each breath as he sat fingering the pages of one of the workbooks.

She wanted to touch him, place her hands on his shoulders and take away his pain. But she balled up her fists instead. Ben didn't want her help or her comfort. Not only that, he didn't seem to want her there at all.

She opened the door and headed back to the refuge of the carriage house.

8

Ben watched through the window as Jenna's darkened form moved toward the carriage house. She opened the door, but before going in, she turned and looked back at the house. After a few seconds, she went inside, and soon the windows of the carriage house turned from plates of black to a warm golden glow.

He smiled wistfully, knowing exactly which lamp she had turned on. He designed that carriage house and knew it like the back of his hand even though he hadn't stepped foot in it for more than three years.

Had it already been three years since that awful day?

His thoughts were jumbled, jumping between the past and present. He took out his phone and looked at the pictures he'd taken with Kate just days ago at Disney World. He stopped at a picture of Kate smiling with her bright green eyes and dark hair all wild and flowing around her. Would her hair be styled with little bows and braids if her mother were still alive?

Sara, why did you have to leave us like that?

Deep down, he had known she wasn't well, but he couldn't forgive her. It was irrational to hate the mother of his child, but she had left him in the worst way possible.

They had met at a party during his last year at the University of Missouri-Kansas City. He was finishing up his master's in architecture while she was completing her undergraduate degree in landscape design.

Sara was petite with shining green eyes and chestnut colored hair that brushed her shoulders. They spent the entire night debating the use of green space in urban planning, and he offered to take her home.

They ended up kissing in his old Jeep Cherokee, and within a few years, that kiss had grown into something much more, and they married.

The first miscarriage came right after their wedding. They blamed it on stress. Ben was starting his architecture firm, Fisher Designs, and Sara had taken a position with a large landscape group in Kansas City. They worked crazy hours and lived on takeout.

But then it was two and then three miscarriages. And it started to take a toll.

Sara stopped working, which meant Ben had to make Fisher Designs profitable. They purchased a 1930s Tudor style home in Langley Park, and Ben moved his office to the town center nearby. He worked long hours, and Sara, often alone, withdrew from the world, only interacting with him and making phone calls to her mother in Arizona.

Ben wondered if that was when Sara began to slip away, but before he could worry about Sara's retreat into herself, she was pregnant again. This would be her fourth attempt to carry a child, and Ben's fourth attempt to try and hold them together.

Sara's mother, Liz, had decided to leave her home in Phoenix and move to Langley Park to be closer to Sara and, God willing, the baby. Ben designed and built the carriage house specifically for her.

But sadness and tragedy found them again. When the carriage house construction was completed and ready for Liz to move in, they received an awful phone call. Liz had died suddenly—a heart attack in her sleep.

Six months pregnant, Sara and Ben traveled to Phoenix to bury her mother. Sara's grief was indescribable. She didn't have any other family, and she and her mother shared a bond like Ben had never seen.

As Ben grieved for Liz, he worried about being the only one there for Sara if she were to miscarry for a fourth time. Ben's family loved Sara, but in her grief, she had distanced herself from them. He was all Sara had, and that terrified him.

Thankfully, the fourth try turned out to be the charm. Despite going through the painful loss of her mother, Sara gave birth to a healthy Kathryn Elizabeth Fisher or Jellybean, as Ben would come to call her shortly after her birth.

The early years with Kate were tough. Like most parents with their first child, they were all about survival. Their lives revolved around feedings and sleep schedules. The time went by like a blur. He had also found his niche in renovating and restoring the beautiful, old homes in Langley Park. He was working harder than ever, building up his business, and taking on more clients. In no time at all, Fisher Designs had grown from a one-man shop into a successful business, employing three architects and an office manager.

He wanted to spend more time with Kate and Sara. He told himself work would eventually slow down. Then he'd be the doting father and husband he knew he could be and find the work-life balance.

Sara seemed to adapt well to motherhood, but she was extremely protective of Kate. They rarely left the house, and Sara limited the amount of time Ben's family could spend with Kate; citing safety concerns over germs and accidents or any other hazard she perceived. Ben didn't fault her for this. After living through the miscarriages, he wanted to do everything in his power to keep his sweet daughter safe, too. So he acquiesced to Sara's demands, and they lived a quiet, solitary life.

Looking back, Ben should have known something was very wrong around the time of Sara's death. It was Mother's Day, and Kate was growing into a precocious three-year-old. They had spent the holiday, like most of their days, at home playing inside. Mother's Day was especially difficult for Sara, but that year she was full of life. She'd kissed him that morning, and it was the first time she'd initiated physical contact in years.

He was at work the next day when his mother called. She wanted to tell him how pleased she was that Sara had brought Kate over for a visit, but voiced her concern regarding her almost euphoric behavior.

Ben had told his mother not to worry and even shared how much more vibrant Sara had become in just the last few days. But after their call ended, he couldn't shake the terrible feeling that something was off.

Despite a light rain, Ben decided to walk home and join Sara and Kate for lunch. He tried to call Sara to see if she wanted him to pick up some sandwiches from Park Tavern, but the call went right to voicemail. This was odd. Sara always had her phone on her. She insisted for safety that it always needed to be charged and ready in case of an emergency. Ben's walk became a jog, and he rushed up the path leading from the sidewalk to their home.

The front door was unlocked. That should have been his first warning. He walked inside his home. It was deathly quiet with only the sounds of the spring rain dancing on the roof.

"Sara? Jellybean?"

No response.

He made his way upstairs to Kate's room and then into the bedroom he shared with Sara when he saw the pill containers sitting in a neat row on Sara's nightstand.

Sleeping pills.

Three empty bottles silently accused him of being the distracted husband, blind to his wife's deteriorating mental health.

Sara's doctor had prescribed the pills for her insomnia, but he didn't know she'd been refilling the prescriptions and stockpiling them right under his nose.

Adrenaline coursed through his veins.

"Sara!"

He ran through the house, checking closets and bathrooms, even going down to the basement. But Kate and Sara were nowhere to be found.

Ben passed through the French doors leading from the kitchen to the back porch, hoping he'd find his wife and daughter in the backyard. It was raining harder now, and thunder was rumbling. But a faint noise drew his attention. He stopped and tried to pinpoint the sound. He glanced at the carriage house, and then it clicked.

Heart pounding, Ben ran. It had to be less than a hundred feet to the garage, but time was moving slowly.

He lifted the heavy garage door and saw Sara's car. He was met by a rush of fumes and the sound of the motor humming. There was something else. A word repeated over and over again.

Mommy. Mommy. Mommy.

It was Kate.

Ben rushed to open the car door and found his daughter glassy-eyed, head lolling against her car seat, her face red and stained with tears. Kate met her father's gaze with sleepy eyes.

"Out, Daddy. Out."

Ben unfastened the five-point harness. He threw back the straps and clutched his daughter in his arms. Looking her over frantically, he carried her from the garage and set her on the wet grass. She was groggy, and the storm didn't seem to faze her, but she was breathing and alive.

"Stay right there, Jellybean. I'm going to get Mommy."

"Sara," he yelled, almost losing his footing on the slick grass as he ran back toward the garage. But before he reached her car, a voice called to him from the sidewalk.

"Is everything all right?"

It was a jogger. She'd heard the commotion and came running up the driveway to offer help.

"Call 911. Tell them we need an ambulance," Ben called out, rushing to turn off Sara's car.

Sara's small body was slumped over the steering wheel. Ben had to reach awkwardly over her just to turn off the ignition. He lifted her from the car and dragged her body out of the garage and onto the grass. She felt as if she was made of lead.

"I called 911. They're on the way," the jogger called out.

Ben pulled his gaze away from Sara to see that the jogger had taken Kate to sit on their covered back porch. Only then did he feel the rain soaking through his shirt.

Ben looked at his wife. Her lips were tinged blue, and her eyes were open and vacant, not blinking back the punishing rain soaking them both. He checked for a pulse and found nothing.

"Daddy, Daddy!" Kate cried out to him, but he had to try and save his wife.

Shielding Sara's body with his own, he kept looking for some sign of life, waiting for the rise and fall of her chest, the sound of her voice. But there was nothing.

"Come on, Sara! I can make this right. I can fix this. You just need to breathe."

His movements were frantic as he administered CPR. He pressed his mouth against Sara's, trying to force air into her lungs. But as he worked, an unbelievable realization took over. His wife no longer inhabited her body.

She was gone.

Then there were people all around him. He heard the crunch of their boots coming up the driveway. Firefighters and EMTs descended and clustered around Sara's prostrate form. A fireman had taken him by the arm and brought him over to the porch where Kate was still sitting with the jogger.

From there, things moved quickly. Kate was loaded into an ambulance with an oxygen mask strapped to her tiny face, and her painful whimpering filled the air. "I want Mommy. Where's Mommy?"

"Just breathe, Jellybean. Just breathe," was all he could say holding her tiny hand as they sped toward the hospital while images of his wife's dead body, sprawled lifeless in the wet grass, flashed through his mind.

Sara was dead, and he was to blame.

. . .

JENNA SAT at the corner desk of the carriage house typing on her laptop. After her tense exchange with Ben, she needed a distraction and turned to work. She finished up an email and glanced out the window. Ben was standing in the middle of the backyard looking up at her.

What could he want?

She opened the carriage house door and walked across the dew kissed grass to where he stood.

"Is everything all right?"

"You can help Kate."

She wasn't sure if Ben was making a statement or asking a question.

"Yes, I can."

A few long beats of silence passed as they stood face-to-face in the darkness.

"It would have to be in the house. I don't want Kate near the garage."

Her pulse quickened. "Okay."

Ben nodded as if he'd just decided something important he'd been silently contemplating.

"Good night, Jenna."

She heard his words, but he wasn't moving. He wasn't retreating from her. It felt as if he had more to say, but he just stood there rooted to the ground. She stared back at him. Her hands twitched. She wanted to touch him, but she held back.

"Good night, Ben," she said, almost taking a step toward him, but turned and walked back to the carriage house.

She glanced over her shoulder before opening the door, but Ben was gone. The Tudor's French doors were closed, and the house was dark. She didn't know what to make of the moment they had just shared, only knowing it was gone.

9

Despite her late night, Jenna woke early and stretched as she glanced out the window. The sun hadn't begun to greet the day yet, and she smiled, loving the stillness of the early morning. Her video conference with the teachers wasn't until ten o'clock, giving her plenty of time for a run.

Walking out of the carriage house, Jenna noticed the Tudor was still dark. She shivered, thinking back to last night and how badly she'd wanted to reach out and touch Ben. Even after all this time, she still felt a connection to him. But if there was one thing Jenna had learned, it was that connection could be a dangerous thing.

Had she just built him up in her mind?

Of course, she had. While he had lived in her sweetest of memories and starred in her most tender teenage daydreams, she was barely a blip on his radar.

Jenna pushed Ben Fisher out of her mind and focused on the sound of her feet crunching on the packed gravel driveway.

She was starting to find her bearings for Langley Park and decided to head toward the lake. She popped in her earbuds and set off, heading south down Baneberry Drive. She loved this time of day when the world around her was still sleeping. The lazy sun was just beginning to cast its light over the tall oaks lining the street as she inhaled deeply.

Her legs were warming up and feeling stronger with each stride as the first notes of pianist George Winston's "Living in the Country" played. Her body in sync and her mind focused on each crisp, deliberate note, she turned left on Prairie Rose Drive and followed it east past the botanic gardens and onto the Boley Lake trail.

While mountain biking was the way she escaped her thoughts by allowing her mind to focus on navigating the terrain, running was how she processed anything weighing heavy on her heart. It was as if her body's physical exertion helped her mind order the chaos into manageable pieces.

Midwest Medical Center came into view as she headed east along the trail, and her thoughts went to Judith. For the first time in many years, she knew where her mother was living. She pictured Judith asleep in her small hospital room and reflected on how strangely their first meeting had gone. She needed to keep her guard up, but that tiny part of her heart that yearned for a mother's love wanted to believe her mother could change.

Jenna rounded the lake trail and headed back toward Langley Park's town center. Pleased to be heading west with the sun at her back, she turned off the main trail and followed one of the narrow dirt paths leading into the dense woods surrounding the lake.

Running hard, she felt the presence of someone behind her and moved to the right to allow the runner to pass. But, after a few moments when nobody went by, Jenna looked back and was surprised to see she was all alone. Unsettled, she increased her pace and turned off the music.

More alert to her surroundings, she debated turning around and running back to where she'd left the main trail. She'd been lost in her thoughts and wasn't sure how long she'd been running on the winding dirt path. Deep in the dimly lit woods, she couldn't quite get her bearings as to which way she was heading.

Just then, Jenna saw something fly through the air. But before she could discount it as a bird, another object came whizzing past her head.

A rock?

Then she felt a stinging sensation on her shoulder blade where a baseball-sized stone had struck her hard.

Her mind was racing. What the hell was going on? The sun was coming up, but it was still quite dim under the thick canopy of trees. Could it be kids? A horrible, mean-spirited prank?

Jenna ran harder, ducking when another rock flew over her left shoulder and hit the ground.

Whoever was doing this was behind her now.

She kept going, thighs burning, as she propelled her body from the shady woods and onto the main trail now bathed in the early morning sun. She slowed to a jog as a group of older women came power walking toward her.

"Did you happen to see anyone coming out of the woods?" she panted, hoping the walkers could make out her breathy words.

The women clustered around her with concern etched on their faces.

"No, you're the first runner we've come across, dear. Are you all right?"

Jenna rubbed her shoulder. "Someone was throwing rocks at me. I was hoping you saw something."

The women all shook their heads.

"We'll keep an eye out. It was probably just children. They start to get a little stir-crazy this close to the end of the school year."

Jenna nodded and tried to smile as she jogged toward the botanic gardens and the Langley Park town center. She checked her phone. It was half past six. It seemed quite early for children's shenanigans, but she shrugged off the encounter. She was only a little banged up but no worse for wear.

She continued jogging and made her way into the periphery of the town center. She hadn't explored this part of Langley Park and noticed several professional businesses lining the southeast side of Bellflower Street, their shingles hanging peacefully in the morning light. There was a dentist, an acupuncturist, a family medical practice, and past the hanging sign for an attorney, one M. MacCarron, was the office of Fisher Designs.

Jenna slowed her pace and walked down the sidewalk as her gaze remained transfixed on the sign's black lettering. It was still early, and all the offices were quiet, their lights off and shutters closed. As she approached Fisher Designs, her pulse quickened in anticipation.

She'd always kept to herself and did her best to seem disinterested in other's personal lives, but she couldn't help wanting to look inside Ben's office. She wanted a glimpse into his life, into who he was now. She chalked up this newfound curiosity to her disconcerting morning run.

She walked up to the window and saw before and after photos of different renovation projects artfully displayed along the glass. Jenna examined a picture of a once dilapidated bungalow now transformed into a charming, vibrant home. She went from picture to picture pressing her fingertips against the glass when she noticed a small desk lamp near the back of the office casting a dim glow.

She peered in to see Ben standing at a desk. His palms were pressed down on the table with a set of blueprints strewn across the surface. He was staring at her, his face unreadable.

How long had he been watching her?

Embarrassed, Jenna smiled and gave a small wave. He nodded. And then nothing else happened. He didn't move a muscle, and she just stood there, her raised hand slowly falling back to her side.

Jenna waited a beat. A friendly person would at least come to the door and say hello, right? But Ben looked down at the drawings and returned to his work.

"THAT ABOUT WRAPS IT UP. The testing data you've submitted looks great. You should all be very proud of the work you're doing. Does anyone have any questions?" Jenna asked, finishing her video conference with the Denver teachers.

"Jenna, if you don't mind. I was wondering if you could talk a little more about that click thing."

She took off her glasses and sat back in her chair. "Sure, but I have to warn you, it doesn't have anything to do with data collection, test scores, or reading levels. I'm guessing that sounds like music to your ears right about now."

The sounds of exhausted laughter came through loud and clear.

"You're finishing up your first year implementing the reading program. This year is full of trying to remember how to teach this new skill or that new skill. You're in your head a lot, and rightly so. There's so much to learn, and it's absolutely normal to feel a little overwhelmed. But as you settle in and become more familiar with the program, you'll find yourself more observant of the subtle changes. You'll find yourself noticing your students' growing confidence in their ability to read and comprehend text. And that's where the click comes in."

Jenna tucked a few strands of loose hairs behind her ear. "This isn't something that happens at a particular reading level or after mastery of a certain skill. Over the years, I've had students click at reading level 4 and then some at 24."

"The click is more of a feeling. You feel the student's confidence growing. You see a child go from anxious to interested when you introduce a new book. You feel the student's growing sense that he's achieving something important for himself. It's kind of like a sixth sense. You're waiting for that moment when it all comes together. When your student's inner voice says, 'I got this.'"

The teachers nodded.

"And with that, I wish you all a wonderful end to your school year. It was a privilege working with you in Denver. I'm sorry I wasn't able to finish out the year, but it looks like you've all *clicked* with the program."

The teachers laughed, and Jenna could see them moving around as they closed their notebooks and laptops. She was about to log off when she heard someone call out her name.

"Jenna, we wanted to ask about your aunt. How's she doing?"

Jenna blinked, and then she remembered the lie. "She's doing well and getting better every day. Thanks for asking."

She logged off and sat back rubbing the heel of her hands against her eyes. In the short time she had been in Langley Park, she'd forgotten how heavy the weight of the lies could be.

AN HOUR LATER, Jenna walked toward Langley Park's town center. Her destination was The Pedal on Honeysuckle Way. She needed a distraction and decided it was time to meet the Yeti Beti.

As she went to open the shop's door, she heard Zoe's voice. "We meet again! The Pedal must be our place! Are you going inside? I've got some time. I'll join you!"

Three tarnished bells made an off-kilter jingling noise as the door opened, and Jenna found herself doing something she never thought she'd enjoy—shopping with another woman. Two weeks ago, the thought of this would have driven her into a tailspin. She would have manufactured some reason to leave. But today, she just took a breath and followed Zoe inside.

The shop was empty except for the faint sounds of "What I Got" by Sublime playing in the background. The store had a pleasant rubbery smell and was filled from top to bottom with bikes, some hanging from hooks in the ceiling and others arranged in neat rows on the floor. Jenna spotted the red Yeti Beti, still in its place, calling to her from the back of the shop.

A young man, lean and lanky, sat cross-legged on the counter with his gaze glued to the phone in his hands. "You ladies looking for the kids' bikes?"

"No, I'd like to see your Beti."

"That's a lot of bike," he said, still not looking up from his phone. He reminded Jenna of the kind of guy who said *dude* a lot.

"I'm all about the SB5c frame, the switch infinity suspension, and, from what I've heard, the drivetrain is the bomb."

"You're serious?" Dropping his phone on the counter, the

formerly lackluster sales associate jumped up and offered her a goofy smile.

"I am."

"I haven't sold anything but training wheels and cruisers in..." He paused to think, and the silence seemed to be stretching into minutes. Zoe and Jenna looked at each other, trying not to laugh.

"A long time," Zoe offered.

"Yeah, a long time. Just give me a second, and I'll get her down," he replied, giving Zoe a grateful smile.

Zoe met Jenna's gaze as the salesman went to retrieve the mountain bike. "Keanu Reeves. *Point Break.*"

Jenna glanced at the salesman. He did resemble Keanu Reeves, and his pseudo-surfer voice tied the whole thing together.

"You are so right!" Jenna answered, trying to whisper but unable to contain a hiccup of laughter.

The salesman wheeled the bike over. "You're going to get so much air with this beauty, and she's great on the skinnies."

"And that means...what?" Zoe asked.

"It's a light bike, good suspension, and handles well on narrow surfaces," Jenna answered as Keanu nodded, agreeing with her translation.

"How'd you hear about the Beti? I don't get many requests for her." Keanu asked, adjusting the seat.

"I was in Colorado for a couple of years and saw quite a few on the trails."

"Nice! I bet you saw some pretty sweet brown pow."

Again, Zoe looked to Jenna as if they were having a conversation with an alien.

"Good trail riding in the mountains," Jenna said to Zoe, who seemed to be getting quite a kick out of this whole exchange.

"You know, you're not in the mountains anymore. But there are some pretty bomb trails not too far from here," Keanu said as if he was letting Jenna in on a secret.

Jenna turned to translate, but Zoe waved her off. "Don't worry. I got that one."

Listening to Keanu tell them about the different off-road trails in the area, Jenna couldn't help thinking how nice it was sharing this moment with Zoe. But all too quickly, echoes of her past crept into her mind.

You have nothing to offer anyone.

Who would want you? You are unlovable.

"I'll take it," Jenna said, interrupting Keanu, needing to speak to silence the painful dialogue racing through her head. She reached into her purse and produced a credit card.

Keanu stopped talking and broke out into another goofy grin. He took her card and walked over to the register. "Killer! Let me just get her all tuned up. Can you come back in about an hour? It may be a little longer if I get swamped." He looked around the store as if hordes of customers were about to start stampeding inside.

Jenna and Zoe glanced around the still very empty bike shop, biting back their laughter. This guy was a trip.

"Sure, that would be great," Jenna replied, feeling herself relax, the disparaging soundtrack not quite so deafening.

"You should join me for ice cream. It's just across the street," Zoe said as Jenna signed the credit card slip.

Jenna looked out the bike shop's window, and sure enough, there was an ice cream parlor. *The Scoop* was written on the glass in bold pink and white lettering.

"I better just head home. I really do have a lot of work to catch up on."

"There's always time for ice cream. That's chick law 101."

"Well, if it's chick law," Jenna said begrudgingly, but she couldn't wipe the smile off her face.

"Seriously, you've got at least an hour till Keanu Reeves has your bike ready. It doesn't make sense to walk home and then come right back. What do you have to lose?"

"They better have cookies and cream," Jenna said as they left the bike shop, resigning herself to the ice cream excursion.

As they crossed the street, a little girl dressed in a Darth Vader costume, sans helmet, ran toward them. Her long brown hair trailed behind her like a cape. The mini-Vader made contact with Zoe, and they both nearly fell over from the impact.

"My little monster niece! I missed you!" Zoe said, picking up the little girl and hoisting her on her hip.

Kathy walked toward them. "Why, Jenna! It's so nice to see you. Kate and I were just going to get some ice cream. The Scoop's got the best homemade ice cream in town—worth every last calorie."

"Jenna's going to join us while they tune-up her bike," Zoe said, pressing a kiss to the little girl's head.

So, this is Kate.

"Who's that?" Kate whispered to her aunt, furrowing her brow.

"That's Jenna. She's the lady who's going to be living in your carriage house this summer."

Jenna smiled at the little girl. "You must be Kate. It's very nice to meet you."

"Oh," Kate said, green eyes wide and unsure.

What Jenna lacked in her ability to maintain relationships with adults, she made up for in the way she connected with children. Jenna took in the little girl's curious expression and remembered the first child she'd taught to read.

Just shy of her thirteenth birthday, Jenna was spending another afternoon in the peaceful safety of the public library when a little boy set the book *Make Way for Ducklings* by Robert McCloskey in her lap.

"Do you like ducks?" she asked, a bit startled.

The boy nodded and met her gaze with inquisitive green eyes.

"Do you want me to read it to you?"

The little boy nodded again and sat down next to her.

Jenna read aloud, but, every so often, she'd point out a word and ask the little boy to try and sound it out.

After several minutes, she looked up to see an older woman watching with a curious look on her face. "I didn't want to disturb you. I'm Barbara, Andy's grandma."

Jenna hadn't even asked the little boy his name and her cheeks heated with embarrassment. She wasn't even sure it was okay to read to a child she didn't know.

"Don't worry, dear! You're not doing anything wrong. You see, Andy won't do a lick of reading for his mother or me. And here he is, sounding out words for you."

Jenna relaxed a fraction. "Andy's very smart. He's a good reader."

"How would you like to tutor Andy? I take care of him while his mom's working, and we're at the library most days around this time. He seems to have taken a shine to you, and I'd pay you, of course."

And that's how it started. That chance encounter at the library changed the trajectory of her life.

Inside the ice cream parlor, Kate scrambled out of her aunt's arms and stared at Jenna. Her gaze had changed from unsure to skeptical. She screwed her face into a scowl and then, as seriously as a six-year-old can, asked, "Empire or Rebels?"

Jenna crouched down so she could be at eye level with the little girl and considered the question. "The Empire has Darth Vader and Sith Lords, and they're pretty powerful."

Kate nodded as if she and Jenna were debating the laws of thermodynamics.

"But the Rebels have Luke, Han, Leia, and Chewy." Jenna tipped her head weighing the options. "If I had to choose, I'd have to say the Rebels are my favorite."

"Me, too! But Daddy said if I wore my Luke Skywalker costume for one more second his eyes would explode."

Jenna chuckled but stopped when she heard a voice come from behind her.

"What's this about my eyes?"

10

K athy was right. The Scoop's homemade ice cream was worth every last calorie. The group had eaten their treats at an outdoor table situated near a small fountain.

Streaks of strawberry ice cream ran down Kate's chin as she sat perched on Ben's lap delighting them with her sweet chatter. Jenna both loved and hated watching these kinds of family exchanges.

For as long as she could remember, her goal was to appear normal. If she studied the interactions of ordinary people, she could emulate their behaviors and, someday, maybe not feel so different. But that day had yet to come.

More often than not, watching these families made her wonder. Had she been brought up like Kate in a loving, safe home, would she have turned out differently? It was a pointless line of questioning, but one that looped over and over in her mind like a scratched record repeating the same string of lyrics, unable to move on to the next verse.

As they finished up their ice cream, Keanu propped open the door of the bike shop and wheeled her Yeti Beti mountain bike onto the sidewalk. He waved and walked the bike across the street. "Here she is! All tuned up and ready to shred."

Ben met her gaze and raised an eyebrow. It was the first time he'd even glanced her way since he arrived at the ice cream parlor.

"Thank you so much. She looks great!" Jenna said, standing to take the bike from Keanu.

"No problemo," he replied, then turned to Kathy. "Hey, Kath."

"We missed you at Sunrise Vinyasa last week, Ted."

Jenna met Zoe's gaze. The fact that Keanu's real name was Ted like *Bill and Ted's Excellent Adventure*, one of Keanu Reeves' other films, was just too funny, and they both picked up on it immediately.

"I missed you guys, too. I was up all night studying and needed to catch a few Z's before my exam."

"Ted's getting his doctorate in astrophysics. Did I get that right?"

"Totally, Kath. I'll be there for class next week. Catch ya later." Ted turned to leave but stopped in front of Jenna. "Did that guy find you?"

"What guy?"

"Some dude. He came in asking about you. I told him you were right across the street. I figured he was a friend of yours."

A prickling sensation crept down Jenna's spine. "I don't really know anyone in Langley Park."

Zoe pointed an ice cream filled spoon at her. "Jenna, you did go to school nearby. Maybe somebody just recognized you. You're in the Midwest. People around here are friendly like that."

Jenna nodded, but she wasn't convinced.

As Ted walked across the street, Zoe looked at her mother. "Are you serious? That guy's getting his doctorate in astrophysics?"

"Yes, he's such a sweet boy."

Holding onto her bike, Jenna turned to Zoe and Kathy. "Thank you so much for letting me join you for ice cream. I'll let you get back to your day together."

"Are you heading out so soon?" Zoe asked, licking the last of the mint chip off her spoon.

Before Jenna could respond, Ben stood and reached for Kate's sticky hand. "We'll head back with you," he said, his voice neutral, revealing nothing. Then, in a softer tone, added, "Say goodbye to Grandma and Aunt Zoe, Jellybean."

"Are you all right? You look a little freaked out," Zoe asked, touching Jenna's arm.

"I'm fine, really," Jenna said as much to herself as to Zoe.

But before Jenna could say anything else, she heard Kate calling, "Come on, Jenna! I'll race you home."

"Stop at the corner, Bean," Ben directed as his daughter bounded up the street.

Jenna walked next to Ben, glad her bike was between them. She didn't know what to say so she went to her default with this man—verbal overload.

"Kate seems like an amazing kid, but I'm sure you already know that. She has your smile. Your real smile, not the one you usually..." she trailed off, mentally cementing her lips together.

They continued walking in silence. Kate would run ahead, and then she'd stop and wait at the corner until Jenna and her father caught up. After the second block of walking in silence, Ben spoke, his gaze trained on his daughter. "You were up early."

She heard his words, but it took a moment for her to understand. "I didn't mean to disturb you."

"You didn't disturb me."

His words hung in the air as they strolled up the street. After a few steps, they both started speaking at the same time.

"I could start working with Kate today."

"How often do you run?"

They laughed, each smiling nervously at their overlapping words. The tension that existed between them seemed to wane a bit.

"I've been running for a long time. I started about ten years ago when I was in Kentucky."

"Is that how it works? You go from city to city for your job?"

"That's right. I spend about two years training teachers and working with students. And then I move on to the next school."

"You don't mind the moving?"

"I love my work, wherever it takes me."

"Is that what you tell people?" he asked, a bit of sarcasm lacing his words.

Jenna stopped. "What kind of question is that?"

"I'd just think you'd want more."

She stared at him. There was a glint in his eye. Did he enjoy trying to set her off? She parted her lips to speak. She wanted to tell him to mind his own business. She wanted to tell him she was perfectly happy with the life she had built for herself.

Ben barely remembered her at all. He had no right to any opinion regarding her life. He was getting under her skin, and that had to stop. Detached and indifferent was the way she protected her heart. She closed her mouth. She wasn't going to give him the satisfaction of knowing he'd upset her.

Kate came running back to them. "Keys please, Daddy."

Ben handed the house keys to his daughter then put his hand on the seat of the bike. "I haven't told Kate that you'll be working with her yet. She's been very resistant to tutors in the past."

Grateful for the change of subject, Jenna looked down at Ben's hand, suddenly recalling how it felt when it was wrapped around hers.

Don't even think about that. He doesn't even remember you.

"We'll take it one step at a time. Let me get my things, and I'll knock on your door in about fifteen minutes."

JENNA SMOOTHED the pleats of her skirt. She released a breath and knocked on the French doors, but nobody answered. She knocked again and peered into the kitchen through the glass. The pile of workbooks, once nicely stacked, now looked as if someone pushed them off the counter in one fell swoop.

A serious-faced Ben finally met her at the door. His posture was rigid.

"Hey," she said, inwardly cringing for sounding so unprofessional. She had to stop letting her memories of this man get the better of her.

Ben glanced into her tote bag. She had all the usual teacher tools like books and paper. But she also had some unconventional items like puppets and a toy telephone. Ben's pinched expression softened, but then a high-pitched wail rang through the house, and his whole body tightened.

"No, Daddy! I hate reading! I hate it! I won't do it! You can't make me!"

"Kate locked herself in the bathroom when I told her you were coming over to help her with reading."

Jenna gave him her best teacher smile. "That's all right. I can work with six-year-olds locked in bathrooms."

Raising an eyebrow, Ben gave her a skeptical look. But his face was also riddled with worry and exasperation.

The bathroom was situated under the staircase just past the entrance to the kitchen. It was easy to find. Jenna just had to follow the sounds of Kate's yelling and crying. She lowered herself to the ground and sat on the hardwood floor directly in front of the bathroom door.

"What are you doing?" Ben asked, looking even more frustrated. But Jenna raised her index finger to her lips and signaled for him to be quiet.

Sitting crossed-legged and leaning against the bathroom door, Jenna selected a book and started to read aloud. Kate continued crying and yelling, but after she'd read only a few lines of text, the little girl quieted.

Jenna had chosen to read the book *Amazing Grace* by Mary Hoffman, a favorite with all the children she worked with and the perfect book to engage Kate.

The story was about a little girl named Grace who loved listening to stories and acting them out, often in costume. Thinking back to Kate in her Darth Vader get-up, she decided this book would be a good place to start.

As Jenna continued reading, she heard a thud from inside the bathroom. Kate had jumped. She must have been standing on the toilet or sitting on the sink. Jenna smiled as she heard little steps and then, looking at the space between the bottom of the door and the wood floor, she watched the light shift and saw little fingers poking out. Kate was stretching her fingers under the door trying to reach Jenna's hand resting nearby.

Jenna moved her fingers, and then they were touching, Kate's little fingertips on hers. As she began to read again, she glanced up to see Ben staring at her with a look of disbelief on his face. She gave him a knowing smile and finished reading the last page.

The story ends with Grace being cast in her class play as Peter Pan even though she's a girl. Children loved how Grace was able to achieve her goal by working hard and believing in herself, and Jenna often chose this book to engage nervous or anxious students.

She closed the book but didn't move her fingers from where they met Kate's. It was quiet for several minutes as they sat there, Jenna leaning against one side of the door and Kate leaning against the other.

Ben hadn't moved either. He was still observing her intently. Over the years, Jenna had done hundreds of teaching demonstrations, and she never felt self-conscious. But today, with Ben watching, she felt his eyes on her. She wasn't able to block him out. And somewhere deep inside, she liked knowing he was there.

Soon the tiny fingers disappeared from under the door, and Jenna heard Kate moving to her feet.

"Do I have to do the workbooks?" Kate's squeak of a voice asked from behind the door.

"Nope, I don't have any workbooks."

"If I do a good job, can we play hide-and-seek after?"

Jenna smiled at the sweet request and glanced up at Ben. He nodded his approval. "It's a deal," she said, her gaze still locked with his.

11

Kate murmured under her breath, enthusiastically using magnetic letters to spell rhyming words. Jenna brought the tutoring session to a close, and a warmth filled her chest. Working with children never got old, and the challenging cases always held a special place in her heart.

"I usually count first when Daddy and I play hide-and-seek," Kate said as she helped Jenna put the magnetic letters back into the bag.

"Is that right?" Jenna asked.

"Daddy says no hiding in the basement and no leaving the house."

"Leaving the house?" Jenna asked and met Ben's gaze.

"Kate had the idea to go hide behind the fountain in front of The Scoop Ice Cream Parlor."

Jenna held back a chuckle. "Oh, no!"

"Luckily, she left the front door wide open, and I was able to intervene."

"We still got ice cream, right, Daddy?" Kate added.

Ben gave a conciliatory groan. "Yes, Jellybean, we still had ice cream."

"All right. I think I've got it. No basement and no going outside."

"You got it, Jenna! Daddy, you're playing, right?"

"Okay, Bean. Start counting and no peeking."

As Kate counted, Jenna watched Ben out of the corner of her eye. This was the most at ease she had seen him. His dark hair was a bit disheveled, and his eyes were bright and lively. He loved his daughter, that was as plain as day to see.

At first, Jenna thought some of this enthusiasm was meant for her, but it wasn't. Ben was simply a relieved parent, encouraged to see his daughter doing well. It would do her no good to think his smile was for anyone but Kate.

"Daddy!" Kate yelled, temporarily halting her count, hands pressed to her eyes. "First hide-and-seek and then sardines."

"All right, Jellybean, but then dinner."

"Jenna!" Kate yelled, overcompensating with volume for her temporary lack of sight.

"Yes, Kate?"

"Sardines is like reverse hide-and-seek. One person hides, and everybody tries to find them. Do you know that game?"

"I do," Jenna answered.

Kate resumed her count, and Ben gestured for Jenna to follow him. He walked through the narrow hallway and into the dining room where two columns of long hanging drapes framed a large picture window. Ben hid behind one of the columns of the curtain while she followed suit on the other side.

Enveloped in the thick fabric, she listened to Kate count. Now in the sixties, Jenna guessed she was going to count all the way to one hundred. Her teacher's brain clicked on, and she was pleased to see Kate's math skills seemed to be right on grade level.

As she stood quietly, her hands went to her long hair. A nervous habit for years, she gathered the strands to one side and began to braid. She used an elastic hair tie she kept on her wrist and tied off the end without thinking.

She glanced over to where Ben was hiding only a few steps away. He was watching her. She wrapped the tail of the braid around her finger. Ben swallowed hard. He glanced up and met her gaze. They stared at each other. There was something in his eyes. His gaze flicked back to her braid. She took a step toward him but stopped as Kate called out, "ONE HUNDRED," at the top of her lungs.

Kate's feet skittered up the steps followed by a series of slams and bangs as she went room to room. Moments later, the footsteps thumped back down the stairs. Kate was talking to herself and giving a play-by-play of where she was going and interjecting audible groans of disappointment every time she'd found a hiding spot empty.

Finally, she made it to the dining room, and her frantic pace slowed as she crept forward, one tiptoed step at a time. She surreptitiously pulled back the curtain with all the elaborate drama a six-year-old could offer, revealing first her father and then moving to the opposite side to uncover Jenna, laughing and squealing the entire time.

Jenna watched, a stupid grin on her face, as Ben lifted Kate up and tossed her into the air. A shiver crept up her spine.

Being with Ben and Kate felt so natural.

"Can we play sardines now, Daddy?"

"All right, Bean. One game of sardines."

"Jenna, you hide first. Daddy and I will find you."

Kate tugged on Ben's hand, pulling him back toward the kitchen. Looking over his shoulder, he asked, "Do you have plans?"

A smile lit her face. "No, why?"

Did Ben feel it, too?

"I just didn't want to keep you from anything," he answered.

Her heart sank, and the dreary soundtrack in her mind clicked on.

You mean nothing to him.

BEN RELEASED A TIGHT BREATH. His response disappointed her. A pang of regret surged through him, but he ignored it. The years of losing baby after baby and then Sara's suicide had left him paralyzed. He couldn't even consider the idea of falling in love again. There was no place for that in his life. He was a father and an architect, and that had to be enough.

But something was changing inside of him. He could feel it.

The orderly life he'd constructed didn't seem as solid anymore, and that had everything to do with Jenna.

As Kate counted, he listened to the sound of Jenna's footsteps above him. He heard her at the top of the steps. The old Tudor had its telltale creaks, and then the sound faded as she entered one of the front bedrooms.

Finishing the count, Kate whispered for him to check upstairs while she looked downstairs. He could suggest Kate check her room and let his daughter find Jenna first, but he said nothing and nodded as Kate went to search the pantry. He walked up the stairs, and with every step, he wondered what the hell he was doing.

He entered Kate's room as the late afternoon sun streamed through the window. The closet door was slightly open, and Ben gave two soft taps to it with his knuckle. Pulling the door open, he found Jenna standing inside the small space among his daughter's dresses. She stepped to the side to make room for him. The closet was a tight fit for two adults. Inches separated their bodies.

Jenna gave him a nervous smile and tugged on the end of her braid. He pulled the door shut, the only light now coming from the narrow space between the door and the frame. She dropped her hands and clasped them in front of her, and his gaze went to the end of her braid where it came to rest near her exposed collarbone. Without thinking, he took her braid in his hand. He twisted the strands around his fingers, and his wrist brushed across her smooth skin.

Jenna's breath hitched. Her body inched closer. It was as if they'd traveled back in time to when they were teenagers, their bodies pressed together against that cold creek embankment. He'd wanted to kiss her then, and he still wanted that, now more than ever.

She rested her hands on his biceps, and her touch ignited a flame inside of him. He slid his hand up past her collarbone to the back of her neck and tangled his fingers in her loose braid.

Cradling the back of her head, he tilted it up. Only inches apart, he gazed at Jenna's lips. She gasped as he tightened his grip in her hair, and his cock twitched. She was so warm, her body molded against his as her perfect breasts pressed into his chest. He was hard and so ready, his body wanting to take what his mind wouldn't allow. God, he wanted to kiss her, taste her, rip off her panties and plunge himself deep inside her.

"Ben," Jenna said, barely whispering but loud enough to break through the haze clouding his mind.

He leaned in and rested his forehead against hers. He needed to slow down. If he kept staring at her, he'd lose himself completely. He closed his eyes and inhaled the lavender scent of her hair, the sweet smell doing little to quell his growing need to have her.

She pulled back and met his gaze.

Could she see that he wanted her? Could she see the pain and darkness that lived in his soul?

His hand still in her hair, Ben turned her head, angling it up to meet his lips. He was giving in to his desire and couldn't hold himself back. He wrapped his arm around her, wanting to feel every inch of her lithe frame. He couldn't even count the number of times he'd envisioned this scenario as a teenager. And then, when she didn't come back to school, he'd worried she was just a figment of his imagination, the fantasy girl of a teenage boy.

He brushed his thumb over her bottom lip, and she melted into his touch. Jenna's sweet breath glided across his lips, and his mind barely registered a faint clomping sound. But as the noise grew louder, he came back to himself. It was Kate running up the stairs, the telltale top step's squeak audibly chiding him for his reckless behavior.

Jenna must have heard it, too. Her body tensed, and her hands fell to her sides. Ben eased back, dropping his arm from around her waist, but his treacherous fingers wouldn't release their grasp of her golden hair.

As the door opened, Kate let out an excited whoop. But upon

closer inspection, she looked pointedly at his hand as he tried to untangle it from Jenna's hair.

A few seconds of silence passed then Kate trained her gaze on Jenna. "Will you braid my hair like yours, Jenna? All Daddy can do is a ponytail."

WITH KATE'S WORDS, the spell was broken.

Taking a breath, Jenna moved past Ben, making sure their bodies didn't touch. "Sure, I can braid your hair. Can you get me a brush?"

Kate skipped over to a white dresser and rummaged in the top drawer.

Jenna's heartbeat was racing, and her body ached to be back in Ben's strong arms. Shaking her head, she forced herself to focus on Kate's room as a distraction.

The space was charming with periwinkle walls and a neat, little desk tucked in the corner equipped with an architect's lamp just like the one Jenna had noticed on Ben's desk. Kate's bed had a beautiful quilt crafted in light blues, greens, and yellows. It was the kind of room that welcomed happy memories and sweet dreams. She walked over to Kate's nightstand unable to tear her gaze away from the framed photo sitting prominently among Kate's treasures.

Kate bounded back, bouncing on her bed and landing next to Jenna. "That's my mommy," she said, pointing to the picture of a woman smiling brightly. "Her name is Sara. And that's me," she continued, pointing to the baby in the beautiful brunette's arms. Her tone was matter of fact, and Jenna knew, with Kate losing her mother at such a young age, she probably didn't have many real memories of her.

What had happened to Sara, and why was she taken so young?

Jenna recalled that Zoe had also been uncharacteristically tight-lipped about Ben's deceased wife.

"You have hair just like your mommy," Jenna remarked, doing her best to keep her voice steady.

Kate nodded and sat down in the middle of her bed. Jenna sat behind her, gently working the knots and tangles from the mass of thick chestnut hair.

Kate called her father over. "Daddy, come watch Jenna so you can learn how to braid."

Ben was standing on the far side of the room, and Jenna didn't dare glance up at him.

As Jenna brushed through Kate's hair, her mind went over what did and didn't just happen in the closet. He had reached for her, right? She thought he was going to kiss her. But that didn't matter. She'd let things go too far. She'd let her emotions take over when what she needed to be, now more than ever, was rational and pragmatic.

Ben walked over and bent down to watch her work, and a shiver ran down her spine. She glanced up at him. His eyes were the dark blue of a stormy ocean at night. But he wasn't looking at her. His gaze was trained on his daughter's hair.

Jenna released a steadying breath and finished the braid. From where they were seated on Kate's bed, she could see their reflection in the mirror above the dresser.

She gestured toward the mirror then smoothed Kate's bangs across her forehead. "What do you think?"

The little girl smiled. "I'm pretty like you."

Jenna returned the smile. "Even better. You're pretty like *you*."

"Thank you, Jenna." Kate turned and wrapped her arms around her neck.

"Anytime," Jenna whispered, trying to keep the emotion out of her voice. She had braided many of her students' hair over the last ten years. The little girls used to flock to her, begging to have their hair done by the reading teacher. But there was something different about Kate.

Kate turned her head from side to side, watching the end of the braid whip around like a horse's tail. Then she bounced on the end of the bed and ran from the bedroom and into the hall. "I'm getting a juice box."

Now that they were alone, the tension radiated off of Ben. He started to speak, but Jenna had to stop him.

"You don't need to say anything," she said, rising to her feet. "But I need you to understand something. I went to six high schools in four years, and the memories all kind of blur together. Except, I always remembered that night when we ran through the creek. I know we weren't even friends back then, but I've held on to that memory. Maybe I've been giving off some silly schoolgirl-crush vibe. I know you don't remember me, and I never expected you to. It was a long time ago."

A beat of heavy silence hung in the air.

Jenna glanced at the closet. "I want you to know nothing like that will ever happen again."

She waited for Ben to respond, but he said nothing. His posture was rigid, and his expression was dark and detached as if a switch had turned off inside him, and the vibrant, laughing man who had touched her so tenderly was gone.

12

A thunderstorm rolled in minutes after Jenna left Ben standing in Kate's room. The rain created a barrier between the carriage house and the Tudor, and she had taken solace in the separation. She needed time to sort out her thoughts. She had to forget the moment in the closet with Ben. But when her mind betrayed her with thoughts of his warm hands and blue eyes so full of want, she turned to work.

Summers were almost as busy as the school year. During the summer months, when she wasn't working in a school, she spent her time synthesizing Gwyer reading data and consulting for several educational textbook publishers. The work was tedious and involved quite a bit of research, but she enjoyed the hours spent reading and writing.

She had spent all of Saturday and the better part of Sunday comparing the benefits of small group instruction versus large group instruction when a brisk knock on the carriage house door broke her concentration.

Jenna made it to the bottom of the stairs expecting to see Ben, Kate, or even Zoe and was surprised to see a tall man with a serious expression dressed in uniform.

A Langley Park police officer.

"I'm sorry to bother you, miss. I'm Officer Clayton Stevens. I tried knocking on the door at the main house, but nobody answered. I saw you up in the window when I was checking the perimeter."

"The perimeter? Is everything all right?"

"Does the black SUV parked out front belong to you? The one with the Colorado plates."

"Yes, I just got into town."

The officer nodded. "I was patrolling, and I noticed all your tires looked flat. I'm sorry to tell you this, but when I took a closer look, I saw they'd been slashed."

Jenna's eyes widened.

"Why don't you come with me, miss. We'll write up a report for your insurance."

The officer took a step back. He eyed her bicycle leaning against the side of the carriage house. "Looks like they got your bike, too." He gestured to the rubber shreds littering the ground.

Who would do this?

Jenna had jogged all through the neighborhood and seen many bikes left on porches or leaning on the sides of houses. She wanted to ask Ben about using the garage, but he never used it and always parked on the street in front of the house. The one time she'd ventured to try and open it, she'd found it locked.

She figured he must have his reasons for keeping it off-limits and after their awkward moment in Kate's closet, she wasn't about to ask him for anything, especially not access to a garage he clearly wanted to remain unused.

Jenna went to her bike and crouched down, picking up a few rubbery strands. It looked as if someone had taken a hacksaw to the tires. She glanced up at the officer and watched as he turned away from her and called in on his radio.

She stood and started to follow the officer when she heard the squeal of tires. Within seconds, Ben was rushing toward her with Kate in his arms.

"Jenna, are you all right?"

Kate stared at the policeman, her bottom lip trembling.

Not wanting to frighten the little girl, Jenna gestured to the officer. "This nice policeman saw that the tires on my car were flat. He stopped to tell me so I could get them fixed. Wasn't that kind of him?"

Kate nodded, but Ben didn't look convinced that this was the only reason a Langley Park police officer had turned up on his doorstep.

Ben set his daughter down. "Kate, why don't you head inside and get our movie started. I'll be in right after I help Jenna with her car."

Kate glanced at her father and then to Officer Stevens who gave her a reassuring smile. After the little girl had made it safely inside the house, Ben met the officer's gaze and shook his hand. "I'm Ben Fisher. This is my home. What's going on?"

The officer filled Ben in on the slashed car and bike tires.

"Did you see anyone?" Ben asked.

"No, sir, I didn't. I was doing a patrol of the neighborhood, and the tires caught my eye."

Ben nodded as he scanned his property.

Officer Stevens turned to Jenna. "Miss?"

"It's Jenna, Jenna Lewis."

"All right, Ms. Lewis. I patrolled a few blocks from the house before I came to your door. I wanted to check and see if any other vehicles in the area had been vandalized, but I didn't see anything out of the ordinary. I called in to see if there had been any acts of vandalism reported recently, but dispatch said there'd been no reports of any destruction of property in weeks. As of right now, it looks like you may have been targeted."

Ben looked at her, a mix of anger and concern in his eyes.

"Ms. Lewis, is there anyone you can think of who may have wanted to damage your property?"

Jenna wrapped her arms around her body. "I don't really know anyone here. I've only been in town a week."

"Aidan Hadley?" Ben asked, meeting her gaze.

He was right. She had endured two run-ins with Hadley in the short time she'd been in Langley Park.

Ben's gaze softened. "But how would he know your name or where you were staying? Sam wouldn't tell him."

"He might know my name. Yesterday, when we were all at The Scoop, Ted brought my bike over and mentioned that a guy had come into the shop and asked about me. Ted may have inadvertently given him my name. I'm not sure. Plus, I've gone for a run almost every day since I arrived in Langley Park. Anyone could have seen me coming or going from the carriage house."

"Who's Hadley?" Stevens asked, taking out a small notepad.

"I thought he was just a creep. I was having dinner at Park Tavern, and I declined some drinks he tried to send over to me the first night I arrived in town. I found him waiting for me when I came out of the bathroom. He grabbed me. He tried to force himself on me, but I was able to use a self-defense move to make him let go."

Stevens frowned. "Did you file a report?"

She shook her head. "No. Sam, the owner of Park Tavern, kicked him out. I figured he was just a nasty drunk."

Officer Stevens nodded as he wrote. "I know Ted over at The Pedal. He's a good guy. He helped me get through calculus back in high school. I'll ask him about Hadley. Anything else seem out of the ordinary?"

Jenna's cheeks heated with embarrassment. "I went for a run around Lake Boley early Friday morning. Someone threw rocks at me while I was running on one of the dirt trails off the main path."

Ben's eyes widened.

"Did you report this incident?" Stevens asked.

"No, I figured it was kids playing a prank or something."

"You should report things like that, Ms. Lewis. It's why we're here."

Jenna twisted her sleeve. "You're right, officer. I didn't want to overreact."

"We'd rather you overreact. It's better to be safe and call it in," Officer Stevens said as chatter began streaming over his radio. "I need to head back to my cruiser and write this up. I'll come and knock on your door when I'm ready to take your official statement, Ms. Lewis."

"She'll be in the house with me," Ben said as the officer nodded and walked back to his patrol car.

Jenna turned to Ben and tried to keep her expression neutral. "I'll be just fine on my own."

"From where I'm standing, it doesn't look like you're doing fine."

Jenna stood there, mouth open, not knowing whether she should slap him or be glad she didn't have to be alone. As much as Ben's words stung, he did have a point.

"All right. I'll come inside until we're finished with Officer Stevens. But not a minute longer."

Ben gestured toward the house, and Jenna straightened her back as she walked, clasping her trembling hands in front of her body. She didn't want him to see how shaken she was by all this. She couldn't be weak. She had only herself to rely on, and if it meant pretending to be brave, then that's what she would do.

Once inside the house, she looked in the den and noticed Kate cuddled up asleep on the couch.

Ben went over and picked her up, and Kate instinctively wrapped her limbs around her father, placing her little head on his shoulder, her dark hair falling in waves over her sleeping face.

"I'm going to put her to bed. Don't leave," he added, pinning her with his gaze.

Jenna didn't give him an answer but walked over to the kitchen table and sat down with her arms folded.

This action seemed to appease him, and he continued up the stairs.

"Bossy," she whispered under her breath. Anger was good. Anger kept her from thinking about his hands, his lips...

Stop it. Right now. That man cares nothing for you.

Ben returned to the kitchen and sat down across from her, pulling her from her thoughts. She watched him from the corner of her eye. He looked like he'd stepped out of a Lands' End catalog in his button down shirt with the sleeves rolled up exposing his muscular forearms. He was so handsome with his angular features and dark hair that she had to physically turn her head away from him to avert her gaze.

She shook her head. Pining over Ben Fisher wasn't an option. Over the weekend, she decided she had to put distance between them. She would continue to tutor Kate while she was in Langley Park, but that would be the extent of her time spent in this house.

"Is Kate feeling unwell?" she asked, telling herself she was only conversing with the parent of a student she was working with, nothing more.

"She's just tired. We were at my mom and Neil's house. Kate was gardening with my mom all afternoon. It always wipes her out."

"It's good to wait until after Mother's Day," Jenna said as she craned her neck to look out the window.

"I'm not sure what you mean."

"Gardening. My aunt always waited until after Mother's Day to plant her flower boxes. Something about the weather, I think."

Ben nodded, and they lapsed into silence.

"Neil's your stepfather?" she asked, internally chastising herself for the slip. These kinds of questions didn't help maintain distance.

"I figured you knew. Zoe didn't tell you?"

Jenna shook her head.

"Zoe and I are half-siblings. My mom married Neil when I was four, and Zoe came along shortly after."

"I wondered why they were all Steins, and you're a Fisher," Jenna replied, then gave Ben an embarrassed smile.

He chuckled, his expression softening. "My father passed away when I was two. My mother was a social worker at North Kansas City Hospital. She met Neil there, and the rest is history."

"I'm so sorry, Ben. I didn't mean to pry."

"It's okay. Neil's a good man. I couldn't have asked for a better stepfather."

Jenna twisted her sleeve. "I'm glad. Zoe and your mother are so kind. I can only imagine your stepfather is a pretty amazing person, too," she added, not sure if that was an appropriate thing to say.

Ben nodded, and another pocket of silence swallowed them up.

He seemed just as unsure as she did about navigating this conversation.

A sharp knock at the front door reminded her that she wasn't sitting in Ben's kitchen to make small talk. Someone had maliciously vandalized her car and her bike.

Officer Stevens had completed the paperwork, and Jenna spent the next few minutes answering some routine questions and providing the officer with her contact information.

As Jenna and Ben walked the officer out, Stevens turned and gestured to the carriage house. "I'd suggest parking your vehicles and bicycles in the garage from now on. You don't want to make it easy for the bad guys."

A beat of silence passed. Jenna glanced a Ben. His posture was rigid, and a bead of perspiration lined his top lip.

Ben released a breath and ran his hand across his mouth. "I agree, officer," said with a slight shake to his voice. "We'll start using the garage."

"And, Miss Lewis, try sticking to the main Boley trail when you're exercising outdoors. Or better yet, you could join a running group. Langley Park is a safe place to live, but you can never be too careful."

"Of course, officer. I'll be more careful."

Officer Stevens gave them a nod and returned to his vehicle. Jenna watched as the patrol car disappeared down the sleepy, tree-lined street. Her mind raced with everything she needed to do.

She would need to have the car towed to a repair shop. The SUV would need new tires, and, hopefully, Ted could bring her Yeti Beti back to life. She had lived the last fourteen years of her life free of drama and chaos, and now each day seemed to bring some new catastrophe.

She rubbed her hands over her face. It felt as if she'd lived a thousand lives in just a week. Had it been only a matter of days since she'd seen Nick? Her world had been turned upside down, and fatigue washed over her body.

Out of the corner of her eye, she noticed Ben with a stern expression on his face.

"Why didn't you say anything to me about the rocks when you were peeking in my office Friday morning?"

His harsh tone ignited something fierce in her soul. She turned on him, eyes blazing. "Peeking inside your office? I wasn't peeking at anything. I had just finished the run from hell when I finally made it to the town center. I was in a part of town that I'd never been to before, and that's when I saw the sign for Fisher Designs."

Taking a breath, she took a step closer to Ben. "And you know what? I liked seeing all those before and after pictures you have posted on the glass. There's something inside me that's really happy to know you've built a successful business. All these years later, I had always hoped you were living a good life somewhere. And again, we're back to the humiliating fact that you meant something to me, while I never meant anything to you."

BEN COULDN'T LISTEN to her go on. He hated that she thought she meant nothing to him, but he didn't have the words to tell her he remembered everything, her touch, her smell, and how desperately he had wanted to kiss her, taste her. He watched her, cheeks flushed and eyes flashing, and couldn't stop himself.

He closed the distance between them, cupped her face in his hands, and kissed her. The kiss started off awkwardly. He was horribly out of practice, and she was midway through a rant, but as their mouths and teeth gnashed together, their lips and tongues soon found a rhythm.

Jenna's hands rested on his chest, and she melted into his kiss. But all too soon, hot tears streaked down her cheeks. Ben pulled back and tried to meet her gaze, but Jenna pushed him away with a hard shove.

Wiping away the remaining tears, she took two shaky steps away from him, then turned and ran back to the carriage house.

Ben stood in the driveway. It was better to let her go. He was glad she'd run from him. Jenna remembered the old Ben, the man he was before Sara crushed his heart. She didn't know the shell of a man he was now. Jenna deserved better, but that kiss told him she wanted him just as much as he wanted her.

Pull it together, Fisher. Thoughts like that don't help anyone.

In the darkness, he saw the dim glow of a lamp from inside the carriage house. She was safe inside. He started to make his way into the house when the sound of an engine pulled him from his thoughts. He looked down the darkened street and watched as a pair of tail lights disappeared.

13

Jenna paced the length of the driveway. Monday morning had come, and her car and bike were still there waiting to be repaired.

She spent the morning having her car towed to a local mechanic's shop. Now she found herself standing at the end of Ben's driveway waiting for Zoe, unable to tear her gaze from the spot where Ben had kissed her last night.

She wanted to resist him. But when his lips met hers, it was like two tornadoes coming together. A wild storm of attraction, desire, and need all tangling her emotions. Jenna touched her bottom lip where he'd nipped and sucked, and she could almost feel the heat of his breath.

"Hey, daydream believer!"

Dropping her hand, Jenna looked up to see a dusty Jeep Wrangler. Zoe was leaning over the passenger seat moving her hand back and forth as if she was trying to wake her from a hypnotist's trance.

Zoe called earlier that morning, wanting to wish her luck with her first family therapy session. Jenna told her about the events of the previous night, leaving out the kiss with Ben. And, Zoe being Zoe, she insisted on driving her to the hospital.

Jenna didn't know what to make of her situation with Ben. Between the vandalism and her concerns regarding her mother, she tried to push the kiss out of her mind, but his taste still lingered on her tongue.

She hopped in Zoe's car and settled herself in the front seat. "Thanks for the ride. I was dreading walking in this heat."

It was the end of May, the last week of school for the children of Langley Park, and temperatures were already in the upper eighties.

"Heat? Just wait until July. And you're welcome. I was surprised Ben didn't offer to take you."

"I didn't want to bother him." Jenna looked away. If she met Zoe's gaze, her friend would see right through her.

Putting the car in gear, Zoe began the short drive to the hospital. "You sure have made an impression on Kate. She talked about you the entire time we were at my parents' place on Sunday."

Jenna smiled. Kate was a wonderful little girl. Then her thoughts slipped back to Ben. Did he like hearing his daughter talk about her? Could he remember what she tasted like, too?

She shook her head. She couldn't let her mind go there. She folded her hands in her lap, trying to gain control. "Kate is one great kid," she said, allowing herself to only focus on the little girl.

"You should come to my mom and dad's place next Sunday. They're just on the east side of Langley Park."

That was not what she was hoping Zoe would say. After what had happened with Ben, she couldn't imagine going to his childhood home.

"I really can't. I have quite a bit of work."

"You sound like Ben. You like to work, right?" she asked, pulling into the Midwest Psychiatric Center's parking lot.

Jenna raised an eyebrow. "I guess you could say that."

"Great! You can help me work the Park Tavern booth at the Langley Park Festival this Saturday."

Jenna started to protest, but Zoe cut in. "All we do is give out popsicles and cookies. There's live music, games for the kids, and then fireworks over the lake. You'd be doing Sam and me a giant favor."

What could she say to that? Zoe and Sam had been more than kind to her since her arrival in Langley Park.

"Okay. Of course, I'd love to help," she said, trying her best not to look too resigned.

"Excellent! Everything happens in the Langley Park Botanic Gardens and around Lake Boley. This is going to be so fun, you'll see."

JENNA WAVED as Zoe's car pulled out of the parking lot. She stared at the psychiatric center's entrance. A bead of sweat trickled down her back, not from the heat but from nerves. She took a deep breath and entered the building.

She signed in at the reception desk and was handed a visitor badge. She looked around the lobby and noticed a heavyset, middle-aged woman standing by the window and a younger man, maybe a college student, staring at his smartphone. They were wearing the same visitor badge as she was just given.

She finished fastening the badge to her top as Eric entered the lobby, and he gestured for her to join him. "Elaine, Dan! It's good to see you. This is Jenna. She'll be joining our group today."

Elaine shook her hand, and Dan gave her a quick nod. Were they as nervous as she was? She tucked those thoughts away and smiled with what she hoped wasn't a hollow expression as Eric led them back into a large room where several chairs were arranged in a circle.

Jenna glanced at her watch. It was five past one. She had fifty-five more minutes to go. Just as she was about to launch into a silent pep talk, she glanced up and saw her mother, an older gentleman, and a young girl walking into the room all smiling and chatting.

Should she hug her mother? Were they expected to sit next to each other?

Luckily, Eric addressed the group. "Welcome everyone. Let's all find a seat in the circle."

Judith walked over to Jenna, smiling in that same disconcerting way as she had during their last meeting.

"JJ, you look so pretty. Oh, my! Another pair of fancy shoes. How nice for you!"

Jenna glanced down at her Marc Jacobs ballet flats and felt a flash of anger. Judith rarely spent a dime on her growing up, choosing to spend lavishly on herself and Travis. Trips, luxury cars, and designer clothes were her mother's staples.

Now a grown woman, Jenna knew there was no reason to feel guilty about purchasing nice things. She, unlike her mother, worked hard for the things she had. But her mother had a way of making her feel guilty about her very existence.

Judith smiled at the older gentleman settling in next to Elaine. "Bob, didn't I tell you my JJ was a beauty?"

"Yes, you did, Judith. She takes after her mother."

Jenna stood there looking at her mother, unsure of what to do. She didn't recognize this woman. Judith was acting like a loving and attentive parent when she had been the polar opposite.

But fourteen years apart was a long time.

Maybe her mother wanted to heal those past wounds. Maybe commenting on her appearance and footwear was the only way Judith knew how to bridge the gap that existed between them.

Eric tapped on the back of two chairs and gestured to Jenna and Judith. Eric opened the meeting, and the young woman, Dan's sister, Amber, addressed the group. Amber only had a few more days of treatment left, and much of the discussion revolved around her and her plans for the future.

Jenna couldn't deny the group members were kind and seemed supportive of one another. Even her mother offered encouraging words, leaving Jenna dumbstruck.

"Let's open this up to the group. Does anyone want to share any concerns they may be feeling about leaving treatment?" Eric asked.

The room was quiet for a moment, and just when Jenna thought she'd been able to make it out of the session without calling any attention to herself, her mother's Alabama drawl filled the void.

"Well, yes, Eric. I have some worries."

Everyone's gaze fell on Judith.

"I've shared with you all that because of my addiction, I did not surround myself with the best people."

The group nodded, listening intently to Judith's every word.

"I'm not sure what I'm going to do after my treatment ends. I'm so afraid of being on my own. No one, not even my own family, wants me."

The group's focus shifted away from Judith and onto her.

Swallowing hard, Jenna turned to her mother. "Mom, I'm here. I can help you get back on your feet after treatment."

"You are such a good girl. I can't tell you how relieved that makes me feel." Judith reached out and patted her knee.

The contact felt foreign and gave Jenna anything but relief.

Jenna met her mother's gaze, and Judith's gentle pat became a squeeze. The group moved on to another topic, but Judith leaned in close to her. "You know, you're old enough now to do whatever you want with your trust."

The comment caught Jenna off guard. But her mother was right. Shortly after her thirty-second birthday several weeks ago, she had received a notification from the trust attorney telling her exactly what her mother had just disclosed.

Before her thirty-second birthday, she could have taken a monthly stipend from the trust, like her mother did, which Jenna had vehemently declined. She didn't want a single penny from a family who wanted to pretend she didn't exist.

Jenna looked at Eric. He must have seen the uncertainty in her eyes.

"We need to be mindful of the time," he said, glancing down at his watch. "I think this was a very productive session, and Jenna, we are so glad you were able to join us."

Eric continued speaking, bringing the session to a close, but Jenna couldn't concentrate on his words. She kept thinking about her mother's comment. As the group members walked toward the exit, Judith held on to Jenna's forearm.

"What is it, Mom?"

"You've been smart with your trust fund, right, sweet girl? You'd be willin' to let me have a little bit, just to get goin'? I only have you now, JJ."

Jenna's mind was spinning. There was too much to think about, and she couldn't get into a discussion about her trust today.

She took a step back. "Mom, we don't need to get into all that right now. I'm here, and I'm going to help you. Just work on getting better. I'm proud of you for leaving Travis. He wasn't a good man. You know that now, don't you?"

"I do," Judith said, gifting her with a tight smile.

But there was something in her mother's eyes that Jenna couldn't read. Was it anger? Was it embarrassment? She couldn't tell.

JENNA LEFT THE PSYCHIATRIC CENTER. She walked down to the Boley Lake trail then headed back toward the Langley Park town center. Anyone trying to throw a rock at her head now would have a difficult time escaping in the bright afternoon sunshine. She needed to think, and the tree-lined path dotted with mothers pushing strollers and midday joggers was the perfect place to try and piece out what had just happened in the group therapy session.

Jenna ran through the things her mother had said. Could it be possible Judith just needed money? Or was her mother just worried about trying to start a new life without Travis? As far as she knew, her mother never worked a day in her life. Maybe the thought of holding down a real job scared her. She wanted to be understanding of her mother's situation, and then she remembered the quiet game.

She was very young, maybe three years old, when her mother had come into the farmhouse while Aunt Ginny was asleep on the porch. Nestled in her favorite rocker overlooking the sunflowers in her front garden, Aunt Ginny could sleep soundly for hours. Jenna was supposed to be napping in her room, but she'd woken up early and gone to the kitchen for a drink.

She was surprised when she saw a pretty young woman opening and closing the tins and jars lining the shelves.

Jenna loved the sounds of jars popping open and the ping of the tin lids being placed quietly on the counter. She started to speak, but the young woman shushed her.

"I'm your mama, sweetheart. I brought you a lollipop. I'll give it to you if you can be real quiet."

It was like a game. She could still see her mother's smiling face as she uncovered a wad of bills from behind a stack of cookbooks.

Her aunt never spoke of Judith. But after the kitchen was ransacked, Aunt Ginny added a line to their nightly prayers.

Dear Lord, we pray for our Judith Jo and ask You to help her find the righteous path.

JUDITH JO LEWIS had been the first and only child of Henry and Adele Lewis. Henry's family had made a fortune in Alabama's oil industry after World War II, and Adele was the lovely southern belle who had caught the young oil magnate's eye. The pair, who started out as Mobile society's most devoted couple, soon met with great tragedy.

Adele died only hours after giving birth to Judith, and Henry was left to raise a child he would never forgive for taking away the love of his life.

As Judith grew older, her beauty mimicked that of Adele's. It was a constant reminder to Henry of his great loss, and as Judith grew, so did Henry's disdain for her.

Rarely interacting with her father, Judith had been raised by a string of nannies. She was a willful child, desperate for attention, and it was rare for any caregiver to last more than a week.

Henry remarried when Judith was ten years old and built a new family with his second wife. By the time Judith was sixteen, her father had four children from his second marriage and no desire to acknowledge his oldest daughter from his first. The only way for Judith to gain her father's attention was by embarrassing the family, and so began the drinking, the drug use, and running around with those her father deemed unsuitable.

At seventeen, an out of control Judith found herself pregnant. If an out of wedlock teen pregnancy wasn't enough to upset Henry Lewis, the fact that his promiscuous daughter didn't know who the father of her unborn child was, became the straw that broke the camel's back.

Judith was sent to live with her mother's aunt, Ginny Barker, on a small farm in Kansas. Aunt Ginny was a fair, no-nonsense woman who had continued working and managing her farm twenty years after her husband passed away. While Ginny didn't condone Judith's behavior, she had loved Adele and wanted to help her daughter.

A month after Judith's arrival, Jenna Jo Lewis was born. A week later, Judith packed up in the night and left, unable to cope with the responsibility of having to care for a newborn. Judith only returned when she needed money, but soon she wanted more.

No longer satisfied with the small bills hidden away in Ginny's tins, Judith contacted her father and demanded money. At first, Henry ignored his daughter's calls and letters. But when she threatened to reveal her situation to his conservative business partners, he acquiesced to her demands.

Henry Lewis, wanting nothing to do with his daughter, created a trust fund from which Judith would receive a monthly allowance under the provision she would never contact him or his family again. Upon turning twenty-one, Jenna learned a trust had been created for her with the same conditions as her mother's. No contact under any circumstances.

JENNA SAT on a bench nestled near an old oak and watched the people passing by on the Boley Lake trail. Her gaze was drawn to a mother pushing a stroller. She listened as the woman spoke to the baby, pointing out this tree and that bird. Jenna smiled as she heard the child babbling back.

As the mother and child passed by, she thought about Judith and what it must have felt like to have her own father pay her to stay away. She let out an audible breath. She knew what she had to do. It was time to put aside the anger and disappointment. Maybe, just maybe, she and her mother could build something new that wasn't marred by the past.

14

Ben walked back to his office pushing Jenna's mountain bike outfitted with two new tires. Jenna would probably be angry and tell him he had overstepped his boundaries by taking it upon himself to have her bike fixed, but he needed to do it. He knew she wouldn't ask him for help, and he couldn't overcome this primal need to keep her safe.

As he wheeled the bicycle inside, his office manager raised an eyebrow.

"It's not mine, Mrs. G," Ben said, giving the gray-haired woman a look that said drop it.

"Is that so?" Mrs. G said, raising an eyebrow.

Ben pushed the bike into the small conference room and rested it against the wall. She knew him too well. That was the curse and the blessing of having your teacher become your office manager.

Rosemary Giacopazzi was Ben's beloved third-grade teacher. When his business started growing, he couldn't manage both the design and day-to-day business side of things. A chance encounter with the retired "Mrs. G" seven years ago, started a conversation that ended with her working in his office. And to this day, decades after leaving third grade, Ben still couldn't call her Rosemary; to him, she'd always be Mrs. G.

Ben walked out of the conference room and over to Mrs. G's desk. Two young architects worked diligently as the sound of keyboards clicking and blueprints rustling filled the workspace.

"I'm guessing you haven't eaten," Mrs. G said, setting a takeout bag from Park Tavern on her desk and nudging it toward him.

"I was going to scarf down some Pop Tarts Kate left in my bag."

"Benjamin! What am I going to do with you?"

Ben gave her an appreciative smile and took a bite of the chicken club sandwich, but he stopped eating when he saw Jenna walking across the street.

At first glance, all he saw was a beautiful woman. But then he noticed she was wringing her hands as she walked. She was upset. That was her tell, her hands, just like back in high school.

"That one's hard to miss," Mrs. G said, nodding toward Jenna.

Ben put down the sandwich, unable to pull his gaze away from her when he caught a glimpse of a white truck driving down the street. The vehicle stayed just out of Jenna's line of sight, but close enough to watch her every move.

"What in the world is that truck doing?" Mrs. G asked. "I thought he was just looking for parking, but look, Benjamin, he's already passed two good spots."

Something was off. Ben opened the door and stood outside his office trying to get a better look at the driver. Jenna and the truck were now almost half a block past him. He walked up the street, keeping both Jenna and the truck in sight.

She was almost to Baneberry Drive where he was certain she would turn right and head north toward the Tudor. He picked up his pace. The truck sped up and signaled to turn right even before Jenna had made it to Baneberry.

Now he knew something strange was going on. The driver seemed to anticipate Jenna's every move. The vehicle's tinted driver side window was cracked about an inch, allowing a steady stream of cigarette smoke to escape. Ben couldn't tell if it was a man or a woman driving. His walk changed to a jog. He had to get her attention. "Jenna! Stop!"

As if awoken from a dream, Jenna stopped and looked toward him and the white truck. In a clumsy maneuver, the truck overcorrected to the left, abandoning the right turn, and swerved haphazardly back into traffic.

A gray sedan slammed on its brakes, screeching and swerving to stop from rear-ending the erratic truck. With a loud honk, the sedan allowed the reckless vehicle back into traffic. Back in control, the truck gunned its engine, tearing down the road and away from Jenna and Langley Park.

Ben ran across the street. "Are you all right?"

"What was that?" she asked, her worried brown eyes looking to Ben for answers. She'd gone pale and was wringing her hands furiously.

"The truck, Jenna," Ben said, taking her trembling hands into his. "It looked like it was following you. Did you see who was driving it?"

She shook her head. "No, I was looking at you and then, all of a sudden, those two cars almost crashed. It happened so fast."

They stood together, neither seeming to know what to say next, as an elderly couple came out of a nearby shop. Hand in hand, the couple gave them a knowing smile. They hadn't witnessed the near accident and only saw Ben and Jenna, her hands clasped tightly in his.

"You hold on to that one," the elderly woman said, giving him a wink as the couple shuffled down the street.

Jenna pulled her hands from his, breaking their connection. He felt the loss of her touch like a thread snapping in his chest and shoved his hands into his pockets. The urge to touch her was almost uncontrollable.

Jenna's hand went to her mouth, and he knew she was thinking about their kiss.

"I better go," she said, clasping her hands.

"I'll walk with you."

She shook her head wearily. "There's no need for that. I'm just going to stop by the bike shop and then head back to the carriage house. I'll be fine."

"I've already been to The Pedal today," he said, watching her demeanor change from exhausted to spirited.

"Why?" she asked, her brown eyes full of fire.

"Your bike is at my office. I had it fixed."

"You did?" She put her hands on her hips and released an audible breath. "I didn't need you to do that."

"I know."

She glared at him. "All right. It looks like we're going to your office."

"HELLO!" Mrs. G said. "Is everything all right? We were watching that odd white truck. My goodness! Wasn't he out to lunch?"

Ben nodded to Mrs. G. He was sure she could sense the tension between the two of them. But the energy in the office shifted, and the tension melted away as Mrs. G left her desk and came to greet them.

"I hug everyone," Mrs. G said, reaching toward Jenna. "I better just hug you now before these phones start ringing."

Jenna looked a bit startled, but she embraced the tiny woman who was at least a good eight inches shorter than she was.

"I'm Rosemary Giacopazzi, Benjamin's office manager."

"Mrs. G, this is Jenna Lewis. She's staying in the carriage house," Ben said, trying to gauge Jenna's response.

Jenna smiled. "It's nice to meet you," she said as Ben watched her fall under Mrs. G's spell.

"You can call me Rosemary. Benjamin started calling me Mrs. G in third grade and hasn't stopped."

"Were you neighbors?"

"Heavens, no! I was his teacher."

Jenna's face lit up, and Ben held back a grin. It was hard to stay angry around Mrs. G. He grabbed a set of drawings and walked into the conference room while Mrs. G told Jenna about the time he used all the rulers to build a house for the class guinea pig.

"It had a pitched roof and everything. I thought he was going to cry when we had to take it all apart to do math. But you know Benjamin, he just smiled and said he'd make an even better one tomorrow. That boy, no matter how many times he had to take that house apart, he would be ready to rebuild the next day."

Ben came out of the conference room with Jenna's bike and met her gaze. The anger in her eyes had disappeared and was replaced with something softer.

"You know, Mrs. G, Jenna's a teacher, too."

That set off another conversation. Jenna spoke animatedly about her work. Mrs. G listened and asked questions, and soon the women were chatting like old friends. It gave Ben time to really observe Jenna. He'd spent time with her, sure, but there hadn't been a time for him to watch the way she turned her head and nodded as she listened, or how her hands gestured when she wanted to emphasize a point.

He had watched her plenty in high school, and while he still saw many reminders of that young girl, seeing her as an accomplished woman took his breath away. Unable to take his eyes off of her, he didn't notice that his phone had started chiming until everyone in the office was looking his way.

"That's you," Jenna said, the side of her mouth quirking into a smile.

"Right," Ben said, fumbling with his phone.

"It must be time to get Kate," Mrs. G said, shifting the attention away from Ben. "You better go. You know our girl doesn't like to be kept waiting."

"You're right about that," Ben said, then turned to Jenna. "Would you like to come with me to pick up Kate?"

She nodded, and Ben worked to conceal his excitement. Had he been alone, he would have done a fist pump.

"See you tomorrow, Mrs. G," he said, rolling Jenna's bike out the door.

"It was so nice meeting you," Jenna said as Mrs. G settled herself back behind her desk.

"Don't be shy. You know where we are now, and I have missed talking shop. We should get lunch together soon."

"I'd love that," Jenna replied as Ben cast a grateful smile to his office manager.

KATE'S SCHOOL was just across the street from Ben's office. Within seconds of the crossing guard ushering them across the road, a bell rang, and a mass of excited children spilled out of the main doors. It was the last week of school, and there was a hum of excitement in the air as children ran to their parents, an extra spring in their step.

Despite the end of the school day chaos, Jenna was at ease.

"Have you ever considered giving up life on the road for this?" Ben asked, gesturing to the teachers who were talking to parents and directing children toward the correct carpools.

"Several of my Gwyer colleagues have left to do just this."

This was the second time Ben asked about the traveling aspect of her job. But this time, she hadn't given her canned response.

Did she want to settle down? Was a life like that even possible for someone like her?

Before either of them could say another word, their attention was drawn to a boisterous voice.

"Daddy!" Kate called out, running toward them, backpack swinging behind her. "Jenna!" Kate added, then turned to her father. "Jenna's here!"

They laughed at Kate's sweet enthusiasm.

Kate looked at her father and then to Jenna. She gave them what could only be described as a Zoe expression which was a cross between "I told you so" and "thank goodness you finally figured it out" look.

"How was your day, Jellybean?"

Kate prattled on about a picture she'd made in art class as Jenna went to retrieve her bike from where they had left it leaning on a nearby tree, and the trio headed toward home. The walk up

Baneberry Drive was starting to feel familiar and a sense of contentment set in as she listened to Kate and Ben chat.

Soon enough, Kate was running ahead of them. Ben and Jenna trailed behind, Jenna pushing her bike and Ben carrying Kate's backpack. They walked in a comfortable silence as Kate skipped from tree to tree, stopping every so often to grab a low-hanging leaf.

"Thank you for having my bike fixed. It was very kind of you." She couldn't stay angry with him. She would be lying to herself if she thought she didn't have feelings for him and, while that scared her, she didn't know how to stop it. She didn't know if she wanted to stop it.

It wasn't like she was a spinster. She would date if she happened to meet a man she was attracted to and even sleep with him if that was what she needed. But before any feelings could develop, she'd end the relationship. She never invited anyone to her home, and it was easy enough to block a phone number if a suitor became overly persistent.

She had crafted a life where there was little risk of having to worry about a jilted lover. And there was always Nick, who wanted nothing from her. This arrangement had worked for nearly a decade. But now she could see everything was different when it came to Ben.

"You're welcome," he said, his voice sounding relaxed as they watched Kate move from tree to tree. "Any news on your car?"

"The mechanic said they'd bring it to the house today after they replaced the tires. Isn't that kind of them? I'd forgotten how friendly Kansans could be."

He nodded, and they lapsed back into silence for a few beats.

"I saw my mother today," she began. "It was our first group therapy session, and it was pretty crazy sitting next to her after not seeing her for fourteen years."

She was surprised at how freeing it felt to tell him that. Despite all her reservations regarding Ben and all the mixed signals he was throwing her way, she wanted to tell him about her mother. She needed to tell him. A desire she didn't quite understand. She was so used to lying about her past, but she couldn't do that with him.

Jenna looked up, making sure Kate wasn't within earshot. "The day after Mother's Day, I learned she'd been at a women's shelter and had threatened to take her life."

Ben was quiet a beat. She thought she'd said too much until he met her gaze and nodded solemnly.

"But I think she's going to be okay. She's left her boyfriend, and I hope it's for good. They'd been together since I was quite young and had a very tumultuous relationship. She was no saint, but he was truly a terrible person."

"Are you her only child?" Ben asked.

"Yes, she had me very young, and I never knew my father."

"Did he pass away?"

"No, well, I don't know."

"What do you mean?"

"My mother doesn't know who my father is," Jenna said as the familiar threads of shame weaved their way into her heart. She knew this shame. It had been her companion for as long as she could remember. But instead of resigning herself to it and masking it with another lie, she continued. "All I know is that back in Alabama—that's where she's from—she was a troubled, promiscuous teenager and ran with a rough crowd. She had the kind of family that didn't tolerate that sort of behavior. They're wealthy society types, very concerned with appearances. So when her father found out she was pregnant, he sent her to Kansas to live with an aunt. That's my Aunt Ginny. She was technically my great aunt. I lived with her until she passed away."

"Your mother wasn't with you when you lived with your aunt?"

"No, she left when I was very small. It was just me and Aunt Ginny."

The sound of footsteps coming toward them got louder, and Jenna glanced up to see a frustrated Kate running toward them.

"Are you two pretending to be banana slugs?"

"What?" they asked in unison.

"A banana slug. You know, the slowest mollusk in the world."

"I thought the sloth was the slowest creature," Jenna replied, sharing a look with Ben.

"That's the slowest *mammal*," Kate answered.

"Is that so?" Ben replied.

"Yes, I learned it at school."

Just then, a light bulb seemed to go off in Kate's head, and she turned to Jenna. "Jenna, can we play school with your books and letters when we get home?"

"Jellybean, I'm not sure that will work," Ben said, then turned to Jenna. "You don't have to work with Kate today. I know you've had a long day."

She met Ben's gaze, and it wasn't aloof or severe, but the one of the boy she had known in high school. That kind boy was in there, or at least a part of that boy still was.

"I can't think of anything that would make me happier," she replied, shifting her gaze from Ben and watching Kate burst into a toothy grin.

"Can I have the keys, Daddy? I want to open the door and get ready to play school with Jenna."

Ben barely had the keys out of his pocket before Kate grabbed them. "I'm going to beat you home, banana slugs," she called out, laughing and skipping the last half block home.

"We'll be right behind you, Jellybean," he answered.

Jenna smiled as Kate sprinted toward the Tudor but froze when something warm slid over her hand. Her pulse quickened. Ben had shifted his hand from where it had been resting on the bike's crossbar and wrapped around her hand holding the grip. His touch triggered every memory of their time in the creek—his body pressed protectively into hers and his warm, steady hands.

She didn't move. It was like being caught between two worlds. She stared at Ben's hand. It was much larger than hers, but they fit together. Ben started to pull back, a tiny movement, but she noticed it immediately. Jenna flicked her gaze to meet his. Uncertainty flashed in his eyes.

She didn't know what she was doing in Langley Park. She didn't know what she was doing with this man she'd never forgotten. But what she knew for certain was that she didn't want him to pull his hand away. Without breaking eye contact, she shifted her fingers and laced them with his and watched as the boyish smile she remembered stretched across his face.

15

Jenna spent the next hour working with Kate. Ben wasn't hovering around them as he did during their first tutoring session. She'd heard him going up and down the stairs, the tell-tale top stair giving a gentle squeak each time he passed. She'd caught a glimpse of him carrying a laundry basket and bit back a chuckle thinking of him folding Kate's little socks.

Kate didn't want to play hide-and-seek when they finished and had instead requested a game of crazy eights. Ben set a pot of water to boil and joined them at the table, dealing out three hands.

At the tender age of six, Kate had all the makings of a card shark, eyeing both Ben and Jenna sharply when they played a card she didn't like. It didn't take long before Jenna racked up the requisite fifty points and was deemed the loser by a cheering Kate.

"I don't know where she gets her competitive streak," he remarked with a glint in his eye while Kate did a victory dance around the kitchen table.

But before Jenna could respond, the timer went off near the stove, and Ben left the table to quiet the beeping.

"Remember, Jellybean, winners clean up," Ben said as he poured the spaghetti into the colander.

"Is Jenna going to eat dinner with us, Daddy?" Kate asked, slipping the cards back into the worn box.

"I better not," Jenna said, looking down at her fingers. Barely an hour ago, they'd been laced with Ben's. "The mechanics should be dropping off my car soon, and I'd hate to interrupt your meal."

She glanced at Ben. His hair was a bit disheveled. He'd slung a dishtowel over his shoulder and was mixing the pasta with the sauce.

"Go wash your hands, Bean," Ben instructed his daughter. "You should stay," he added with a boyish grin and handed her three plates.

She set down her bag and gave him a little nod. As Jenna reached for the plates, her fingertips brushed past Ben's. A surge of electricity shot through her hands. Butterflies erupted into flight inside her belly.

Get. It. Together.

She bit her lip, and Ben's gaze lingered on her mouth. It was too much. He was too much. She turned away and took a steadying breath.

Kate tugged on the hem of her skirt and was quick to school her on how to set the table. The precocious six-year-old gestured for Jenna to take the seat next to her father as she chattered on about the last week of school, and soon they were all enjoying good old spaghetti.

Ben shook his head and smiled, reminding his daughter to breathe and chew with her mouth closed.

"Jenna, you're lucky Daddy made spaghetti. He tried to make a whole chicken once, and it caught on fire. We had to go to Park Tavern for dinner that night."

"It didn't catch on fire," Ben said, a slight blush on his cheeks.

Jenna tried to stifle a laugh.

"Daddy, it was all black and tiny."

Ben shook his head. "I set the heat too high and then forgot to turn on the timer."

"The chicken was all smoky and stuck to the pot. The fire alarm went off, remember, Daddy?"

Jenna and Kate were laughing as Ben feigned horror, and then he laughed with them. "It was pretty bad. I just threw the whole thing, pan and all, in the trash."

"You certainly get points for trying," Jenna said, reaching over to touch Ben's arm. But she stopped herself and pulled her hand away awkwardly.

Kate took a sip of milk and narrowed her gaze. "Jenna, how long are you going to live with us?"

She was caught off guard by Kate's question, and Ben looked perplexed as well. It was the first time Jenna had seen Ben at a loss for words with his daughter.

"That's a good question," she answered, watching Ben from the corner of her eye. "My mom is in the hospital, so I'm here until she gets better. Is that all right with you?"

Kate chewed on a bite of pasta. "Is Grandpa Neil your mom's doctor?"

"I don't think so," Jenna said, looking to Ben.

"My stepdad's a surgeon at Midwest," he said, then turned to Kate. "Jenna's mom has a different doctor, Bean."

Kate nodded, and Jenna could almost see the wheels turning in the little girl's head.

"Jenna," Kate began, "can we keep playing school? I like playing school with you."

"You know what, Kate? I love playing school with you, too. How about if we play school a little bit every day?" She turned to Ben. "It would be best if I could work with Kate for an hour every day, Monday through Friday."

He nodded. "During the summer, Kate spends the mornings at the Langley Park Community Center's day camp and then she's with my mom in the afternoons. Could you do this time, right before dinner?"

"Please say yes, Jenna!" Kate jumped up and threw herself into Jenna's arms.

"Okay, then! We'll play school every day before dinner."

Jenna had to work to keep her face neutral, but inside she was doing cartwheels. She was going to get to spend a little bit of each day with these two people. It was both terrifying and exhilarating.

"Do you want to come jump rope with me, Jenna?"

"Jellybean, Jenna and I are still eating. Bring your plate to the sink, and then you can jump rope in the backyard."

"Will you watch me jump, Jenna?" Kate asked, balancing her glass and fork on her plate.

"Absolutely."

As Kate walked past them, she reached over and touched her father's face. "Daddy, you're messy."

Jenna looked over at Ben and had to bite her lip to keep from chuckling. "Kate's right. You've got a little sauce on your cheek."

Ben blushed and dabbed at his cheek with his napkin, but he missed the sauce completely.

"No, there," she said, trying to direct him toward the offending sauce.

After watching Ben wipe without success, she leaned in, and, with the pad of her thumb, wiped the small bit of sauce off his face. He was warm, and his beard stubble tickled her finger. She could barely register the faint sound of Kate singing a jump rope chant as time seemed to slow down. She started to pull back, but Ben put his hand on hers, keeping it in place.

She met his gaze. "Thank you for dinner."

"Anytime," he replied, smiling that boyish smile.

BEN FELT weightless as he stared into Jenna's haunting brown eyes. She was like the sun, and he was locked in her orbit. Bringing her hand to his lips, he pressed a kiss to her palm. She inhaled sharply, and the sound ignited something primal inside him, making him want to drag her over to the nearest flat surface. Completely bewitched, he cupped her cheek with his other hand.

"Daddy! Jenna's car's here! And there's a tow truck! A giant tow truck!" Kate called from outside.

"I think your car's here," he said as he ran his thumb over Jenna's bottom lip. It trembled beneath his touch.

She held his gaze and nodded.

"I'm going to go look at the tow truck," Kate called from outside, her voice trailing off.

"I think my car's here," Jenna echoed, her voice sounding like it was caught in a dream.

"I think I just said that."

He felt like a lovesick teenager. She made him feel complete, made him feel like he could grab onto life with both hands and really live.

A knock came from the front door and, reluctantly, he released his hold. He followed Jenna toward the front door. But just as she was about to turn the doorknob, he took her hand and pressed her back against the door.

"I have to kiss you first," he whispered, pressing his lips to hers.

She was so sweet. She released a contented sigh, and her mouth opened, allowing him to deepen the kiss. He wanted to take his time, but his body had other plans. Within seconds, his hands were everywhere—cupping her face, running down her neck, then finding their way into her hair. With every touch, he was coming back to life. He was a man waking up from a coma, all his senses rebooting.

After Sara's death, the only way he could keep going was to live a controlled, orderly life focused on Kate and his work. But as he listened to Jenna's breaths come faster and felt the rise and fall of her chest against his, he knew he wouldn't be able to sleepwalk through life anymore. He slid his hand down, cupped her ass, and pressed his cock against her belly. Jenna released a low moan and threaded her fingers into his hair.

There was no beginning and no end, just his mouth on hers, his teeth gently biting her lip. He'd never known anything like this before. He slid his hand under her skirt and dipped a finger into her panties. Wet heat greeted him, and his cock twitched.

Another tentative knock came, and Ben could feel the vibration through the front door. Jenna tensed, and he removed his hand from her panties. They pulled apart and stood there for a moment, breathing hard and smiling at each other like teenagers caught kissing under the bleachers. She was gorgeous. Her hair, a golden tussled mess. Her lips, cherry red from his kisses. Her eyes, swimming with desire. A possessive urge coursed through his veins. He liked knowing he'd done this to her.

"We should probably open the door," he said, taking a step back but leaving one hand on her hip. "We're pretty trusting in Kansas, but I don't think they'll release your car to a first grader."

Jenna leaned into his touch. "Probably not."

A third knock came, and Ben shrugged his shoulders. "I better open it."

Jenna nodded and stepped away from the door.

"Sorry to bother you," a young mechanic said, giving Ben and Jenna a bit of a double take. The thin lines of grease visible on his neck and cheek weren't enough to hide the embarrassed blush creeping up to his face. He gestured toward the street. "Don't mind the tow truck, we got a call to go pick up a stalled car but wanted to drop your vehicle off first. She's in great shape, all fixed up and ready to go."

Jenna tucked a few strands of her disheveled hair behind her ears and quickly smoothed her skirt. A pink blush bloomed on her cheeks. She was even more beautiful when she was flustered.

"Thank you so much," she said, finding another errant curl and tucking it back.

He was sporting a stupid grin, but he didn't care. He had Jenna's taste on his lips and was covered in her lavender scent.

She glanced up at him from under her eyelashes and gestured toward where her car was parked on the street. "We should probably go check the car," she said with the world's sexiest smile stretched across her lips.

The mechanic gave an exaggerated nod, and Ben and Jenna followed him over to her car now fitted with four shiny new tires.

"Do you want me to park it in the garage?" the young mechanic offered, removing Jenna's keys from his pocket.

Ben's body tensed. The garage. Christ, he hadn't even considered parking her car in there. But after what had happened, what choice did he have.

"No, I'll do it," he said, retrieving the keys before Jenna had a chance to answer.

He could hear Jenna speaking with the mechanic. Kate had joined them, and his daughter was asking the man questions about the different parts of the tow truck. Their conversation blurred as his heart rate kicked up. He put the key into the ignition and started her car. Slowly, he maneuvered the vehicle onto the gravel driveway. The crack and crunch grated his nerves. Each pop sounded like cannon fire. He blinked, trying to push back the memories of Sara's death.

Ben pulled the car up and cut the ignition. His movements were sharp and deliberate as he walked over to the garage door and pulled out a set of keys. A drop of perspiration fell from his chin as his gaze settled on the small silver key that unlocked the garage door.

He stared at the key. It was just a piece of metal, and this was just a garage. It was merely a physical space he had designed himself, but his trembling hands told him his body disagreed. He inserted the key into the lock hoping that the years of being left untouched may have rendered it unworkable. But the key slid inside smoothly and with a quick turn, the lock disengaged.

He could feel the blood pumping through his veins and whooshing in his ears. After Sara's death, Neil had cleaned and emptied the entire garage. In the days after Sara's funeral, needing to do something other than sit and be idle, he went and purchased wood and materials. Letting his mind focus on the measuring, hammering, and sawing, he built a small shed on the side of the house to accommodate things like the lawn mower, a few snow shovels, and his tools. To this day, the garage remained unoccupied and was empty except for an old broom Neil had left propped in the far corner.

Kate and Jenna were chatting behind him, but he wasn't able to focus on the content of their conversation. He heard Kate say things like "fairies" and "dancing." But his addled mind could only focus on thoughts of Sara and her lifeless body. He held the silver t-bar in his hand and lifted the garage door, each little click sounding like the macabre lowering of a coffin. His hands shook. A chill passed through him.

He turned. He needed to see Kate. He needed to know she was alive and breathing. But instead of finding his daughter, all he saw was Jenna.

Concern clouded her eyes. "Are you feeling okay, Ben?"

He opened his mouth to speak, but nothing came out. Time felt like it was folding in on itself. He stared at her face, trying to piece together the present and the past. But Jenna's look of worry changed to one of delight as she gazed over his shoulder into the opened garage.

Ben turned to see Kate, green leaves now adorning her braided hair, twirling inside the center of the garage. The garage faced west, and the setting sun cast an ethereal glow into the space. As Kate danced in the sunlight, Ben's first thought was that his daughter looked like a celestial pixie spinning barefoot on tiptoes. Her yellow dress billowed out and caught each ray of sunshine.

But then his paternal instinct kicked in. He ran into the garage and grabbed ahold of his daughter, scooping her up mid-spin. Kate's arms, still in motion from the twirling, knocked him in the face as he hurled both of them out of the garage and onto the grass.

Looking back and forth, a sick sort of déjà vu came over him. This was the exact spot where he had held Kate, drowsy from the carbon monoxide, three years ago when his wife had not only taken her own life but had tried to take their daughter's as well.

"Kathryn Elizabeth Fisher, you are never, never to go inside that garage. Do you understand me?" His voice shook with fear and relief. "Kathryn, say you understand."

This was the first time he had raised his voice to his daughter. Eyes wide, she stared at him as if she was looking at a stranger. A beat passed, and her eyes filled with frightened tears. She sobbed against his chest.

Jenna ran over to them. "Ben! Ben! You're scaring Kate."

He ignored her and focused his attention on his daughter. "Promise me, Jellybean. Promise me you will never go inside the garage," he said, softening his tone as Kate cried in his arms.

"Okay, Daddy," she answered, her little voice wobbling. "I won't go in the garage. I promise."

He closed his eyes and cradled his daughter in his arms. Something touched his shoulder, and he recoiled.

"It's just me," Jenna said, holding her hands up defensively. "What can I do to help?"

Ben pulled away from her touch and came to his feet with Kate still in his arms. She'd stopped crying, but her head was burrowed into his shoulder. His gaze bounced from the garage then back to Jenna or was it Sara standing in front of him. He blinked. He needed to get away. He needed the nightmare to end.

"Please, let me help."

Hands shaking, Ben reached into his pocket and took out the spare garage door key. "This has nothing to do with you," he said, tossing her the key. "Keep the garage locked at all times. No exceptions, Sara. Do you understand?"

A perplexed look crossed her face. She parted her lips to speak, but he cut her off.

"Good night," he said over his shoulder as he headed into the house and left her standing next to the garage.

16

A week had passed, and not a word had been spoken regarding Ben's outburst. Jenna hoped to bring it up with him, but he never gave her the chance. When she knocked on the French doors this week to tutor Kate, it was Kathy, not Ben, who let her in.

Now it was Friday, and Jenna was just finishing up her session with Kate. Ben might as well have been a ghost. The only glimpses of him she had caught this week had come late at night. She would be working at the corner desk, and every time she looked up from her computer, her gaze was drawn to the main house. There were a few times when she thought she saw him standing by his bedroom window. But every time she tried to take a closer look, the form in the window would vanish.

Was that Ben? Did he think about her?

She couldn't let her mind go there. Ben's absence had made his feelings loud and clear.

"I know he's got a lot going on at work," Kathy said as Jenna packed up her tutoring materials, and Kate ran outside to jump rope.

"I'm sure he does," Jenna answered, trying to sound pleasant but indifferent.

Kathy had been a social worker for many years, and she started teaching yoga after she retired. Both jobs fit her perfectly. But her usually calm, serene manner seemed off as she fingered the small tree of life necklace dangling around her neck.

"Mrs. G says they're swamped at work, and they're even thinking about hiring someone just to do the drafting."

Kathy sounded more like she was trying to convince herself of something rather than make small talk.

Her gaze moved to the carriage house. "Have you seen Ben much this week?"

"Not really. But I've been working quite a bit myself."

Kathy's gaze lingered on the garage.

"Ben was kind enough to let me use the garage after my car was vandalized," she said, wishing she knew why everyone seemed so preoccupied with that space.

"Your bike, too?"

"Yes, they got my bike as well."

"That's what Zoe said. I'm so sorry, Jenna."

"Luckily, it was an easy fix for both."

Kathy nodded, glanced once more at the carriage house, and started chopping vegetables.

The front door opened and Ben walked in. His messenger bag was slung over his shoulder, and it looked like he hadn't shaved in a few days. He gave his mother a tired smile, and then he noticed Jenna.

"I wasn't sure if you were working with Kate today," he said, in lieu of a greeting.

Jenna gave him a curt nod. "Kate didn't seem to mind it being the last day of school and even reminded me that we agreed to work together Monday through Friday."

"Friday, already?" He said the words as if he was discussing a prison sentence.

"Ben, you know we've got the Langley Park Festival tomorrow. You're supposed to set up the jumpy castle like last year, honey," Kathy called over her shoulder.

Like magic, the words "jumpy castle" summoned Kate from the backyard and into the kitchen.

"Daddy, can I help set up the jumpy castle?"

"Jellybean, you just want to be the first jumper," Ben said as he planted a kiss on the top of her head.

"I can help you, and *then* I can be the first jumper."

Ben released a tired chuckle. "All right. You can help."

"Jenna, are you still helping Sam and Zoe?" Kathy asked, eyeing her son as he grabbed a Boulevard Pale Ale from the fridge.

"Yes, I'm just helping them hand out popsicles and cookies. Nothing too involved."

"Just you wait and see. With all the Langley Park kids running around, the cookies and popsicles are a pretty big deal. You may be busier than you think."

Jenna nodded. "Well, I'm off."

Kate ran over and clasped her little arms around Jenna's waist. She knelt to give Kate a proper hug, then pulled back and tucked a few strands of Kate's hair behind her ears.

"You worked so hard today, Miss Kate. You're a reading machine," she said, wiping off a bit of dirt from Kate's cheek.

Jenna looked up to see Ben watching them. A shadow of longing passed over his face, but it disappeared as he hardened his features into one of casual indifference. That callous look sent daggers through her heart. The Ben who had kissed her just days ago, the Ben who had looked at her as if she made up the entirety of his universe, wasn't the man standing in front of her now.

Rising quickly, Jenna picked up her bag and passed through the open French doors. She knew his eyes were on her. She felt the heat of his gaze nearly boring holes into her back.

Don't turn around. Just keep putting one foot in front of the other.

But she couldn't help herself. Jenna stopped and turned to find Ben standing in the doorway. They looked at each other for one beat, then two, before he turned away and closed the doors.

. . .

Saturday turned out to be a beautiful day. Some clouds had formed to the east of them, but the weather was mild, and all of Langley Park and the surrounding towns had come out to enjoy the weather and the festivities.

The festival had grown over the years. What was once a gathering of neighbors selling a few knickknacks and baked goods, had turned into hundreds of vendors and artists showcasing their wares. The festival stretched from the actual park of Langley Park and into the Langley Park Botanic Gardens. Tables and tents were spread out over the thick zoysia grass, and oak trees provided shade from the late spring sun. A large play structure situated near the center of the park was teeming with children, sticky from ice cream and popsicles while music from the bands floated through the air.

Kathy wasn't kidding about it being busy. The Park Tavern booth was hopping from the moment the first cookie left the tray. Jenna, Zoe, and Sam were handing out cookies and popsicles as fast as they could to a chorus of cheers and squeals of delight.

"These Langley Park kids *do not* mess around with free treats," Zoe joked as she brought out another large tray filled with deliciously gooey chocolate chip cookies.

Jenna passed two cookies to a set of twins, and then she caught sight of Ben helping a group of men string lights inside the pavilion. She had watched him all day setting up jumpy castles, assisting an elderly couple with their marmalade booth, and even hanging a gong for his mother to use during her yoga demonstration. He seemed to be everywhere except near her.

She'd barely been able to work this past week. Her treacherous thoughts kept going back to that kiss. It had to have been more than just kiss. Everything about it seemed so real. But then again, what did a girl whose life was based on lies know about what was real?

"How are things with Ben and Kate?" Zoe asked.

Jenna dropped a cookie. "What do you mean? I mean...they're fine. Did he mention anything to you?"

"I just meant, how's everything going with the tutoring and living in the carriage house. I know Ben can sometimes be a douche-canoe. I'm hoping he's been on good behavior with you."

"A what?" Jenna asked, tossing the ruined cookie into a trash bin.

"You know, like a jerk but on a grander scale."

"Watch your language, Zoe Christine Stein," came an amused voice.

Just then, Kate ran up to the table and grabbed the hand of an older gentleman smiling and shaking his head.

"Dad, you taught us to speak our minds," Zoe said, leaning over the table to kiss the man's cheek.

"Jenna, this is my dad, Dr. Neil Stein, aka the language police."

Jenna smiled and shook Neil's hand. "It's so nice to meet you. Kate talks about you all the time."

"Likewise," Neil answered, meeting Jenna's smile with one of his own.

Kate jumped up and down. "Jenna, will you take me to get my face painted? I want to look like a butterfly."

"I'm not sure I can, Kate. I'm helping your Aunt Zoe and Sam with the cookies and popsicles."

The little girl's face fell.

"I could take you, sweetheart," Neil said, giving Kate's hand a little squeeze.

"I wanted Jenna to take me."

"How about this," Neil said, looking from Kate to Jenna, "I help out with the cookies, and Jenna can take you to get your face painted?"

"Deal! Deal! Deal!" Kate cheered.

"As long as it's all right with you?" Neil asked, giving Jenna a warm but apologetic grin.

She took off her apron and handed it to Neil. "Looks like we've got a date with a face painter."

BEN LOOKED on from the pavilion as Jenna and Kate made their way, hand in hand, through the growing crowd. Everything about them seemed so natural. Of course, he'd seen his mother and sister interact lovingly with Kate, but there was something about seeing Jenna and his daughter together that made his heart ache.

He watched as Kate hesitantly sat down in the face painter's chair. His daughter probably begged to have her face painted, but now, when it was time to do the deed, she wasn't quite so brave. Jenna bent down next to Kate and put one arm around her then extended her other hand, palm down, to the face painter. Kate watched as the artist painted something on the top of Jenna's hand, and then she smiled and nodded her head.

Kate and Jenna emerged from the face painting tent with a colorful butterfly on his daughter's cheek, and what Ben guessed was a matching butterfly on Jenna's hand. He followed them, studying the protective way Jenna would bring Kate in close to her when large groups passed. He noticed the way Jenna's skirt swayed as she twirled Kate around when they passed a tent full of people square dancing. He'd never seen anything so beautiful yet so painful in all his life.

The clouds that had stayed east of them for most of the day rolled in obscuring the sunset and bringing with it a cool breeze. Ben watched Kate and Jenna peruse the artists' stalls when something in his periphery grabbed his attention.

Earlier in the day, a man wearing a baseball cap had lingered nearby while Kate and Jenna were at the face painters' tent. There were several artists painting designs on eager children, and he just assumed that the man was waiting for his child. But it did seem odd how the man's gaze was locked on Jenna.

Now, much later, he was almost sure the same capped man was still watching them. In the dim light, he couldn't make out much about the man other than that he was of medium build, but there was something about the man that seemed off.

As Kate and Jenna stopped to watch a magician surrounded by a large crowd, the man moved closer to them. Jenna picked up Kate and was holding her on her hip so she could see the show. The capped man pushed through the crowd and stood behind Jenna. Ben's pulse jumped as he raised his hand then dragged his fingertips across Jenna's back, pausing to finger a few strands of her hair before melting back into the crowd. Jenna turned her head slightly. She probably thought it was just a person pushed forward by the jostling crowd.

Ben had seen it as clear as day and set off to confront the man. "Hey! I saw what you did back there," he called out, following the man as he darted past stalls and tables.

Between the growing crowds and the darkness, it was difficult for Ben to track the man. Weaving through groups of people, he tried to keep the man in his sights, but the labyrinth of tents and tables kept him just out of reach.

Sidestepping around an elderly couple, it was as if he was moving against the current. The ball cap seemed to be moving farther and farther away when he collided with someone and looked down to see it was Zoe.

"Jesus, Ben! Where's the fire?"

His gaze darted between his sister and the man.

Zoe frowned. "What happened?"

He wiped the sweat from his brow. "There was some guy following Jenna and Kate." His heart was jumping in his chest, and he could hardly believe it when his sister laughed.

"Ben, look around." Zoe gestured to the pavilion where Jenna was now dancing with Kate and a few other little girls.

She was smiling and laughing, and she looked so beautiful that he had to remind himself to breathe. He couldn't tear his gaze away from the slim lines of her body beneath her skirt and her golden hair now up in a messy bun with loose tendrils falling on her neck.

"Hey," Zoe said with a wry grin.

"What is it, Zoe?"

"I hate to break it to you, big brother, but everybody's looking at her."

Ben scanned the crowd around the pavilion. His sister was right. Several men threw glances, some more obvious than others, Jenna's way. Even women were watching her.

"Are you sure Jenna and Kate were being followed? It's a madhouse around here."

Ben blew out a frustrated breath. "Maybe, maybe not?"

The crowd had grown considerably in the last hour. The fireworks were set to start after sundown, and things at the festival were always a little haywire before they began.

Dusting cookie crumbs off his shirt, Sam joined Zoe and Ben. "She's like the Pied Piper of Langley Park," he said, gesturing to Jenna and her gaggle of little girls.

Jenna glanced away from the children and met Ben's gaze. She gave him an embarrassed smile as the little girls danced around her.

"Looks like we might get some weather," Zoe said, motioning to the lightning in the distance.

"It's that time of year," Sam replied with a yawn.

"All right, lazy bones, why don't we give poor Jenna a reprieve," Zoe said, taking Sam's hand and joining Jenna and the children on the pavilion dance floor.

Sam picked up Kate, and Zoe ushered the remaining little girls over to watch a woman making balloon animals. Jenna was left standing alone as the first few notes of Eric Clapton's ballad "Wonderful Tonight" began to play.

Jenna turned to leave, and Ben's heart rate kicked up. His limbs twitched. His body was nearly vibrating. He needed to be close to her. Unable to hold himself back, he walked up the steps to the pavilion and cut off her departure.

She stopped and met his gaze, confusion clouding her eyes.

He offered her his hand. Jenna looked at it warily as if he were handing her a stick of lit dynamite.

She shook her head. "I don't think—"

"It's just a dance," he countered, knowing that was a lie.

She bit her lip. He could tell she was turning something over in her mind, but she put her hand in his.

Several people had gotten up to dance, and soon the pavilion was full of couples swaying under the twinkling lights.

He gathered Jenna into his arms and inhaled, smelling the faint lavender scent of her shampoo. She shivered, and he wasn't sure if it was because of his touch or the cool breeze that picked up and caused the hanging lights to sway as if they too were moving to the beat.

"Are you cold?" he asked, pulling her in closer.

She studied his face as if she were trying to decipher a code. "Why are you dancing with me?"

He released a pained breath. "Because I couldn't stay away from you any longer."

"I don't know what you want from me. Did I do something to upset you?" Her brown eyes were full of questions.

"It's not you."

"It's something," she whispered.

A chorus of giggles erupted nearby, and Ben and Jenna looked over to see Kate and her friends sitting on the steps of the pavilion. Their hands were cradling their little chins as they watched them dance.

"I think we have an audience," he said, then raised his arm and slowly twirled Jenna around to the little girls' delight. He finished the turn and brought Jenna back to him.

"She's amazing, you know?" Jenna began.

"Who?"

"Your daughter, she's wonderful."

Ben smiled. It was the first real smile to grace his lips all week. He'd been fighting his demons since the episode in the garage. Memories of Sara haunted his dreams, and he tried to block out the torment the only way he knew how—by spending his time focused on his job and his daughter.

But it wasn't working.

Looking over at Kate, he saw how she was staring at Jenna. "I think we're both falling for you."

"Ben, I don't understand, I..."

But she wasn't able to finish.

The ping, ping, ping, sounds of rain echoed on the tin roof of the pavilion, and a sharp crack of lightning followed by the angry rumble of thunder caused the band to stop playing. Another bolt of lightning struck, and lights in the pavilion went dark as the wind whooshed through. The sound of cups and plates crashing to the ground filled the air.

Cell phone flashlights broke out through the darkness and moved erratically as the rain fell harder. Jenna felt little arms grab around her waist.

"Pick me up," Kate cried, grabbing a fistful of Jenna's skirt.

Ben turned on his cell's flashlight and shined it down on Kate. "It's all right, Bean. Remember, it's springtime. We get lots of storms this time of year. I'll carry you."

"No, I want Jenna."

"It's all right. I've got her," Jenna said, pulling Kate in close.

Kate trembled in Jenna's arms. Ben tried to reassure his daughter, but his words were drowned out by an eerie mechanical sound penetrating the crackling air.

Tornado sirens.

17

———

"We need to get home," Ben said, wrapping an arm around Jenna while Kate cowered in her arms.

"Isn't your office closer?" she asked.

"No basement. We need to go home."

"What about Zoe and Sam and your mom and Neil?"

"They'll be okay. I'm sure they're on their way home right now. We need to get Kate home. She doesn't do well with storms."

Jenna tightened her grip on the little girl. "All right. Let's go."

They walked down the slick pavilion steps and were met with sharp wind and biting rain as the sirens added an extra layer of urgency to their movements.

Walking with Ben's arm wrapped around her, Jenna turned into him hoping to shield Kate from the relentless wind. Police officers were directing the anxious crowd, but Ben and Jenna found themselves at a standstill, huddled with other families trying to leave the gardens.

"I know a better way," Ben said, ushering them away from the crowd and onto a narrow stone path. "We'll come out right across the street from the firehouse."

The firehouse was off Prairie Rose just a block or so from

Baneberry Drive. From her morning runs, Jenna knew it would take them less than ten minutes to get home from there.

A bolt of lightning illuminated the layered clouds hovering ominously above them, followed by a palpable rumble of thunder. The stone path narrowed and changed to one of packed gravel, giving Jenna an opportunity for better footing compared to the slick stones. But with the rapid downpour, each step was like trudging through the shallow end of a pond with mud and water splashing up on her calves.

She glanced up at Ben. He was navigating the twisting path, doing his best to pull the branches, dancing deliriously in the wind, out of their way. Kate was uncharacteristically quiet through the whole ordeal, but Jenna could feel her little heart beating a mile a minute.

Finally, they made it to the north gate leading out of the botanic gardens and onto Prairie Rose Drive. The old wooden door, barely used, creaked loudly, and Ben had to give it an extra shove before it opened wide enough to allow them to pass through.

Jenna was glad to be out of the gardens. But out on the open sidewalk, they were without the dense, protective foliage and had to endure the full force of the storm.

"Let's cross over to the firehouse," Ben said, shielding his eyes.

Soaked to the bone, they stood under the firehouse awning taking a brief respite from the pelting rain. Ben stroked Kate's back, looking her over, then turned his gaze to Jenna and tucked strands of wet hair behind her ear.

"Do you want me to take her?" he asked, raising his voice over the gusts of wind.

"I don't think she's going to let go."

"We just need to get her home. We're not far. Can you make it?"

Jenna nodded, and Ben wrapped his arm around her. They walked up Prairie Rose past the community center and then headed north on Baneberry Drive.

As they neared the house, Ben released his arm from around her shoulders. "I'm going to run ahead and open the door. I'll be right back."

"Here we are," she whispered to Kate. "I can see your house now. We're home safe and sound."

Ben jogged back and guided them up the brick walkway and into the safety of the darkened house.

He ran a hand through his soaked hair. "Looks like the power's out here, too."

Jenna hadn't realized the true force of the storm until they were inside, and she heard the wind whistling through the old home as pellets of hail battered the roof and windows.

They'd made it back just in time.

Ben put his hand on the back of Kate's head. "We're home, Jellybean."

Kate didn't answer.

"Head down to the basement," Ben said, handing Jenna a flashlight. "There are candles and some bottles of water down there. I'll go get some towels and dry clothes for us."

The adrenaline was beginning to subside, and Jenna felt the fatigue in her arms set in as she held Kate propped on her hip with one arm and gripped the flashlight in the other. Step by step, she went down the staircase and entered the cozy basement. Shining the light around the small space, she saw an old blue couch and matching love seat arranged in an L-shape in the middle of the room.

"I'm going to set you down on the couch, Kate. I just need to light a few candles."

Kate didn't reply, but she loosened her grip and allowed Jenna to set her down. Kate rested her head on the bolstered arm of the old couch as Jenna shined her flashlight and found a bookshelf containing candles, more flashlights, and bottles of water. She found the matches on the highest shelf, lit the candles, then placed them around the basement. An old side table sat where the couch and love seat met, and Jenna put several candles on it, illuminating Kate's pale face.

A few minutes later, Ben came down the basement stairs. Lit only by the candlelight, she had to remind herself to breathe. His hair was wet and tousled, and he was wearing some worn sweatpants and a t-shirt as the candlelight illuminated his strong arms and broad chest.

Stop. Just stop. She had to silence those silly schoolgirl fantasies.

"Here, it's the best I can do." Ben handed her a towel and one of his old t-shirts along with a pair of boxer shorts.

He went over to Kate and took off her wet clothes, then helped her put on a pair of dry pajamas. He spoke softly, and she complied with his requests but remained silent.

Jenna took the clothes and walked over to a corner where she was partially obscured by a hot water tank and stripped off her soaked outfit. His shirt was soft and well-worn. It was several sizes too big and the boxers threatened to fall off when she tried to walk, but they were blessedly dry, and that trumped fit tonight.

After hanging her wet clothes on an old drying rack, she walked over to the couches and sat down on the love seat. Ben was sitting next to Kate on the larger couch with his laptop balanced on his knees.

"See, Bean. We can watch the storm pass by on radar cast. It looks like the worst of it is south of us. I thought this might help you feel better during the storm."

Kate paid no attention to her father's computer screen and made a beeline for Jenna on the love seat and curled up in her lap like a frightened cat.

Jenna patted Kate's back. "Did I ever tell you that when I was a little girl, I was terrified of storms?"

Kate shook her head ever so slightly. She still refused to speak or make eye contact.

"I lived in an old farmhouse with my Aunt Ginny in a teeny-tiny little Kansas town called Ballentine. I bet you've never even heard of it, have you?"

Kate shook her head again. The little girl shifted and now had her head in Jenna's lap, looking up at her.

"The farmhouse didn't have a basement, so when it stormed we would go down into the root cellar."

Kate furrowed her brow

"I bet you're wondering what a root cellar is. It's a funny word."

Kate didn't respond, but the ghost of a smile crossed her face.

"A root cellar is a little room, kind of like a basement, built underground. People usually store food inside of them, but they're also a safe place to go when there's a big storm."

Kate gave her a tiny nod.

"To get to the root cellar, we'd have to run over to the side of the house and open two big red doors. And do you know what was behind those doors?"

Kate shook her head.

"There were these old wooden stairs that went down, down, down into the root cellar, and it was full of all sorts of things. Jars of pickles and jams. Jars of zucchini and asparagus."

Kate wrinkled her nose, making Jenna chuckle.

"My Aunt Ginny would tell me, 'If you could grow it, you could probably put it in a jar and pickle it.'"

Now Kate was smiling, hanging on her every word.

"We'd go inside the root cellar with all those jars and close the big doors behind us. My aunt would light candles, just like we did tonight, and we'd cuddle up together on a little mattress. Then we'd play a very special game. Do you want me to teach it to you?"

Kate nodded.

"I'm going to draw a shape on your back with my finger, and you have to guess what it is. But you have to focus all your thinking on what I'm drawing. Are you ready?"

Instead of answering, Kate shifted her body to expose her back.

Jenna started to draw a shape.

"Circle," came the whisper of a voice.

Ben gasped.

"Is this okay?" she asked, meeting his gaze.

Eyes wide, Ben nodded.

Jenna smoothed the little girl's hair. "You got it, Kate. Now I'm going to try to trick you."

She drew the next shape.

"It's a triangle. Make it harder."

"All right," Jenna said, smiling down at the little girl. "How about letters?"

Jenna traced along Kate's back.

"It's a K. It's a K, Daddy. I'm good at this game."

"Yes, you are, Jellybean," Ben answered, his voice thick with emotion.

Jenna continued making letters and numbers on Kate's back. With each correct guess, Kate became more animated.

Soon the storm was forgotten, and Kate grew sleepy as Jenna traced the outline of the letter Z on her back for the third time, then the fourth, then the fifth.

"I think she's asleep," Jenna whispered.

BEN LOOKED ON IN DISBELIEF. This was the first time Kate had spoken during a storm, and it was all because of Jenna.

He could see Kate's connection to Jenna deepening, and he couldn't deny his own feelings. Avoiding her this week had been a living hell. Just catching glimpses of her working through the windows of the carriage house at night or coming back from an early morning run had made his limbs twitch. He was like a man going through withdrawal, and his entire body ached to touch her.

"Ben, I need to ask you something," Jenna said, her words breaking into his thoughts.

He lifted his gaze from his sleeping daughter.

"The day Kate went into the garage, you called me Sara."

"I know."

He'd realized he'd made the mistake nearly the moment the word escaped his mouth. He rubbed his hands over his eyes and leaned forward.

He needed to say more, but he didn't know where to start or how to convey the significance of that garage. And he didn't want to make Jenna feel responsible for causing his outburst.

"I wish you'd tell me what happened. I've never seen you act like that."

He looked at her, surrounded by the glow of the candles and wearing his old t-shirt. It had been so long since he'd talked about Sara's death. Of course, he thought about it. The events of that day were always close to the surface for him. He only had to look at Kate to be reminded of almost losing her, too.

"The garage is where Sara died and where I almost lost Kate."

"What do you..." Jenna began, but then a knowing expression crossed her face. "Kate lost her mother and was exposed to carbon monoxide at the same time."

Ben nodded.

Jenna's eyes filled with tears as she put together the pieces of Ben's shattered life.

"Sara took her own life and tried to take Kate with her?"

He nodded again.

"Was it raining that day?"

Ben released a breath. "Yes, with thunder and lightning."

Jenna placed a hand on Kate's head; then she reached her other hand out toward him. They were sitting catty-corner to each other with their knees almost touching. Her hand was so close to him now. He was sitting on the edge of the couch with his elbows on his knees and his fingers laced tightly together, but he felt them loosen and disengage as her hand drew closer to his.

He took Jenna's hand into his. Her touch was a lifeline. He was a drowning man, and she had just thrown him a rope.

He let out a breath. "Some days, I can't stop going over what I could have done differently. I loved Sara, but I don't know how to forgive her."

Jenna gave his hand a gentle squeeze, urging him to go on.

The story of his life with Sara came slowly at first, but he found that as he opened up to Jenna, every word he spoke brought him closer to a peace he hadn't known in years.

18

Ben and Jenna talked for hours, and her hand had stayed securely clasped in his. He told her everything: the good and the terrible, the beautiful and the tragic.

The candlelit basement had become his refuge from both the storm outside and the internal storm he weathered every day, not fueled by wind or rain but guilt and shame. He could have spent his whole life on that couch holding Jenna's hand and watching his daughter sleep peacefully in her lap.

He tried to ignore the rattle and click of the ice maker and the whispers of the air conditioner forcing cool air through the vents. These were the unmistakable sounds of restored electricity. A signal that their time in the basement had come to an end.

She looked down at her hand, still clasped in his, and he knew she was just as reluctant to let go as he was. His chest tightened as Jenna smiled and her gaze moved over Kate.

"We should probably get this sweet girl up to bed," she said, stroking Kate's hair.

"That's probably a good idea."

He was different now. For many years, he was like this house in a storm, still standing but dormant on the inside. Jenna had brought him back to life.

He turned her hand over to expose the remnants of the butterfly that had once matched Kate's. He traced the outline, his touch making her tremble.

His daughter shifted on Jenna's lap, reaching out her little arms in her sleep. He smiled down at his brave little girl and smoothed back her chestnut locks of hair.

"I'll blow out the candles," Jenna said softly.

Ben took one last look at the faded butterfly on Jenna's hand before carefully lifting Kate into his arms. The room darkened around them as Jenna blew out the candles.

He stopped at the foot of the steps. "Are you ready?"

WAS SHE READY?

Ben was only asking if she was ready to go upstairs, but Jenna was reading more into those three words.

Was she ready for what came next? And what exactly did come next?

She nodded. If she tried to speak, her voice would reveal the depth of emotion she felt for him.

She followed Ben up the basement stairs watching Kate's head bob up and down with each step. She turned toward the French doors leading out to the carriage house. But just as Ben was about to start up the staircase, Kate opened her eyes languidly and focused on her.

"Jenna, don't go. Tuck me in," Kate said, her voice groggy with sleep.

Jenna glanced toward the carriage house. Her first impulse was to run. She needed to be alone to think. She needed time away from Ben and the swirling emotions twisting through her body. But then Kate gave her a sleepy grin, and she knew her escape was going to have to wait.

"Okay, sweet girl. Let's get you up to bed," Jenna said, falling into step with Ben.

The three of them climbed the stairs lit only by the golden glow of a nightlight. She felt raw and exposed. It terrified her how natural this felt. It was as if the three of them were meant to be together, and she couldn't deny how much her body ached to be back in Ben's arms.

She followed Ben into Kate's room. He turned on the lamp next to the bed, and the room filled with a pink pool of light. Jenna turned down the covers as Ben placed Kate in the center of the bed. He tucked the blanket in all around her, making her look like a little burrito, snug and safe.

Jenna sat on the edge of Kate's bed opposite Ben and touched the little girl's cheek. "You were very brave tonight, Miss Kate. Sweet dreams."

Kate smiled and blinked her sleepy eyes. "Daddy, I wasn't scared of the storm."

"No, you weren't, Bean. You are such a big girl."

Kate looked back and forth between her father and Jenna, her eyes closing as her face relaxed into sleep.

They sat there for a beat watching Kate sleep. Jenna looked up and met Ben's gaze. She had never known another person the way she now knew Ben. She knew his pain and wondered if she'd ever be brave enough to speak about her past.

What would he think if she told him everything?

Ben's gaze darkened, and his wanting eyes wiped all thoughts of the past out of her mind. Jenna stood to leave and felt Ben behind her. There was an energy pulling them together. He closed Kate's bedroom door, and they were now, for the first time in hours, all alone.

"You probably want to go check and make sure the house is okay," Jenna said, looking away and trying to ignore the desire she'd seen swimming in his eyes.

Ben didn't reply. He moved closer to her in the darkness. The chemistry between them was undeniable as every nerve in her body started crackling, vibrating with anticipation.

He cradled her face in his hands. They were just the right amount of rough, and Jenna's nipples tightened in response to his touch. Her vision adjusted to the dim light of the hall, and she looked into his eyes and recognized the need and longing she was sure he saw mirrored back in her own.

"The only thing I want right now is you," Ben said, then his lips descended onto hers in a scorching kiss.

She kissed him back, sighing into his mouth as he moved one hand into her hair while the other skimmed the hem of her t-shirt. He walked her backward, kissing and caressing her until her body pressed up against his bedroom door. She was warm and soft against his sharp angles. He kissed her earlobe, and she gasped. She was losing control.

Her thoughts seesawed wildly between wanting Ben, wanting a life with him, but knowing it wasn't possible. She didn't want to hurt him. But she was falling for him and for the life he shared with his daughter.

It couldn't be real, could it? Liars didn't deserve all this.

But just as the soundtrack of second-guessing and self-loathing nearly became too much to bear, Ben whispered her name like a prayer, hot and heavy in her ear, forcing her mind to focus solely on him.

"I have wanted this for a lifetime," he breathed, taking her earlobe between his teeth.

She was desperate for him to be closer, for his kisses to be deeper. She wanted to memorize each touch, each brush of skin on skin. Reaching under his shirt, Jenna let her hands explore the expanse of his back, feeling his taut muscles flex beneath her fingers.

She felt her way down, inch by glorious inch, to the waistband of his pants. The heat between her legs was growing to a near inferno as his male scent fed her desire. Jenna twisted her fingers into the fabric of his pants. Ben responded by cupping her ass and lifted her up and against the door. He pressed the heat of his erection into her core, and her legs wrapped around his torso, bringing them eye to eye.

Jenna brought her hands to Ben's face and forced herself to pull away from his kiss. She had to make him understand her time here was only temporary. She had to give him the choice to stop and walk away before things went too far. "I don't know if we should be doing this. There's so much you don't know, and I'll be leaving as soon as..."

But she couldn't go on.

His voice was thick and low as he leaned forward, his lips pressing a whisper of a kiss to the corner of her mouth. "I don't want to talk about how long you're here or when you're leaving," he said, then licked a hot trail along her jawline. "I want you for as long as I can have you."

His mouth descended on hers with a desperate growl, and he kissed her with the intensity of a starving man who had just been offered a feast.

"Okay," she breathed, unable to deny herself any longer.

Jenna's pulse hammered in her throat as she reached down and turned the doorknob, letting Ben know exactly where she wanted him to take her.

He ushered her inside and closed the door, gently setting her back on her feet. Now inside the confines of his room, Jenna turned from him and looked over toward the window. The blinds were slightly open allowing for the light from the carriage house's outdoor lamp to cast a dim glow.

"You can see right in, can't you?" she asked, gesturing with her chin.

But Ben didn't react to her teasing comment the way she thought he would. His face became earnest as he ran his thumb across her bottom lip, then cupped her face in his hand.

"I like knowing you're so close. I like watching you work at night. You still twirl your hair around your finger when you're concentrating, just like you did back in high school."

Jenna's world shifted. He did remember. She had been so embarrassed by what seemed like their one-sided connection. She assumed that he'd forgotten her. Her eyes shined with tears. She thought she needed distance to figure things out. But now she knew, she was right where she belonged.

Fierce arousal coursed through her body as she thought of him watching her, night after night.

She went to the window and positioned herself in the pale beams of light. She raised her t-shirt over her head and let it fall. The boxer shorts came next and joined the shirt in a small heap on the floor.

Ben's gaze moved greedily over her naked body, taking in the fullness of her breasts, her lean torso, and those long, toned legs.

"You are so beautiful," he said, adding his shirt to the pile of clothing on the floor and taking her into his arms. "I can't believe you're here, and you're mine."

Mine.

Gazing into his eyes, she surrendered. Being with a man had never been like this. For Jenna, sex had always been about the release and those precious seconds when she would disappear inside herself, the wretched soundtrack of her mind put briefly on hold. But this, this was so much more. Her mind was spinning, her body humming. There was no turning off the soundtrack. Now Ben was the soundtrack. Instead of filling her head with all her faults and weaknesses, her mind was flooded with a happiness flowing through her body, mingling with lust and desire and creating a storm of emotions where he was her shelter.

"Ben," she breathed.

He removed his pants and sank to his knees in front of her. He pressed his lips to her stomach, kissing and licking. "You taste so good," he moaned, cupping her ass as he worked his way up her body.

Jenna closed her eyes. Each brush of his lips sent a rush of heat to her core. He kissed a trail up her stomach to the space between her breasts then took one tight peak into his mouth. She released a breathy sigh.

"I like turning you on," Ben whispered into the darkness, his words sending shivers up her spine.

He kissed a line across her collarbone then gathered her into his arms and guided her onto the bed. He covered her body with his. Each point of contact felt like a thousand tiny electrical pops. He pressed up onto an elbow and smoothed back a lock of her hair. His cock pressed against her entrance as he gazed down at her. Jenna licked her lips, and Ben's cock twitched between her legs.

"Do we need a condom?" he asked, his expression going from carnal desire to one of hesitant uncertainty.

Jenna had been on the pill for years, but she always used condoms. Yes, it was the smart thing to do, but she didn't only use them for the physical barrier. They also provided her with an emotional barrier. Until now, she needed the reassurance that sex was just sex, a biological need, not something that bordered on intimate contact or attachment.

"I'm on the pill," she whispered, then nudged her hips into him and inhaled sharply as his cock pressed past her delicate folds.

Arching forward, Jenna let her hands glide down the planes of his back, acutely aware of his strength as his muscles flexed above her.

For a beat, neither of them moved.

Jenna brought her hands to Ben's face. "It's really you. This is all real."

He smiled. "This is the most real thing I've ever known."

Her fingertips traced his jawline until they found the nape of his neck. How many times had she daydreamed about this man?

His gaze darkened. "Put your hands above your head," he said in a commanding growl.

Jenna complied, hardly able to stop herself from bucking up into him, wanting desperately for him to start moving. But Ben had shifted one of his hands to her hip and held her still, forcing her to keep her desire at bay. With his other hand, he trapped her slender wrists above her head, then pulled himself back and drove his cock in hard.

Jenna bit her lip and tried to keep a gasp of pleasure from escaping as Ben began grinding against her sensitive bud, his hand gripping her hip as he set a steady pace thrusting deep inside and filling her completely.

She'd never been with a man like this, face to face, his body hot and heavy, pinning her down. The thought of this vulnerable position used to terrify her, but not now, not with Ben. She was completely at his mercy, and it was making her body sing with pleasure.

She was so close. With each thrust, she soared higher. She closed her eyes, rolling her head back, her orgasm ready to break through, but Ben stopped her.

"Open your eyes. I want you with me when I make you come," he said, doubling his pace as sweat from his exertion dripped onto her breasts.

She complied, his words igniting all her senses like adding gasoline to a wildfire. Moving in perfect synchronicity, they went over the edge. Their release rocketed through their writhing bodies as they rode out each sweet wave of pleasure.

Ben dropped her wrists, and her hands went to his face. She needed him to stay right where he was, his body on top of hers, making her feel so safe and so protected.

He lowered his head and pressed a kiss to her neck. "Thank you," he whispered.

"For what?"

"For bringing me back to life."

JENNA DIDN'T LET herself fall asleep. It would have been easy to succumb to slumber, warm and safe in Ben's embrace. She closed her eyes and focused on the sound of him breathing and sighed as she felt his breath against her cheek.

It was still dark out when the sound of birds greeting the day signaled it was nearly first light. She stroked his hair while paying particular attention to the way it curled around his ear, and then she kissed his lips. She smiled at the thought of those lips kissing her breasts, her thighs, and making her body come alive. His eyes opened, and he gave her a sweet, sleepy grin.

"Hey," he said, his gaze focused on her face while his hand caressed her hip.

"Hey," she echoed. "I better go. I don't want Kate to find me here when she wakes up."

Ben's hand tightened on her hip. She could feel the disappointment radiating off of him.

"Kate's crazy about you. I think she would be thrilled to have you at the breakfast table. I know I would." He didn't wait for her to respond and kissed her.

"Ben, I think it would be too confusing for her," Jenna said as resolutely as she could. She had to leave. But she couldn't help picturing the three of them lounging in their pajamas, Ben at the stove making pancakes as she and Kate sat at the kitchen table. But before that fantasy could firmly take hold, Jenna remembered the first time she'd awoken to find a man in her mother's bed.

THE NIGHT after Aunt Ginny passed away, Jenna found herself in another world. A frightening world. Judith's world. While her aunt's home smelled of baked bread and warm stew, her first night with her mother reeked of cigarettes and stale beer. Memories of the acrid scents were still as fresh now as they were years ago.

She'd woken up scared and hungry in a place she didn't recognize. The ranch-style home Judith rented was large but sparsely furnished. There were no knickknacks or personal touches. This made the few pieces of furniture look like icebergs floating in a swimming pool, filling the space but lacking in warmth.

As she went from room to room searching for her mother, her little feet stepped over abandoned beer bottles and red solo cups partially filled with stale beer and spent cigarettes. She ran her finger through powder dusting the surface of the kitchen counter and formed a perfect J in the feathery-white film.

The last door she opened revealed a master bedroom with a large four-poster bed. Her mother was sprawled on the bed with a man sleeping next to her. His thick arm draped across her naked stomach. The room reeked of liquor and tobacco, but there was something else in the air. Jenna paused as an unfamiliar, sweaty tang taunted her nostrils.

She nearly backed out of the room, unsure of what to do, but her growling stomach pressed her forward.

"Mommy, I'm hungry," she said, taking a few tentative steps toward her sleeping mother.

The occupants of the bed remained silent. Jenna walked a little closer. "Mommy, I'm hungry," she said again, a bit louder, then recoiled as the man sat up and swung his legs over the side of the bed.

Rubbing his bloodshot eyes, he shook his head and beckoned her over. Jenna complied but kept her gaze focused on her mother's motionless form. A little voice inside her head begged her to run back to her room, but she ignored it and continued toward the bed.

"You're up early." His voice was rough.

She smiled as relief flooded her body. Maybe this man would fix her breakfast.

"I'm hungry," she said, her gaze trained on her bare feet.

The man narrowed his eyes. "You woke me up because you're fucking hungry?"

The man reached out and grabbed her by the hair, making her shriek and gulp for air. Any semblance of kindness he'd previously exuded had disappeared as he stood and held her head at an unnatural angle. Maintaining his punishing grip, he walked her to the door as she whimpered under his brutal hold. He pushed her out of the room with a violent shove that caused her little body to hit the floor with a harsh thud.

"You bother me again, bitch, and then you'll really be sorry."

The bedroom door slammed behind her as she crawled back to her room. There would be no breakfast that day and for many days to come.

. . .

JENNA CARESSED BEN'S CHEEK. "It's better if I go," she said, vowing never to make any child go through even a fraction of what she had endured.

A crestfallen look appeared on his face. Jenna leaned in to try and kiss the worry away when an idea crossed her mind.

"You may want to take a peek out of your window after I leave. You might like what you see."

He smiled against her lips. "Is that so?"

With one last lingering kiss, Jenna left the warmth of the bed and dressed in the boxer shorts and t-shirt Ben had lent her. She opened the door then felt Ben come up behind her.

"Jenna, this is good. We're good."

She was smiling like a schoolgirl. "The window," she mouthed.

"Wait." He stood close to her as his hands found her face. "Come with us to Sunday lunch at my parents' place today. I won't take no for an answer," he added, peppering feather-soft kisses on her lips.

"All right," she sighed, loving the feel of his lips on her skin.

BEN STOOD at his window and watched as Jenna crossed the yard and entered the carriage house. A light flicked on inside, and the darkness transformed into a golden beacon. Jenna came to the window. She turned away and piled her hair on top of her head in a loose bun to expose the graceful curve of her neck.

She lifted her shirt to reveal the soft lines of her hips, her slim waist, and the smooth expanse of her toned back, and his pulse quickened. Jenna held out the t-shirt, arm extended, and dropped it dramatically to the floor. She turned toward him with her arms wrapped seductively around her body, covering her breasts. But her expression changed when she looked away from his window and out toward the driveway.

No longer playing the part of the temptress, she wrapped her arms around her chest protectively. Ben watched with confusion as Jenna's body dropped to the floor. He could only see her head through the window, and it was still looking away from the house and down the driveway.

He pulled on his pants. There had to be someone out there. Not just someone out for an early morning jog, but someone who was purposely looking in at her. He ran down the stairs and out the front door to head off the unwelcomed visitor when he heard the sound of squealing tires.

It took him a moment to orient himself toward the sound. He turned and saw brake lights about five blocks down the street. Barefoot and shirtless, he ran down Baneberry Drive toward the Langley Park town center. He had no idea if that was the pervert, but it was the only car on the road this early in the morning. He'd made it a block or so before he heard Jenna calling out from behind.

He stopped, his heart racing, and turned back to look at her. Her cheeks were pink from running, and he gathered her into his arms.

"Who was that, Jenna? Did you get a good look?"

She shook her head against his chest. "I couldn't tell. He was wearing a hat. But Ben, he wasn't just standing there. I think he had his hand down his pants. Do you think it was that Hadley kid? I mean, I know he must have been angry when Sam threw him out of Park Tavern, but would he take a grudge this far?"

"I don't know," Ben answered somberly. "But when we get home we're calling the police."

Heading back toward the house, he wrapped his arm around her. She leaned into him and rested her head on his shoulder as her staggered breathing returned to normal.

Anger surged through his veins.

He was done playing games with Aidan Hadley.

19

"We'll see you for lunch in a couple of hours," Kathy said as she and Kate walked down the path to her car. "This little garden helper is going to be in charge of watering all our petunias."

Kate was beaming as she carried her junior gardener bag. "Bye, Daddy! Don't forget to bring Jenna to lunch."

"I won't," Ben answered, then mouthed, "Thank you," to his mother.

He'd called the police station earlier that morning requesting to speak with Officer Stevens but was told his shift didn't start until nine. A blessing in disguise, this gave Ben time to contact his mother and see if she could pick Kate up early so he and Jenna could speak with Stevens alone.

It was now half past eight, and the house was quiet, too quiet. Even though Jenna was only a stone's throw away in the carriage house, he wanted her here. Despite pleading with her to stay in the house with him, she was adamant about not wanting Kate to know she had spent the night. He understood she didn't want to confuse his daughter, but he couldn't stop his growing need to keep her close.

He was in his study when he heard a gentle knock come from the back of the house and then the French doors opening.

"Ben, it's me," Jenna called out.

He found her in the kitchen pouring a cup of coffee with her back to him. She was humming, and he watched her skirt sway as she reached for a mug. When he looked at her, it was as if the shattered pieces of his life were coming back together. He wasn't some mannequin playing the part of father and architect. He was a man, flesh and blood, with real emotions and real desires.

He walked up behind her, wrapped his arms around her waist, and pressed a kiss to her temple, inhaling the lavender scent of her shampoo. Jenna leaned into him, and their eyes met in the window's reflection.

"Did everything go all right with Kate and your mom?" she asked.

"They just left," he answered, pressing another kiss behind her ear. "Kate made me promise I wouldn't forget to bring you to lunch."

"I wouldn't miss it for the world."

Jenna set the mug on the counter then reached up and touched Ben's cheek.

"What is it?" he asked, still watching her reflection.

"Those dimples," she said, moving her hand from the back of his neck to his dimpled cheek. "I never forgot your smile."

He ran his hands down the sides of her body, and she sighed, making him want to take her right there in his kitchen.

The events of the past twenty-four hours had been an emotional roller coaster. But he knew one thing for sure—what they had together was real.

"Ben," Jenna breathed.

He kissed her neck but kept his gaze locked on their reflection in the window. She arched into him and reached her arms around his neck. Her fingers weaved into his hair. He loved how this position granted him full access to explore her torso and breasts.

"You taste so good," he whispered and nipped at her earlobe.

Jenna pushed back into him, and his hard length rubbed against her ass. She gasped as he pressed her more firmly into the counter. She moaned when he slid his hands from her hips past her stomach and under her blouse, appreciating the perfect weight of her breasts through the thin lace of her bra.

Ben caught their reflection and watched as Jenna surrendered to his touch. His mind went back to just hours ago when he had her in his bed with his cock buried deep inside her.

Last night he'd made love to Jenna, savoring each delicious inch of her. The fact that there was someone out there watching her and possibly trying to hurt her made his need for her deeper, more primal. She belonged with him, and he wanted to protect her. But this morning, he wasn't going to be taking anything slow. He lifted her skirt and trailed his fingertips along her smooth thighs.

"I love all these skirts. Do you even own a pair of pants?" he teased as his hand moved across her thigh and inside her panties. She was already wet, and a torrent of lust swept through him.

He pushed one finger, then two into her tight center as the heel of his hand pressed against her sensitive bud. He rocked his hand, listening to her breath catch. Jenna dropped her hands from where they were grabbing fistfuls of his dark hair and braced herself on the counter. He knew she was close.

She called out his name as her core clenched around his fingers, and her body rode wave after wave of her climax.

He caught her gaze in the window's reflection, and she gave him a sated smile. She reached back and cupped his hard length through his pants while he unfastened his belt. Within seconds, he was buried inside her, taking her from behind.

He gripped her hips. "You feel like heaven."

Ben moved slowly, savoring the sensation of pushing deep inside her and feeling her body respond and tense as if she never wanted to let him go. Then he pulled out, his cock instantly missing her warmth. It was pure pleasure and excruciating pain.

Jenna craned her neck to look at him. Her eyes were filled with so much of everything he never thought he'd have in his life. He saw his future reflected back at him, and, with one hard thrust, he buried himself deep inside her again.

But it wasn't enough. He pulled out and deftly turned Jenna to face him. Then he lifted her up to perch on the counter. He needed to look at her, needed to be able to see what was going on in the depths of her brown eyes.

Face to face, they came together, mouths crashing as Jenna twisted and tugged the hair at the nape of his neck sending sharp pulses of desire straight to his cock. He growled and assaulted her neck with wet kisses. Shirts were hastily removed and, unable to wait any longer, Ben pulled her body forward and entered her. His pulsing cock wept with joy to be reunited with her delicious heat. He moved faster and thrust harder. He dug his fingertips into her hips and was on the brink of losing control.

Lost in the sounds of Jenna's soft moans, he met her gaze. "You are everything."

Jenna gripped him with her core muscles, and he couldn't hold back any longer. She met him thrust for thrust, and they went flying over the edge.

A knock at the door brought them back to reality. There was still someone out there targeting Jenna, and they needed to get to the bottom of it.

"I bet that's Officer Stevens," he said, dropping a string of soft kisses along her jawline.

"Oh, Ben, first the poor mechanic and now Officer Stevens," she answered.

He pondered her words. "I think I need to put a 'Keep Out' sign on the door. We do keep getting interrupted."

Jenna swatted his chest. "Could you hand me my..." she pointed to her blouse which was draped over the blender.

"These shirts won't do," he said, smiling mischievously as he handed her the garment. "What happened to those wrap dresses? Much better access."

Jenna shook her head, but a sexy smile graced her lips.

"I wasn't kidding. I've never seen you in pants. You even run in little skirts."

"Aren't you the observant one," Jenna answered as a second knock echoed through the house.

"Be right there," Ben called out toward the door. He turned to Jenna and held her hands. "Whatever Stevens tells us, we're in this together. It's important to me you know that."

Jenna bit down on her lip. He could tell she was used to handling everything life threw at her on her own.

She let out a breath and met his gaze. "All right."

"MY DISPATCH SAID you had a disturbance, someone on your property?" Stevens took out his notepad as Ben gestured for him to take a seat at the kitchen table.

Jenna nodded. "I saw a man standing in the driveway. He was looking at me through the windows." She glanced up at Ben. He was standing next to her, his hand placed protectively on the back of her chair.

"And you have reason to believe it wasn't someone out exercising? Maybe a runner who stopped to catch his breath?"

A chill went down her spine. "No, it wasn't someone out for a morning run. It looked like he may have been touching himself while he was watching me."

"About what time was this, Ms. Lewis?"

"Early, around five this morning. It was still pretty dark."

"Can you tell me anything about this man? Build? Height?"

"No, not really," she answered, releasing a frustrated breath.

Ben sat down in the chair next to her. "Officer, have you been able to speak with Aidan Hadley? He's the only person that we can think of who could be holding a grudge, real or imagined, against Jenna. There have been too many strange occurrences for this all to be a coincidence."

"I wanted to speak with you about Mr. Hadley. I haven't been able to track him down. He has an apartment near the Country Club Plaza, and his roommate hasn't seen him since the nineteenth of May."

Jenna met Ben's gaze, and then she turned to Stevens. "That was just two days after I arrived in Langley Park."

"That's right. It was the night we saw him at Park Tavern, and he confronted you," Ben added.

"Nobody's seen him or heard from him since then?" Jenna asked, trying to piece it all together.

"Not that I know of, Ms. Lewis, but I was able to speak with his parents a few days ago. They'd been vacationing in Europe for the last two months and had recently returned. They reported that they didn't have any contact with their son while they were gone."

Officer Stevens closed his notepad and folded his hands on the table. "After speaking with his parents, it's my understanding he's had issues with drugs and alcohol in the past. He's disappeared before, and then he resurfaces when he needs money. His parents are going to disable his credit cards. They say that usually brings him home."

Ben reached into her lap and took her hand in his. "Does he have a history of harassment or violence? We need to know what we're dealing with here."

Stevens rubbed his hand across his chin. "His juvenile records are sealed. As an adult, he's had several arrests for public intoxication, and there was one charge of aggravated assault last year. But in all cases, the charges were dropped."

"Officer," Ben broke in, a tinge of anger in his voice. "Is Aidan Hadley related to J. Bonner Hadley?"

"J. Bonner Hadley is Aidan's father," Stevens replied, nodding his head almost apologetically.

"Who's that?" Jenna asked, her gaze shifting from Stevens to Ben.

"He's one of Kansas City's most prominent defense attorneys and probably the reason why Aidan Hadley has no record," Ben said, shaking his head.

"Then what do we do?" Jenna asked, anger replacing any fear in her voice.

"She could file a complaint, right?" Ben asked, looking to Stevens for confirmation. He turned his attention back to her. "He tried to attack you. Sam saw it happen."

Stevens nodded. "You could. He clearly harassed you, and by putting his hands on you, that is considered assault."

"But none of that will matter, will it? It sounds like his father would make sure of that," Jenna said, rubbing a kink in her neck.

"It's your decision, Ms. Lewis. You're well within your rights to file a complaint."

"I think you should, Jenna," Ben said, giving her hand a gentle squeeze.

"I'll think about it," she replied, trying to keep the anxiety out of her voice.

She knew she should file a complaint, but the part of her that ran, the part that left everything behind wanted her to let it go. She'd be gone soon enough, what would it matter? She didn't need a legal issue tying her to Langley Park. But just as the thought crossed her mind, she looked at a picture tacked on the refrigerator of Ben and Kate at Disney World. Her chest tightened. She was kidding herself if she thought she was going to be leaving Langley Park with a clean break.

20

It was the kind of morning Jenna usually loved, overcast and just enough chill in the air to add a spring to her step. But this morning, she didn't notice the weather. As she and Ben walked Officer Stevens out to his cruiser, her mind raced, and her muscles twitched.

She needed to run.

In a matter of weeks, her life had become unrecognizable. She needed time to clear her head, and for that, she didn't turn to a therapist. She turned to the trail.

For nearly fourteen years, she'd focused on her work. And now she had Aidan Hadley, her mother, and Ben all swirling around in her head.

She wasn't even sure who she was anymore. The person she had pretended to be for all those years was fading away, the façade peeling off layer by layer. Anxiety coursed through her body. She didn't even know the person hidden behind the layers of lies and half-truths.

"You let me know if and when you want to proceed with that complaint, Ms. Lewis," Stevens said, standing next to his cruiser. "And believe me, we're going to be keeping an eye out for Aidan Hadley. I plan on checking in with his family every couple of days. I'll let you know as soon as I hear anything. You've got my card, and you can always call Langley Park PD."

"Thank you," Jenna said, shifting her weight from foot to foot.

"Are you okay?" Ben asked, wrapping his arm around her waist.

Her body was vibrating, begging her to lace up and run. "When do we need to get to your parents' place?"

"Around one. Why?"

Jenna glanced at her watch. It was only a little past ten. "I'd like to get a run in before we go."

"I'll join you."

She stepped back and crossed her arms. "I need to run, Ben. Really run. This isn't going to be some Sunday morning jog in the park."

He smirked. "And you don't think I'll be able to keep up?"

She held his gaze. "I guess we'll see. I'll meet you out front in five."

HER CHEEKS FLUSHED and legs pumping, Jenna pushed her body toward the trailhead. She ran close to a six-minute mile, and while this speed usually left her passing most runners, Ben matched her demanding pace. She felt the endorphins taking over, but instead of focusing inward on her thoughts as she usually did, she found herself attuned to the hum of the outside world. Her mind focused on the sound of their feet hitting the pavement in unison, the beat rhythmically changing to a satisfying crunch as they moved onto the gravel trails that surrounded the lake.

Jenna glanced over at Ben. She pushed her body harder and positioned herself in front of him, leading him down a narrow path that weaved deeper into the thick foliage. The trail was only wide enough for them to continue on single file, and she thought she'd find peace in passing him. She thought she'd find comfort in knowing she could get away from him. But instead, the opposite happened. A sense of calm came over her knowing Ben was close behind. If she stopped running, he'd be right beside her.

Her watch gave off a tiny ping, notifying them they'd reached the eight-mile mark. "That's it," she said, slowing down to a walk.

Ben matched her pace. The trail widened, and he came up alongside her and held her hand. His touch was like being anchored in a safe harbor during a storm.

He gave her hand a gentle squeeze. "Where are you?" he asked, smiling down at her.

"What do you mean?"

"I can tell you've got something on your mind."

Jenna nodded. They walked a few more paces as she gazed up at the sky. The trees swayed in the breeze, their stretched limbs whispering thanks to the sun for delivering them from the dormancy of winter.

She released a long breath. "When I run, I feel like I'm running away from something. It's like I'm trying to order all the chaos by escaping it. But today was different for me."

"What are you running away from?" Ben asked.

"My past. My mother. My childhood. I left Kansas right after I graduated high school. I had to."

"Didn't you have any family that could help? I know you didn't know your father, but what about your mother's family?"

"My mother's family made it clear they wanted nothing to do with me. Many years ago, they set up a trust in my name. There's quite a bit of money in it. But you see, the money comes with strings, well, one string."

"What's the stipulation?" Ben asked.

"If I want access to the money, I can't contact them."

Ben stopped walking and met her gaze. "That makes no sense. You're a good, kind person. You're a teacher for Christ's sake. Who in their right mind would pay someone like you to stay away?" There was an edge to his voice, something protective and fierce lingering just below the surface.

"That's just the way it is, Ben."

The anger in his eyes softened. "Post tenebras lux."

She furrowed her brow. "What does that mean?"

"It's Latin. It means light after darkness. That's what you are to me. You've brought me back to life. You've helped me see the beauty in this world again."

And with those words, Jenna knew that with Ben it was going to be all or nothing. She couldn't lie to him, even if knowing about her past meant he never wanted to see her again.

"I've never told this to anyone, Ben. I've been awful, deceitful. I've lied about my past. I've pretended to be someone else, something else for so long. And now that I'm back, and I've seen my mother, I've had to face who I am. But I'm not sure who that is. And then there's you and Kate. I've never felt so..."

Ben closed the distance between them. "You don't have to pretend with me, Jenna. I want every part of you. All of it. The good and the bad. There's nothing you could say that would ever change the way I feel about you."

Looking into his dark eyes, she was lost. Love. Was this love? She knew the answer, knew it in her heart, but her mind wasn't ready for what that meant.

She pressed up on her toes and kissed Ben with a desperate fury. The kiss opened a floodgate inside of her, and everything came tumbling out—her fierce need for him, the pain and confusion she felt about her mother, the anger over Aidan Hadley. The uncertainty and chaos that had engulfed her life came pouring out as she clawed at his t-shirt.

She needed him inside her. That was the only thing that made sense. She knew Ben could feel her need, feel her urgency. It was as if he was able to read her mind.

He pressed her back against a tree trunk and deepened their kiss. Her hands went to the nape of his neck and threaded into his hair. She twisted the dark locks, and Ben growled against her lips, a low, possessive sound that sent a jolt of heat to her core. He reached under her running skirt and pushed the fabric aside. Lowering his track shorts, he grasped her ass and lifted her into his arms. She tilted her hips, rubbing her delicate folds against his cock. Ben found the perfect angle of penetration and thrust inside her. Lust and relief flooded her system. Each thrust felt like a promise. Each kiss strengthened their bond.

Jenna let out a ragged breath. "Don't stop. Please, don't stop."

Ben met her gaze, his eyes filled with conviction. "Never. I will never stop."

THE DRIVE over to Kathy and Neil's only took a few minutes. When they arrived, Jenna was confused when Ben jumped out of the vehicle, until he crossed in front of the car and opened her door.

"You know, you don't have to do that," she said, trying to mask how much she liked this sweet act of chivalry.

"You'll have to take that one up with my mother. She's had me opening car doors and carrying old ladies' groceries for as long as I can remember."

"I'll have to thank her. You didn't turn out too badly."

The run and then the after-the-run lovemaking had left her feeling more at ease. There were so many unknowns in her life right now. But with Ben at her side, it all seemed manageable.

"Not *too* bad," Ben replied, reaching for her hand.

Jenna gazed past Ben to see an elegant red brick Colonial style home. It looked like it belonged in the pages of a storybook. Three white dormers adorned the roof, and the shutters affixed to each side of the nine windows were painted a welcoming Kelly green to match the front door. The yard was wide and lush with pink and yellow flowers lining the brick path leading up to the house.

"This is where you grew up?" Jenna asked, unable to hide the wonder in her voice.

Ben gave her hand a light squeeze. "See that tree over there." He pointed to a shady oak on the west side of the property. "When I was nine, I tried to build a pulley system in it so I could bring materials up to build a tree house. Long story short, I fell out. Spent the whole summer with my left arm in a cast."

She smiled at the thought of a young Ben, running carefree and climbing trees.

As they approached the front door, her body tensed. She started going over the lies she usually told when she was headed into a new social situation. But a strange feeling came over her. Ben's family already knew about her mother. This gave her some peace, but she was still unsure about how to navigate this new life.

She was worried about Kate's feelings and didn't want to do anything to confuse or upset the little girl. She didn't even know what to call what she and Ben had become. The word "girlfriend" sounded too adolescent.

She stopped walking. "I don't think we should say anything about us or..."

"Or about all the sex?" Ben said, flashing the boyish smile she loved.

"Ben!" she whispered as a shiver ran down her spine.

"Your naughty school teacher side is safe with me," he said, then pulled her in for a quick kiss.

Ben opened the door and let her in ahead of him. The heady, warm scent of pie baking in the oven filled the air, and Jenna's mind went back to her Aunt Ginny's kitchen.

One of her earliest memories was standing on one of her aunt's sturdy kitchen chairs, sprinkling flour on the worn butcher block counter. She would move her hands through the cool powder, around and around in tiny circles as the smell of pie filled the air.

Jenna clasped and unclasped her hands. She wasn't even aware she was doing it until Ben's hands engulfed hers.

"It's going to be okay, Jenna. I promise."

She met his gaze and nodded.

"Hello?" Kathy called out from inside the house. "Is that you, Ben?"

"Yes, Mom, it's just us," he answered with a wide grin.

Jenna loved seeing that easy smile on his face and promised herself she wouldn't let the ghosts of her past spoil the day.

"We're in the kitchen," Zoe added.

They entered a gorgeous kitchen that opened up to a covered patio. Beyond that, a fenced in backyard full of shady trees led to a tidy garden tucked into the back corner. A badminton net had been set up in the grass right off the porch where Sam and Kate were attempting to volley back and forth. Neil was close by cheering them on from his post at the grill.

"Hey, you two," Kathy said, pulling Jenna into a warm embrace. "How are you, honey? You had quite a scare this morning."

Jenna nodded. She glanced out into the backyard. Neil was hitting the birdie back-and-forth with Kate and Sam. She didn't want Kate overhearing their conversation.

"Officer Stevens was very helpful, and we think we may know who's been targeting me. Unfortunately, the police haven't been able to locate him."

"It's J. Bonner Hadley's son, Aidan," Ben said, his voice ripe with disdain.

Kathy nodded. "I'm just glad you're all safe. I'm sure the police are doing everything they can."

Zoe frowned. "This makes me so angry. The chances that Aidan Hadley will see the inside of a jail cell are slim to none with his daddy always swooping in and bailing him out of trouble. You know, he's been a problem at Park Tavern for a while now, but he's never lashed out at anyone until you, Jenna." She said the last part sheepishly, giving Jenna an apologetic smile.

"I don't want anyone to go to jail. I just want him to leave me, leave us, alone," she added, glancing at Ben.

"I agree," he said, placing his hand over hers and giving it a reassuring squeeze. "The kid is clearly troubled. The last time we saw him at Park Tavern, he looked terrible, completely strung-out. The best thing for everyone would be for the police to find him and get him some help."

Kathy and Zoe looked down at Ben's hand which was still

wrapped protectively around hers. Jenna saw mother and daughter share a look, a knowing twinkle in their eyes.

She was about to pull her hand away when she heard her name being screeched like a hawk about to swoop down on its prey. Seconds later, an excited Kate was bounding onto her lap, and Ben's hand was knocked away in the commotion of Kate's greeting.

"Have you been having fun today, Jellybean?" Ben asked, kissing the top of Kate's head.

"Yes, Daddy! I pulled weeds and watered the petunias all by myself."

Kathy patted Kate's hand. "She was quite a helper. She even read to me out in the hammock. She's come a long way in the short amount of time you've been working with her, Jenna."

"Well, she's pretty fun to read with," Jenna said, smiling and tickling a squirming Kate in her lap.

"Daddy, can Jenna and I go read in the hammock?"

"Sure, Bean. As long as it's okay with Jenna."

"Only if there's nothing I can do to help with lunch," Jenna said, turning to Kathy and Zoe.

"We've got it under control in here. My children can help me in the kitchen just like the old days."

"And by the 'old days' she means last week," Zoe said, earning herself a playful swat from her mother.

"Go on, you two," Kathy said, ushering Jenna and her granddaughter out onto the porch. "Lunch will be ready in about twenty minutes."

BEN WATCHED as an eager Kate took Jenna by the hand and led her outside to an old green hammock hanging between two sturdy oaks. Kate grabbed a few books and settled herself next to Jenna. The sunlight streamed down through the leaves, illuminating the pair in patches of light and dark. The hammock swung back and forth in a lazy arc as Kate read aloud, her sing-songy voice trailing away on the breeze.

"Kate may be more in love with her than you are," Zoe said, a challenging look in her eye.

Ben walked over to the cutting board and began slicing strawberries. "I'm trying to remember when I asked for your opinion on my personal life?" he replied, giving his little sister a warning glance.

"Children," Kathy said, her tone pleasant but firm.

Ben and Zoe, used to this motherly rebuke, shared a wry smile.

Kathy picked up a dish towel and wiped some flour from the counter. "You know, Benjamin, it's been more than three years since Sara's death. You are allowed to be happy. You're allowed to love again."

He didn't reply.

Kathy joined him at the cutting board, taking up a small paring knife. "Often, honey, all the things we need in this life, the important things, are right in front of us. We just have to open our hearts and let them in."

His usual response to his mother or sister nosing around his personal life was to respond with a sharp barb or ignore the comment altogether. But he didn't want to fall back on the callous ways that had kept him cocooned in his pain. He glanced outside at Jenna and Kate reading and swinging in the hammock.

"I know, Mom," he said giving his mother a grateful smile. "I can see exactly what I have right in front of me."

"REMATCH!" Kate called out, smiling up at her father with a thin rim of vanilla ice cream from her slice of apple pie à la mode still coating the top of her lip. She'd held the badminton birdie all through lunch and kept reminding everyone of the game that was to take place after their meal.

Ben tousled her hair. "All right, Jellybean. Just as soon as we get the table cleared."

"Why don't you all start playing," Neil suggested. "I think Jenna and I can finish up."

"Absolutely," Jenna replied.

The group positioned themselves on the badminton court with Sam refereeing. Ben and Kate teamed up to play against Zoe and Kathy.

Jenna smiled as she watched Ben adjust Kate's grip on the racket while she and Neil collected plates and glasses.

"Ben's not too bad with a racket. He went to state for tennis his senior year of high school," Neil shared.

"I think Ben's probably good at just about everything he does," Jenna replied, giving Neil a warm smile.

They walked into the kitchen and Neil chuckled. "He certainly works hard for what he wants. He's always been like that."

Neil set a dish on the counter. "Kathy mentioned you lived in this area when you were younger."

"I wasn't here for very long. We rented a house near the high school for a few months during my sophomore year."

"Your family moved a lot when you were growing up." It was more of a statement than a question. Neil sat down on a barstool and motioned for her to take the seat next to him.

Jenna took the offered barstool. "We did. It was just my mother and me."

She wasn't going to mention Travis.

"I don't think Kath's told you about my father?"

"No, Kathy's never mentioned your father to me." Jenna met Neil's gaze. His gray eyes were kind and reassuring.

"He was a good man, an officer in the Air Force. He was hurt in a training accident when I was thirteen years old. After that, he wasn't able to serve and was honorably discharged. That's when we moved from Maine to Kansas City to be closer to my mother's sister. But we weren't here two months before my mother passed away."

"Neil, I'm so sorry."

"She had a rare heart condition and, back in those days, we didn't have the technology or the knowledge to diagnose or even treat it like we do today."

"That had to be hard for you and your father."

"It was hard on him, and he didn't deal with it well. He drank to

numb the pain of losing my mother and losing his identity as an officer. By the time I was sixteen, he was an entirely different person. He
became violent and abusive. After going to school with one too many
black eyes, the authorities intervened, and I was sent to live with my
aunt."

A wave of sorrow churned in her belly while thoughts of her
mother, Travis, and Aunt Ginny filled her head. "I'm so sorry you had
to go through that."

"I didn't tell you this to upset you. I may be overstepping here, but
I think you and I may have grown up in similar circumstances."

A lump formed in her throat. If she tried to speak, her words
would have come out all broken and cracked.

"Jenna, I can see you care deeply for Kate and Ben."

Jenna gave Neil a genuine smile, her teary eyes betraying her
control. "I do care for them, so very much."

Neil patted her hand. "When I met Kathy and Ben, I knew I
wanted to spend the rest of my life with them. But I was afraid. I'd
closed off my heart. I told myself I'd never let anyone hurt or reject
me the way my father did. So I pulled away, frightened by all that
love. I didn't know if I could take it if they ever decided they didn't
want me. And thankfully, Kath called me on it."

Laughter broke out in the backyard, and Neil paused. Kathy and
Zoe had bumped into each other, each going for the birdie, and Ben
and Kate were fist pumping and high-fiving after winning the point.

"What did Kathy tell you that made you change your mind?"
Jenna asked.

A smile crept across his face. "She told me that what I was doing
wasn't living; it was merely surviving. She said that all the walls I'd
constructed to protect my heart might be keeping out the possibility
of pain, but they were most certainly keeping out the love. So, I took
the greatest risk of my life. I opened my heart, and I chose. I chose
Kath and Ben, and the rest is history."

Neil rose to his feet and gave Jenna a fatherly pat on the shoulder.
He walked out of the kitchen and greeted his wife and daughter who
were still laughing about their collision on the last point. Jenna

watched as Kathy lovingly touched Neil's cheek as they exchanged a few words. Her gaze left Kathy and Neil, and when she looked at Ben, she found that he was watching her, his smile wide and lopsided.

She met his gaze and whispered, "I choose," then walked out of the darkened kitchen and into the light of the backyard.

21

It was Tuesday morning, and Jenna had to remind herself that the past few days weren't a dream. The early morning sun peeked in through the blinds of the carriage house bedroom as she stretched under the cozy blankets.

She'd been with Ben and Kate nonstop and could barely remember what her life was like before them. Warmth surged through her body fueled by absolute happiness. But then, like a reflex there to protect her heart, her defenses kicked in along with the punishing soundtrack.

They'll only hurt you in the end.

The rapid beating in her chest and the sheen of sweat on her brow were jarring reminders that a lifetime spent protecting her heart couldn't be so easily erased.

Jenna closed her eyes. She took in a breath and slowly exhaled.

You can do this. Remember what Neil said and choose.

She focused on her breathing and let her thoughts drift back to their time together on Memorial Day. Her group therapy appointment with Judith had been rescheduled for Tuesday, due to the holiday, which gave her the entire day to spend with Ben and Kate.

It was a gorgeous day, and they'd spent hours riding their bikes around Lake Boley. Exhausted from the exertion of racing home, Ben had rolled out an old quilt in the backyard, and they plunked down like three sleepy sacks of potatoes.

With Kate lying between them, they stared up at the clouds drifting languidly through the sky. Every so often, one of them would point out a cloud that resembled an animal or some object. Ben and Jenna laughed when Kate had sworn she had seen a two-headed unicorn.

Holding on to Jenna's hand, Kate produced a howling yawn, then wiggled to use Ben's shoulder as a pillow. Her chattering voice had grown quiet except for the occasional softly spoken reference to a cloud or a passing bird.

The gentle breeze had brought with it the far-off rise and fall of voices from a barbecue a few houses down that lulled them into a late afternoon nap. But before closing her eyes, Jenna turned toward Ben and found him looking at her.

"This is..." was all he said, his eyes warm and sparkling blue, before reaching his free arm over Kate and taking Jenna's hand into his.

She shifted, and their joined hands were now resting on Kate as she napped contentedly between them.

Jenna knew what Ben meant. What they had together, this was special. This was real. And this could be forever.

Jenna nodded. "This is the click," she murmured, a soft smile lingering on her lips.

Their clasped hands moved with the rise and fall of Kate's breathing. Jenna closed her eyes, feeling safe and at peace.

Now Tuesday morning, Jenna needed to get a run in to clear her head and ready herself for group therapy with her mother.

As she slipped on her sports bra, she ran her hands down her torso while delicious thoughts of her run with Ben flooded her mind in a wave of near-tangible desire. She could feel him all over her, inside her, consuming her.

She closed the carriage house door and braced herself against the garage to stretch. There was a palpable shift in the air, and she sensed

Ben behind her even before she felt the warmth of his body. She released the wall and leaned back, melting into him as his strong arms encircled her waist. He pressed a kiss to the base of her neck, eliciting shivers that had nothing to do with the temperature.

"Good morning," he whispered into her ear.

She turned to face him and wrapped her arms around his neck. She smiled and gazed into his deep blue eyes. Her hands found the place that was starting to feel like home—her fingers entwined in the hair at the nape of his neck. But then she remembered Kate and tensed, hesitantly looking past Ben's shoulder and into the house.

"Kate's brushing her teeth," he chuckled, bending down to kiss her nose. "And she's the reason I'm here. Kate wanted to see if you had time to walk with us to the rec center."

"Kids Camp," Jenna said, remembering that Kate spent mornings at the Langley Park Community Recreation Center and afternoons with her Grandma Kathy during the summer break. She didn't need to think twice. "I'd love to."

THE LANGLEY PARK Community Recreation Center was only a short walk from the house. Located at the corner of Baneberry Drive and Prairie Rose, it was situated next to the fire station and across from the Langley Park Public Library. Jenna had run past it almost every day since she'd arrived.

As they walked down Baneberry Drive, Kate positioned herself between her father and Jenna, and the trio walked down the sidewalk, hand in hand.

The little girl focused on their shadows and moved their hands up and down. "We look like we're all stuck together."

"We sure do, Jellybean," Ben said with a smile in his voice, sharing a glance with Jenna.

"What's going on at Kids Camp today, Kate?" Jenna asked.

"It's Tuesday. We go swimming, and then we get to play trash."

"Trash? That's a game?"

"Finally! Something I get to teach you about kids." Ben gave her a playful wink. "The goal is to get the balls, or trash, off your side of the gym and throw them over to the other team's side."

"We get three minutes and the team with the least amount of trash wins!" Kate chimed in.

"I see. So, no real trash like old banana peels or moldy bread?"

"Yuck! No way!" Kate squealed as they turned the corner.

"We could make our own version of trash in the backyard. We could use all my old tennis balls."

Kate's face lit up. "Could we do it today after Jenna and I play school?"

Jenna smiled. She loved that Kate didn't see their work together as a chore.

"Sure," Ben answered as the rec center came into view.

Jenna nodded, but her attention was drawn to the center's entrance. "It's a beautiful building. It reminds me of an old barn." She admired the entrance with its white stone pillars connecting a large arch, created by using distressed wood. It even sported a copper weather vane with a rooster.

"I think that's what they were going for. We may be more progressive in Langley Park, but we're still in Kansas, Dorothy."

"Daddy made it," Kate said.

"What?" Jenna asked.

Ben met her gaze. "A few years ago, the building needed some structural updates and several spaces reconfigured. I was able to make the numbers work that also allowed us to renovate the main entrance."

"It all goes together perfectly. It's caught my eye each time I've gone past it," Jenna said, glancing up at the arch that mimicked the clean lines and curves of a barn. The beautiful, distressed quality of the wood added subtle charm to the modern looking facility.

But before Ben could reply, Kate called out, "Hi, Madison," and ran over to a little girl with long pigtails standing next to a willowy older woman.

"Hi, Lynn," Ben said, shaking the woman's hand. "Jenna Lewis this is Lynn Ramsay, Madison's grandmother and—"

"My principal," Kate added with enthusiasm, hugging the woman's legs.

The adults chuckled, and Kate released her principal then went to talk with Madison. The little girls perked up when a counselor blew a whistle, signaling it was time for camp to start. The girls said their goodbyes in a flurry of hugs and kisses, and then they ran to join the other children preparing to enter the building.

"How's your summer going, Lynn?" Ben asked.

"It's going well, but I'm actually headed over to the school now. That's the thing about teaching," Lynn said with a grin, "there's always something to get done even when the kiddos are out on summer break!"

Ben nodded. "Jenna's a teacher."

Lynn's eyes lit up. "You wouldn't happen to be Jenna Lewis from the Gwyer Reading Program?"

"I am," Jenna answered, a bit surprised.

"I thought so. My teaching staff spent last year doing a book study on the Gwyer program. We watched your teaching tutorials on YouTube every week during our faculty meetings."

"You've got a YouTube channel?" Ben asked with a wry grin.

"No, there are videos of me and the other trainers demonstrating different teaching techniques. They're there to help illustrate how to implement the Gwyer teaching protocols," Jenna said, catching a mischievous glint in Ben's eye.

"You're being modest," Lynn said. "As a staff, Jenna was our favorite to watch."

"I hope they were helpful."

"Quite helpful," Lynn said as an inquisitive look crossed her face. "Jenna, are you in town working with a school district?"

"Actually, no," she answered. She wasn't sure what to say next.

A beat of silence passed, but Ben was quick to jump in.

"Jenna's in town visiting family and friends. She and Zoe went to school together."

Lynn nodded. "That's lovely. Langley Park is wonderful this time of year. I'd hate to take up any of your time during your visit, but if you ever have a free moment to grab a cup of coffee, I'd love to meet with you and pick your brain a bit."

"Of course," Jenna said, giving Ben a grateful smile. "Let's exchange contact information. I've got my phone right here."

BEN STEPPED BACK as the women pulled out their phones. He hadn't really understood what Jenna's job entailed and how many children and teachers she was helping. She was good at what she did, his daughter's progress alone spoke volumes. But there was something about witnessing this interaction that made him feel like he was seeing a whole different side of her.

They said goodbye to Lynn, and Ben took Jenna's hand in his as they made the turn onto Baneberry Drive and headed home.

"Busy day?" Jenna asked.

He looked down appreciatively at her running attire. Another little running skirt. "I'd love to join you for a run."

"Would you?" she replied with a glint in her eye.

Ben's face fell. "I've got to head out to Lawrence this morning. I have a meeting with a client, and then I was going to meet Zoe for lunch."

"How about we try for tomorrow? We could walk Kate down to Kids Camp and go from there?" Jenna offered with a wicked grin.

"I'd like that."

He felt like a lovesick teenager. He wanted to tell her that he'd like that for the rest of his life, but he didn't want to scare her away with talk of forever.

He knew she wanted to be with him, wanted a life with him and Kate. He could feel this as real as the sun shining on his face. But he needed to tread carefully. Jenna had to figure things out with her mother, things he wished she would share with him.

They walked hand-in-hand as the familiar sounds of Langley Park waking up filled the air.

"I'll see my mother this afternoon for family therapy."

"At one?" Ben asked, hoping to ease Jenna into a conversation about her mother. He wanted to understand more about their relationship.

"Yes," she answered.

"How's she doing?"

"She seems to be doing well. It's so strange, so surreal, seeing her after all this time. When I was a kid, even a teenager, I saw her so differently."

"How so?"

"She seemed so much more powerful back then. I told you we moved a lot. But what I didn't tell you was why."

Ben pulled her closer, releasing her hand and wrapping his arm around her shoulder. A warm sensation filled his chest as her arm came around his waist.

"My mother was involved with this man. A man named Travis Mayer. It wasn't a healthy relationship. They drank, partied, and argued all the time. Whenever they had a really big blowout, my mother would pack us up and leave town. We always rented furnished homes, so there wasn't much to take. But Travis would always find us. It was like some kind of cat and mouse game to them. They both thrived on the chaos."

"Were you always in Kansas?"

Jenna nodded. "Travis and my mother have a lot in common. Neither of them ever held a real job, and they both depended on family money to survive. Travis' grandmother owned quite a bit of farmland in southern Kansas. She did well financially growing soybeans and wheat. But things really changed when they found oil. She's been a very wealthy woman ever since. So, as long as Travis stayed close and played the obedient grandson from time to time, she kept him flush with cash."

"And this Travis? He wasn't a good guy?"

"No, he wasn't." She let out a shaky breath. "Can I tell you why I had to leave?"

"You can tell me anything, Jenna. Anything."

"It's not a pretty story."

"It doesn't have to be. I meant what I told you. I want to know all of you. I want everything."

JENNA BLINKED.

1:13 a.m.

She blinked again. The number three on her digital clock changed to a four.

1:14 a.m.

She'd woken up to the sound of car doors slamming. Jenna shook her head, groggy from sleep and listened to her mother and Travis laugh, fumbling to open the front door in a drunken haze.

The door opened and slammed shut. Jenna flew from her bed and crawled over to the vent in the floor. She pressed her ear to the metal slats and listened. Her heartbeat raced as she tried to decipher the voices from down below.

This had become a ritual, laying on the floor, straining her ears as she listened to their drunken banter, trying to make out if she was going to be left alone. She didn't know which was worse, the moments she spent on the floor listening or what often came next.

"Music! You know what I want to hear, don't you, baby?" Judith slurred.

The slam of cabinet doors and the clinking of glass liquor bottles echoed through the vent.

"Make me a Jack and Coke, Jude. And yes, I do know what you want," Travis answered.

Jenna listened to his heavy footfalls cross into the living room toward his newest toy.

Travis didn't treat many things with care, but he treasured his Pioneer PL 400 turntable with diamond stylus needle. A recent gift from his grandmother, Travis had set it up in Judith's house to Jenna's dismay.

"Dammit, what happened to it?"

"What the Sam hell are you yellin' about, baby?" Jenna's mother cooed back.

"Your bitch of a daughter, Jude. Get her ass down here."

Jenna froze. She crept back to her bed and crawled under the covers. Her mother opened her bedroom door and stumbled into the room.

She grabbed Jenna's hair and yanked. "JJ, get up! We know what you did."

Jenna looked up at her mother, fear pulsing through her body. "What is it?" she asked, trying to keep her face blank.

"What is it?" Judith parroted back, mocking her daughter's words. "Did you break Travis' record player?"

"No, I didn't touch it."

"Well, it's not working. So, if I didn't break it, and Travis didn't break it. It had to be you."

Jenna wanted to remind her mother of all the people who were at their house partying last night, all taking turns playing records on Travis' new toy.

Travis loved the band The Police. Over and over again, the lyrics of "Every Breath You Take" and "King of Pain" echoed through the house. The notes drummed into Jenna's mind as she tried to study for her calculus final, the last test of her senior year of high school.

"I promise. I never touched Travis' record player, Mom."

But before Judith could answer, Travis was barreling his way into her room. He flicked on the light and yanked her up by her arm. Then he tossed her, face down, back onto the bed.

"Hold her down, Jude. JJ needs to be taught a lesson. For such a smart girl, she's pretty fucking stupid when it comes to showing some goddamn respect for other people's property."

Jenna shifted and tried to put as much distance between herself and Travis as her mother pressed her body into the mattress. But Jenna froze like a beaten dog when she heard a sound, that sound. The sound that had become all too familiar over the years.

The slight jangle of metal on metal, then a quick whoosh.

Jenna had a strange thought, lying there, torso pressed into the mattress, head turned to the side at an awkward angle. She could barely breathe with her mother pushing on her back and her face crushed into the side of a pillow. But at that moment, she realized she'd only ever heard the sound of Travis taking his belt off. She hadn't a clue what it sounded like when he put it back on.

Travis hauled up her nightgown, holding the fabric near the nape of her neck. The belt cut a sharp hiss through the air as Travis landed the first blow across her back.

"You know you had this coming." He punctuated his rebuke with a second hit that landed with a sickening slap.

Then the third strike and a fourth.

The coppery taste of blood invaded her mouth as she bit down on her cheek, willing herself to stay quiet. She'd learned long ago that any sound, even a whimper, elicited a more severe beating.

Her mother had left somewhere between the fourth and fifth strike, and Jenna wasn't sure if she was hallucinating when she heard the first few notes of "Every Breath You Take." The pause in Travis' assault was the only indication he'd heard the music as well.

"Baby! It was unplugged. I fixed it!" her mother called, her voice light and jovial over the music.

The lashes on her back throbbed and burned, but Jenna tried not to move. She kept her eyes closed tight and counted her breaths.

Inhale. Exhale. One.

Inhale. Exhale. Two.

Travis stopped hitting her, but his hand still rested between her shoulder blades.

Jenna stopped counting.

Travis' hand slid down her back, passed over her fresh lashes toward her buttocks.

"Looks like you didn't break it. Let's just say these lashes are for being such a jailbait cocktease." His voice was thick with want as he slid his fingers along the waistband of her panties. "But wait a hot minute, you're not jailbait anymore, are you, Jenna Jo?"

He was right. She had turned eighteen nearly a month ago. The day had come and gone as it always did, unnoticed by her mother.

Jenna couldn't move. While Travis was cruel and would beat her, he'd never touched her like this. Just as his hand slipped inside her panties, she heard her mother call up from downstairs.

"Baby, come on down and have your drink. I'm bored all by myself."

Travis dug his fingernails into Jenna's buttocks, his grip bruising the tender flesh. "We're not done here. I'm coming back for this pretty ass, JJ, and then I'll be teaching you a real lesson."

22

"He didn't," Ben began. "You weren't..."

Back at the Tudor, Ben and Jenna sat on the front stoop.

"No, I wasn't. I sat up all night waiting. Travis and my mom passed out around four in the morning, and then I left."

Worry creased his face. "Where did you go?"

"I figured I'd go to Iowa, to Gwyer. But I knew I couldn't leave without saying goodbye to one of my teachers. Her name was Mrs. Grady."

"I don't understand? Did you stay with her?"

"No, she did something even better for me."

Ben gave her a quizzical look, but Jenna took his hand and gave it a gentle squeeze. "I was in her Honors Lit class my senior year. One day after class, she asked me to stay behind. She'd seen me tutoring children at the public library and asked if I wanted to become a teacher. I told her I did, but I was worried about getting into college because I'd attended so many schools, had to track down so many transcripts. She asked about my parents helping me, and I told her I had to do it all on my own."

"You didn't tell her about Travis?"

"No. Looking back now, I'm sure she knew there was something off about my home life, but she didn't pry. Plus, I would have lied about it even if she'd asked. Instead, Mrs. Grady helped me pull everything together for my college applications and suggested I apply to Gwyer."

"That's how you found Gwyer?"

"Yes, but you see, I wasn't expecting to have to leave so abruptly. I told myself I'd get to Gwyer and find a job. I had some money saved up. I was hoping I could rent a room somewhere. But I was ready to sleep in my car if I had to."

Ben's hand flinched, but she went on. "I knew I had to see Mrs. Grady before I left, just to say thank you. I waited until it was a halfway decent hour and knocked on her door. It was a small town, and everyone knew Mrs. Grady lived across the street from the high school."

"Was she able to help?"

"Yes, and here's where everything changed for me. The best part. The part I thank my lucky stars for every day. Mrs. Grady's sister-in-law was a researcher in the education department at Gwyer. Mrs. Grady called her, right there on the spot as I sat at her kitchen table drinking cocoa. Until that moment, I wasn't sure why she'd suggested I apply to Gwyer. It would have made more sense to go somewhere in-state. She never confirmed this, but I think she used her connection to Gwyer to help me get in and to help me get a scholarship."

"Why did she call her sister-in-law? I don't understand that part. You were already accepted to Gwyer by then, right?"

"To help me get a job. Her sister-in-law agreed to hire me for the summer. It was just doing data entry, organizing files, grunt-level stuff, but I would have washed floors, scrubbed toilets, whatever it took. That summer job allowed me to live on campus rent-free."

Ben squeezed her hand.

Jenna smiled as she remembered Mrs. Grady's snug little kitchen with the smell of cinnamon buns and the hum of NPR playing in the background.

"Everything changed for me that morning, Ben. I told her I didn't know how to thank her. Do you know what she said to me next?"

He shook his head.

"She said, 'Your life is ahead of you now. You get to choose your path. You decide which road will lead you home.'"

They sat quietly for a beat.

Jenna blinked back tears. "And she was right. That was the summer I met the researchers I work for today."

"And your mom? She never contacted you? She didn't try to find you?"

"No, she didn't. She didn't know anything about Gwyer College and probably had no idea where I'd gone. But by then I was eighteen, an adult. I didn't try to contact her either. It wasn't until I turned twenty-one and the trust attorney found me that I started asking him to forward my contact information to her. My mother moved around a lot, but she always made sure the attorneys knew where to send the check. So, through him, I made sure if she ever wanted to contact me, she could."

"The same attorney oversees both your trusts?"

"Yes, well, his office. They're out of Mobile."

Jenna looked away, and then a thought crossed her mind. "Ben, what do you think about the attorney in the office next to yours, M. MacCarron, right?"

"Michael MacCarron?"

"Do you know him well?"

"I do."

"I'd like to have an attorney of my choosing look over the trust. Would you recommend him?"

"I would. Michael and Zoe have been friends since they were kids. He's a good guy. He helped with the will after Sara's mom passed, and then he took care of all the legalities when Sara died. You can come by my office, and I'll introduce you to him."

"I'm surprised we've never seen him at Park Tavern or around town."

"He used to be a pretty outgoing guy when he was younger, back when I remember him palling around with Zoe in high school. But not so much anymore. He does quite a bit of volunteering in the community. Other than that, he mostly keeps to himself."

Jenna nodded. She knew plenty about keeping to one's self.

Ben pulled her closer, wrapping her in his arms. "What do you think your mother wants from you now?"

She'd been asking herself the same question. "I'd like to think she realized Travis was a bad person. She'd been staying in a women's shelter. Maybe he was violent with her. We haven't gotten to talk much about why she went to the shelter in the first place."

"Travis wasn't abusive toward her?"

"No, he never hurt her, just me, and usually with her help."

"Jenna, I'm so sorry you had to go through that."

She tried to give him a reassuring smile. "It wasn't always like that. The times after she'd leave him and we'd move away, there would be at least a few days, sometimes a few weeks, where it was just the two of us. She was pretty depressed during those times, sleeping a lot. But when she was up for it, we'd play cards and watch movies. She even took me to a carnival, once."

He cupped her face in his hands. "I'm not going to let anyone hurt you ever again."

She knew he meant it, and, for the first time in a very long time, she felt safe and cherished. Ben pressed a kiss to her lips, and the world seemed to fade away, filled with only kisses and caresses until the sound of a car door closing floated through the air. But that concern melted away as Ben kissed a line across her jawline and down her neck.

"I'm sorry to disturb you," a voice said, followed by a nervous cough.

Officer Stevens stood only a few feet away, a blush creeping up his neck.

"Oh my gosh," Jenna said, trying to stand and nearly toppling over if not for Ben's steadying hand at her elbow.

"Again, I'm sorry to bother you this early, but I have some news about Aidan Hadley."

"Would you like to talk inside?" Ben gestured toward the house.

"That won't be necessary. This won't take long," Stevens replied, the blush on his neck receding. "I spoke with one of Hadley's friends yesterday who recently got back into town. He was camping in Colorado last week and said he'd run into Aidan at a bar in Denver this past Wednesday. Unfortunately, he wasn't sure how long Aidan had been in Colorado."

Jenna exchanged a look with Ben. "There were six days between when my tires were slashed and when I saw someone looking in my window."

Ben nodded. "It's only about a ten-hour drive to get from Langley Park to Denver. Theoretically, he could have left after he slashed your tires and then made it back to Langley Park before the storm."

"That's what I was thinking," Officer Stevens added. "Until we know more about his whereabouts, it's hard to knock out a timeline. I've let the Denver Police Department know he's a person of interest to us. If he shows up on their radar, they'll contact me."

"Thanks for keeping us in the loop," Ben said.

"Yes, thank you. Just knowing you're on top of this brings me so much peace of mind. And, I'm sorry you had to find us..." Jenna trailed off.

A sheepish grin crossed the stoic officer's face. "You don't have to apologize, Ms. Lewis. I just proposed to my girlfriend in the middle of the town square in front of about twenty strangers. I never thought I'd be that guy. I guess when you've found the person you want to start forever with, you want forever to start as soon as possible."

"Congratulations!" Jenna said as Ben shook the officer's hand.

He nodded respectfully. "You folks, enjoy the rest of your day."

"So, WE JUST WAIT?" Jenna asked, watching the cruiser pull away.

"We stay vigilant," Ben countered. He took Jenna's hand into his. "I wish you'd stay in the house with Kate and me."

The look she gave him let him know that wasn't going to happen.

"I know, I know," he said, reaching into his pocket as his cell phone buzzed. "I had to ask."

Ben looked at his phone and frowned. "I nearly forgot about my meeting in Lawrence."

"Your meeting! Of course, you should go. I hope I haven't made you late."

He gathered Jenna into his arms. "You haven't. And it wouldn't have mattered if you did. You're so important to me, Jenna. I..." Ben rested his forehead on hers. Her breath was soft against his cheek, and he inhaled the sweet lavender scent of her hair. He wanted to tell her how he felt, but he didn't want to scare her off with talk of love. He pulled back and met her gaze. "Thank you, Jenna. Thank you for telling me about your past, for trusting me with it."

She was wringing her hands.

"Jenna, it's okay. There's nothing that could ever change the way I feel about you."

"I think you're beginning to learn all my tells, Mr. Fisher," she said with a nervous laugh.

"Nope, I've known this one since you were fifteen. That night, hiding in the creek, you were wringing your hands. That was the first time I held them."

Ben kissed the knuckles of first her right and then her left hand.

"Ben, I think that I'm, I mean I know that I..." she broke off.

A grin lit his face. "I know. Me, too."

The moment hung there, sweet and perfect, as if they were teenagers again, wrapped up in their shared past, pressed against the bank of the creek until his cell phone buzzed again.

He glanced at his phone. "It's Zoe. She's probably just calling to confirm lunch."

"Take the call. I'm tutoring Kate today, so I'll see you tonight."

Ben's phone continued to buzz, but he slid it back into his pocket. He reached for Jenna, sliding his hand into her hair then pressed his lips to her ear. "Until tonight."

JENNA SAT in her car staring at the entrance to the Midwest Psychiatric Center while glancing down at the digital clock on the console every few seconds. It was five minutes to one. Time to go inside. Time to see her mother. She had spent so much of her life trying to avoid Judith. It felt foreign to be seeking her out.

During their last meeting, her mother had told her she'd left Travis and even seemed pleased to see her. Jenna tried to shake off the nagging feeling that something about this was off, that her mother's selfish ways hadn't just disappeared. But her mother had been staying in a women's shelter. Knowing her mother, and her love of pampered days at the spa, expensive clothes, and fancy cars, a shelter had to have been a last resort.

The glimmer of hope in her heart grew.

She had found Ben and Kate. She had found a life and love in a place she never expected to return to again. Could her mother be a part of this happiness? Could their fresh, Travis-free start be possible? Her thoughts raced as she entered the psychiatric center.

"Don't you look lovely with that smile on your face."

"Sally, right?" Jenna asked, remembering the friendly nurse who had come to her mother's room during their first visit.

"That's right, honey. You have an excellent memory. Are you coming to see your mother?"

"We have family therapy, but I don't see Elaine or Dan."

"There's a good reason for that. Eric's daughter had her baby this morning, and he's not coming in today."

"Oh," Jenna said, wondering if she'd missed an email or voice message. She didn't even know Eric had a daughter.

"Nobody called you?"

"No, I don't think so." Jenna looked at her phone. No new calls, but there was a new text message.

From Nick.

Are you still in Kansas City?

Just six words. A simple question. But when Jenna looked back at Sally, she was momentarily stunned, caught between the past and the present.

"Are you all right, honey?"

Shaking her head, Jenna placed her phone back in her bag. "Yes, of course, I'm fine."

"Lucky for you, I know your mother doesn't see her therapist until later." Sally turned to her computer screen and tapped a few keys. "She's free until two, so you two can have some girl time this lovely afternoon. Let me call back and let them know you're coming."

Girl time?

Then it clicked. She was going to be alone with her mother.

After making the call, Sally walked Jenna back and had her put her purse into a locker. This was different from when she'd seen her mother for group therapy. Today, nobody would be monitoring them. This time, she'd be alone.

"You know, I'd hate to disrupt my mother's schedule. Maybe I should go and come back when Eric's available."

"I'm sure it's no trouble, honey," Sally replied, her kind words doing little to quell Jenna's growing apprehension.

The nurse gestured down the hall. "And look, here's Judith now."

23

And there she was.

Casually walking down the hall, wearing gold sandals, a pair of fitted white capris, and a sleeveless flowing top, Judith was still the beautiful, careless woman Jenna remembered floating through life, blind to responsibility, looking for the next good time. How strange that even in rehab her mother seemed somehow above it. Almost as if everyone's sole purpose in this facility was to cater to Judith Lewis' whims.

"Let me look at you, little girl," Judith said as her gaze flicked to Sally.

"Judith, I think your little girl's all grown up. There's nothing little about her anymore. Now you ladies have a nice visit. Nurse Lori is going to come and get you when it's time to see the doc."

"Thank you, Sally," Judith said in her most syrupy Alabama drawl.

Judith could fill up a room, always pulling the light to shine brightest on herself. Jenna remembered how she too would get pulled into Judith's orbit during those times when Travis wasn't around.

"Sit down, JJ. That was quite a storm the other night. I heard those sirens goin' off and couldn't help thinkin' of Ginny and her sweet little farm."

"Yes, it was quite a storm." Jenna stared at her mother. The woman had never spoken of Aunt Ginny.

"Dear, Aunt Ginny. I've been thinkin' a lot about her and how kind she was to me. I was too much of a wild child back then to know it, but now I see how good she was, takin' us in all those years ago."

"She was a very good person." Jenna couldn't say anything more. Talk of Aunt Ginny only made her feel vulnerable, and she needed all her defenses at the ready.

"JJ, bein' here has got me thinkin' about how you and I need to be there for each other. Help each other."

"I'm here to help you," Jenna answered, trying not to let her heart get too carried away with hope.

"I know you are, darlin'. And I can't tell you how much that means to me."

"Mom, I need to ask you something."

"Ask away, baby girl."

"What happened? Why did you go to the Rose Brooks Women's Shelter?"

"Jenna Jo, isn't it obvious? I was tryin' to leave Travis, and he started breakin' things in the house, punchin' holes in the walls. It scared me half to death. I threw a few things into a bag and went to the shelter. I'd seen a little blurb on the news for Rose Brooks on the television. I think some professional athlete's wife had gone there."

Jenna nodded, urging her mother to go on.

"I knew it was really over between the two of us. And I had to go somewhere he couldn't get to me. That's the long and short of it."

Jenna stared at her mother. Judith Lewis was so good at getting what she wanted. Jenna had seen her manipulate men and women alike to get her way. But things were different with Travis.

Travis and Judith were the Bonnie and Clyde of narcissism and irresponsibility, moving from town to town, living only for themselves. Their relationship was always tumultuous, like a roller coaster about to fly off the rails at any moment. But now, knowing that Judith suffered from bipolar disorder, Jenna could better understand her mother's behavior as well as her attraction to Travis. They both lived for the high and needed a constant stream of drama to survive.

From place to place, especially in the smaller, working class towns, Travis and Judith always found people who envied their easy wealth. The two of them must have seemed like celebrities, no jobs, no responsibilities, and always with money to burn. Their only occupation was having a good time.

And then there were the schemes. Travis was always trying to work an angle. It was no secret he hated pandering to his grandmother to fund his exploits. He would throw his money, as well as Judith's, at any half-cocked business venture. There were partnerships in restaurants that went under in a matter of months, a chain of tanning salons that went bust, and a tech company he swore was going to be the next big thing only to fizzle into nothing but a heap of debts.

And with each failed venture, there was the hope that gambling could recover the money they had so recklessly thrown away. It was just a quick jaunt over the Kansas border into Missouri where casinos and riverboat gambling, glossy and exploding with neon lights, promised the chance of big jackpots.

Judith shifted on the couch and folded her hands in her lap. "They were so kind to me at Rose Brooks. They couldn't believe I had a daughter your age when I told them about you."

This was the opening Jenna needed. "You gave them my contact information. Why didn't you just call me if you needed help?"

Judith crumpled like a wounded bird. "You left me, JJ. What kind of daughter leaves her mother without even a goodbye. I didn't know if I could count on you."

That was it. The familiar twist of guilt tightened around her heart like a vice.

"I'm sorry. I didn't want to leave like that, but I was scared that Travis was going to—"

Judith put up her hand. "That's all in the past. What matters now is that we're here, together."

Jenna wanted to tell her mother about Travis' threat, about why she had to leave right then and there, but her mother's next words stopped her right in their tracks.

"Now tell me about this man. I hope he's not after your money."

"About what? What man?"

"Look at your face! The man that you must be seein'. Anyone can tell that you've got a beau in your life with that rosy glow on your cheeks. Remember, I am your mama. You can't hide anything from me."

Jenna wasn't sure what to say. She couldn't remember a time when her mother had known anything about her life. The familiar memories of her dreary childhood threatened to replay, but she forced her mind to stop.

Maybe this was her mother trying to connect with her. Men, and being seen as attractive by men, had always been important to Judith.

"I have met someone. Not really met but reconnected."

"That's wonderful! But you need to protect your trust, JJ. Does he know about it?"

"The trust?"

"Of course, the trust, baby. We have to think about what we'll need to start over."

"Mom, I have a job and my own money. You don't have to worry about the trust. I have a good idea of what to do with it."

Judith smoothed out a crease on her capri pants. "You know I was never good with money. I don't even know what's going on with my trust fund. All those different businesses that were supposed to be such good investments..."

"Don't worry, Mom. I have plenty to help you get you back on your feet. But you should think about getting a job. You'd have something to do, a schedule, and I'm sure you'd meet friendly people."

"Yes, I think a little job would be very sweet. Maybe helpin' other women at Rose Brooks?"

Jenna had spent a lifetime guarding her heart against her mother's cruelty. But she couldn't hold back the tears of happiness trickling down her cheeks.

"I think that's a wonderful idea. I'd like to do something for Rose Brooks, too," she said, smiling through her tears.

"Judith," came a voice calling from down the hall. "Sally said I'd find you here. It's time for your session, dear."

"Looks like our time's up," Judith said, meeting her daughter's teary gaze. "I'll see you in a few days, baby girl."

Judith stood and took a few steps toward the nurse, but then she turned back to face her daughter. "You know, I talked to the attorney in Mobile. Like I said, I'm having a little trouble workin' out some issues with my trust right now. But he did say you could grant me access to yours. Then we could do all this fun future plannin' together."

"Don't worry about a thing, Mom. I'm going to speak with my own attorney about the trust. I'll get everything figured out."

"Come give your mama a hug."

Jenna closed her eyes and wrapped her arms around her mother's tiny frame. All the broken pieces of her heart were starting to come together. A real life without lies and deceit was possible. She could stay here in Langley Park with Ben and Kate. She could help her mother start a life without Travis. This could be the happily ever after she had always wanted.

JENNA SAID goodbye to the nurses at the psychiatric center's front desk and headed outside. She pulled her phone from her purse only to have it start ringing in her hand.

It was Zoe.

"Hey, Zoe!" she answered, wiping back one last happy tear.

"Jenna, I'm so glad you picked up. I've been trying to call people, but nobody's answering their phone. I wasn't sure what to do."

"Slow down, Zoe. What's wrong?"

"It's my mom. She just called. She and Kate were in the backyard. She lost her footing, and she thinks she may have broken her ankle. My dad's in surgery. Sam's not answering. Ben just left to head back to Langley Park, but he's at least an hour away. I even texted my friend Michael, but I haven't heard back. I hate to bother you with this."

"Zoe, it's no bother at all. I'm leaving the hospital. I'll head over there right now."

"Thank you so much, Jenna. My mom sounded pretty bad on the phone. She was trying to stay calm for Kate, but I could tell she was in terrible pain. I know she doesn't want to upset Kate by calling an ambulance."

LESS THAN TEN MINUTES LATER, Jenna pulled up in front of the Stein's home.

"Hello?" she called out, opening the door after a few tentative knocks.

"We're back here, Jenna," Kathy answered from the patio.

The house was dark, but Jenna could see straight through and directly onto the back porch. Kathy was sitting on a patio chair, her leg propped on another chair while Kate stood inspecting her grandmother's ankle.

"Hello, Jenna. It looks like I've done it this time," she added with a chuckle that turned into a grimace of pain.

"Let's get you to the hospital so they can take a look," Jenna said, then turned her attention to Kate. "Are you ready to be a super helper?"

Kate jumped to attention. "I'm ready! Grandma, do you want me to get your purse?"

"That would be very helpful, sweetheart," Kathy said as Jenna helped her to stand.

A knock came from the front door. "Mrs. Stein, it's Michael."

"Oh, for Pete's sake! It looks like Zoe's called in the cavalry."

Jenna's gaze followed Kate as she ran to the front door toward a tall man entering the house.

"Hey, Miss Kate! Where's your grandma?"

Kate spoke rapidly, bringing Michael up to speed. As Kate led him back to the patio, Jenna had to do a double take.

Sharing the same dark auburn hair and green eyes, Michael could have been Sam's brother. But, while Sam's features were soft and rounded, Michael's were sharper and more angular. He looked as if he had been plucked from a GQ magazine spread with his crisp suit and jacket folded neatly over his arm.

Kathy reached out and clasped his hand. "Michael, thank you for coming to help me."

"It's no trouble, Mrs. Stein. The text came in from Zoe just as I was finishing with a client."

Michael glanced over at Jenna and nodded.

"I'm not sure if you've met Jenna, yet," Kathy said.

"Jenna Lewis," Jenna said and shook Michael's hand. She noticed that while he and Sam shared the same emerald eyes, Michael's were muted. Not that he looked depressed, but they held a hint sadness she recognized.

"I'm Michael," he answered with a kind smile.

"One day, Michael," Kathy said as she tried to stand, "you're going to have to start calling me Kathy." But her ankle proved too weak for even the slightest pressure, and Kathy lost her balance.

Michael was quick to intervene, and soon they had Kathy upright and securely standing with the bulk of her weight on her good leg.

"Thank you both so much," Kathy offered again as they went to Jenna's car. "I don't know what I would have done if you hadn't come so quickly. How can I ever repay your kindness?"

"How about you make us one of your apple pies, and we'll call it even," Michael said, settling her in the car as Jenna retrieved Kate's booster seat and buckled up the little girl next to her grandmother.

"I can agree to those terms, counselor."

IT WAS a quick drive to the emergency room with Michael following behind them in his car. He had insisted on coming along. A nurse had given Kate some coloring books, and the three of them sat at a small table in the ER waiting area while Kathy was back with the doctors.

Jenna was finishing up a text to Zoe when Michael met her gaze. "This may be a strange question, but are you Ben's Jenna?"

"I'm sorry, Ben's what?"

"Ben sent me an email this morning about looking into a trust for someone named Jenna. I'm no genius, but I don't think it's a coincidence that your name is Jenna and you just happened to be at the Stein's helping Kathy."

"You're M. MacCarron, the attorney?"

"I am."

"You know, you look like you could be Sam Sinclair's brother. I'm sure people tell you that all the time."

"You're close. Not brothers, cousins."

"Sam and Michael are the coolest gingers in town," Kate said, not even looking up from her coloring.

"Who told you that, Kate?" Michael asked with a chuckle.

"Aunt Zoe did. She said that you and Sam are her favorite boy gingers, and Em is her favorite girl ginger." Kate paused and looked up from her coloring book. "What's a ginger?"

Jenna couldn't help laughing but noticed out of the corner of her eye how, even though Michael laughed, his good-natured ease had been replaced with a subtle rigidness.

Kate went back to her coloring, having forgotten her question.

"It looks like we're going to be here for a while. We could discuss your trust right now if you'd like?" Michael offered, seeming to brighten with the change of subject.

"That would be great, but I don't have any of the documents with me. You see, I'd like to gift a majority of it. Could you look into that and see if that's even possible?"

"Sure, just send everything you have to my office with a note as to what you'd like done with the funds. I'm happy to check into it for you."

Jenna reached for her purse. "That's so kind of you. I can write you a check up front to cover the costs."

"That won't be necessary," he said, waving off her check. "I have a proposal for you. How about you ask Ben to look at some architectural plans for my staircase, and we'll call it even?"

"I can't promise anything, but I'll see what I can do."

Just then, Kate looked up and waved wildly at someone behind them. Jenna turned to see Neil coming out of the ER accompanied by Kathy who was walking with crutches, her ankle wrapped in a bandage.

Kate ran to her grandparents. "Grandma, did you have to get a big shot? I hate shots. Did they fix your leg? I was hoping you'd get a big pink cast, and we could all sign it."

Neil patted his granddaughter's head. "Slow down, little one. Grandma's going to be okay. No shots and no cast."

Kate inspected her grandmother's ankle as Michael and Jenna walked over to greet them.

"Thank you for bringing Kath in," Neil said, still wearing his hospital scrubs.

"Not broken?" Michael asked.

"No, just a sprain. There will be no downtown-dogging it for about a week or so."

"It's downward facing dog, and you know it," Kathy said, her laughing gaze meeting her husband's.

The emergency room doors opened, and a worried looking Ben came rushing in. "I'm sorry. I had my ringer turned off. I saw all the calls and texts when I stopped for gas."

"Hey," he said, meeting Jenna's gaze.

But before she could answer, he cupped her face and pressed his lips to hers, as if kissing her hello was something he did every day. The kiss was quick, lasting only a second, maybe two. But it was the kind of kiss that spoke of intimacy. The kiss between two people, deeply connected.

"Hey," Jenna echoed, momentarily transfixed.

Ben hadn't seemed to notice he had done anything out of the ordinary and joined Kathy and Neil, who were speaking with the ER doctor.

Jenna let out a sigh, relieved no one seemed to have noticed their kiss. Kate had been entertaining herself at the water fountain, and the doctor had just come out and was speaking with Neil and Kathy. But Jenna's smile disappeared when she caught Michael giving her a knowing look.

She knew what he was thinking, and warmth bloomed inside her chest. All she could do was meet his teasing gaze and shrug her shoulders. Michael was right. She was Ben's Jenna.

She wanted to give Ben and his family privacy while they spoke to the doctor and left to tidy up the table covered in Kate's drawings. As she was collecting the crayons, she heard Kate call out.

Kate had left the water fountain and wandered over to investigate several vending machines lined up near the exit.

The adults turned their gaze toward the little girl who was quite angry. She was looking out the doors as a man hastily exited the building, a ball cap pulled low over his head. Ben moved past a few nurses toward Kate with Jenna following close behind.

"What's wrong, Jellybean?"

"That man, Daddy," Kate said, a scowl on her face. "He was taking pictures of Jenna cleaning up the table. I could hear the click, click, click from his phone. I said, 'You better stop it. That's not okay. You don't know her.' Remember how they told us at school that people we don't know shouldn't be taking our picture?"

Ben nodded. "Are you sure he was taking pictures of Jenna? Smartphones make a lot of different noises."

"I was watching him. I could see because I was standing by the soda machine. He was taking your picture, Jenna. Lots of them. Click, click, click."

Kate pantomimed the movements while holding an imaginary phone, her thumb flicking up and down.

Click, Click, Click.

Could it have been Aidan Hadley?

Jenna's senses sharpened. She noticed the hum of the fluorescent lights and the coppery scent of blood intermingled with hand sanitizer. She looked outside, scanning for anyone resembling Hadley, only to see two elderly women walking out to the parking lot. Her heart was racing, but she wasn't frightened.

Whoever this person was, he was only inches from Kate, and that brought out a protective instinct like nothing Jenna had ever known.

She was done letting Aidan Hadley call the shots.

"I'm sure the man must have mistaken me for someone else," Jenna said. But the look she shared with Ben said the exact opposite.

24

Ben pulled into the driveway, shifted the car into park, and glanced at Kate asleep in the backseat. Jenna had beat them home, and he watched her close and lock the carriage house garage door. The late spring sun was beginning to set, and it cast her in a warm glow.

The garage didn't hold the same emotional weight now that Jenna was using it. Images of Sara didn't hijack his thoughts when he looked at the structure. He cut the ignition, got out of the car, and lifted his sleeping daughter into his arms.

Jenna met him at the car and rested a hand on Kate's back. "You've had a long day, haven't you, sweetheart," she whispered.

They walked up the path, and Ben shifted Kate to one arm and opened the front door.

He glanced down at his daughter. "I think she's out for the count. I'm going to put her to bed."

Jenna nodded and smoothed Kate's chestnut locks. "I'll be in the kitchen."

It didn't take him long to get Kate tucked in. Closing her door, he headed down to the kitchen, his thoughts drifting back to the hospital. As he neared the end of the stairs, he heard Jenna speaking in hushed tones.

"I tried to call Officer Stevens," she said, setting her phone on the counter.

He gathered her into his arms. It took him a beat to follow her words, her lavender scent and the feel of her body momentarily making him forget the events of the day.

"He wasn't on duty?" Ben asked, moving his hands in slow circles across her shoulder blades.

"Not just that, he's on his honeymoon. Didn't he tell us that he just got engaged?"

"Well," Ben said, resting his chin on her head, "when you've found everything you want, you want all that everything to start as soon as possible. Isn't that the gist of what he told us?"

An easy silence hung between them. It was the kind of comfortable quiet that said there's no place I'd rather be than right here.

"Did they say anything else?" Ben asked, taking a lock of Jenna's hair between his fingers.

Those weren't the words he wanted to say. He wanted to tell her that *she* was the everything he wanted, but this wasn't the time.

"The desk officer said I could talk to someone else or leave a message, but I didn't do either. We're not even sure what Kate saw. Plus, Stevens knows the situation better than anyone. I'd feel silly reporting a person who may or may not have taken my picture—and all of that coming from a worn-out little girl."

Jenna looked up and met his gaze. "The desk officer said Stevens is expected back next week. What happened today was weird, but after thinking about it, I don't believe that it's urgent. Do you?"

He wasn't sure how to answer. There were too many odd coincidences, too many events that pointed to someone, if not stalking Jenna, then at least watching her. And even more disturbing was the episode in the woods where someone was throwing rocks at her. Whoever was doing this wanted to hurt her. Could all this be Aidan Hadley's doing? Something wasn't adding up.

"Hey," Jenna said, running her finger down his jawline and pulling him from his thoughts.

"No, I agree. Let's wait until we can talk with Stevens." He paused. "What if it's not Hadley? I know the kid's a creep, but he's also young and spoiled. I'm sure his ego got bruised when you put him in his place, but to keep coming after you? You remember what he looked like when we saw him at Park Tavern. The kid was blitzed. He could barely put a sentence together. All these incidents seem like a lot of work for someone who's used to things coming easy."

Jenna bit her lip. "If not Hadley, then who?"

"I don't know. But whoever it is, we'll figure it out. We're in this together."

THE LAST FEW breaths of late-day sunlight illuminated the kitchen. It was dim, but Jenna could still make out Ben's beautiful face, gazing down at her with such devotion. Even amidst all this craziness, his touch made her feel a sort of solidness, a permanence.

Her whole life had been one change after the next. Different schools. Different cities. She had lived in all these places, but she'd never made a life anywhere.

Up to this point, her life had been like a theater production. Once the show finished, all traces of the performance would vanish. But not Langley Park. This place would always hold a piece of her heart.

But what if she didn't have to leave?

"Ben," she said as if saying his name would make him more real. Her life revolved around so many lies. She needed to know everything her heart was telling her was the truth.

"Hmm?" He kissed the crown of her head.

"What if I stayed?"

He stilled. "You don't mean just stay the night, do you?"

"No," she whispered. "The forever kind of stay."

Before she could take another breath, Ben's mouth was on hers, kissing her with such tenderness her lips trembled.

He met her gaze. "There's nothing I want more than for you to stay. You're mine, Jenna. You've always been mine. You've lived in my heart since I was seventeen years old. And now that I have you back, I will never let you go."

She couldn't speak, but her hands moved down Ben's hard stomach and found their way to his belt. Her fingers worked quickly, and before she knew it, Ben was lifting her up on the counter. Their mouths locked in a kiss so full of wanting, she thought she might implode into a million tiny pieces.

"Wait! I don't want Kate to..."

Ben read her mind and carried her into the small kitchen pantry. He closed the door to the tight space, and they were hidden away.

Jenna inhaled the scents of oregano and Pop Tarts and home. "Here?" she asked, her voice a laughing whisper.

But all thoughts of laughter were extinguished, and a rush of desire flooded her body as Ben pushed her panties aside. She reached up, knocking over a box of cereal and tried to steady herself.

He cradled her sex as one long finger slipped inside while he rocked his palm against her sensitive bud. As Ben's hand ignited a firestorm of want and need, her body bucked forward begging him not to stop. She ran her nails down the length of his back. He kissed her neck, her earlobe. She rode his hand, hips circling and swaying as her core tightened around his finger.

"Ben, please," she whispered between kisses.

His breath came in hot pants against her neck. "I don't want anything coming between us."

He released her, gripped her panties, and pulled.

Rip.

Hot, wet, lace scraps fell to the ground.

Jenna gasped. Lust clouded her mind. He slid two fingers inside her and set a steady pace, working her swollen bud. Her hands went to his pants, her urgent fingers moving deftly at his fly. She pushed his pants down and took his cock into her hands. She stroked him in long smooth lengths, matching his pace as he continued to work her. She was on the edge, her body humming with pleasure.

"Reach back and hold onto the shelf," Ben commanded.

She released his cock and gripped the shelf. He palmed her ass and lifted her up. Jenna reflexively wrapped her legs around him as he positioned himself at her entrance and thrust inside her. But he didn't move. He paused, and they stayed connected like that, silent in the darkness.

She caressed his cheek and felt a tremor pass through him.

Ben bent his head forward and rested it against hers. "I can't imagine a life without you. I love you, Jenna. I love you with everything I am."

Those words, his words, broke any last resistance she had. All her doubts about her ability to love or to be loved by this man came crashing down.

"Ben," she breathed. "I want my life to be here, with you. I love you. I've loved you since I was fifteen years old."

The words filled the darkness. Engulfing them. Embracing them.

Her body took over, and she rotated her hips in a slow circular motion.

Ben groaned, a primal sound that cut right to her core.

Holding onto the shelf, she pulled herself up, feeling the loss of him, only to slide back down, the bliss of his fullness causing her to gasp. They were nearly fully clothed, but now it was their souls that were completely exposed.

Ben's grip on Jenna's ass tightened as he thrust, their lovemaking going from sweet and slow to wild and frenzied in an instant. Each thrust, each gasp proving this was real, that their love was real. He moaned her name as he worked them toward release.

Their mouths became a tangle of lips and breath as they came hard, two bodies becoming one, moving fluidly together as if they were the ocean itself crashing and rippling with no beginning and no end.

They caught their breath, wrapped around each other, safe in the darkness.

Ben kissed the corner of her mouth. "I will never stop loving you, Jenna. You are the love of my life."

"And you're mine. You've always been mine," she whispered.

He set her feet on the floor. Their arms shook from the exertion, and Jenna rested her head against Ben's chest, listening to his heartbeat, steady and strong.

He released a sated chuckle.

"What is it?" she asked.

"I knew putting in this pantry was a good call."

Jenna wrapped her arms around his neck and laughed. It was a girlish laugh, an easy laugh. The kind of laughter that comes out when you can't imagine ever being so perfectly happy. Then she stilled, a sound grabbing her attention.

"Did you hear that, too?" Ben asked.

They listened as the sound came again.

Knocking.

The front door.

BEN FASTENED HIS BELT, and Jenna righted her dress, both of them tucking and smoothing like teenagers caught making out.

"Who could it be?" Jenna asked as they went to the front door, only to see it start opening.

Zoe stepped inside carrying a paper bag and dropped a set of keys into her purse. She gave him a playful punch to his shoulder. "Ben, you never texted me back," she said, handing him a bag.

"Kate's asleep. What's all this?" he asked, inhaling something heavenly.

"Sam picked up barbecue, and mom had the idea of coming over here to eat. Aren't you guys starving?"

Zoe turned to Jenna, and she pulled a Cheerio out of her disheveled hair. "I see you've been enjoying some breakfast cereal."

Her gaze flicked back to her brother, and she plucked a Cheerio from his shirt collar. "Lots of Cheerios fans here on Baneberry Drive."

Ben opened his mouth, ready to throw a sharp comment in response, but he shook his head and smiled sheepishly. "Sorry I missed your text, Zoe. We were organizing the pantry."

"Is that what the kids are calling it these days?" Zoe asked.

Sam entered the house, and Zoe's playful ribbing was cut short. He was carrying two large bags smelling even more delicious than the bag he was holding. "Your mom and dad just pulled up," he said, giving them a nod.

"What's going on with the Cheerios?" Sam asked. "Were you guys planning on doing breakfast for dinner?"

"No, they were organizing the pantry," Zoe said, her voice laced with hints of doubt.

"Good times," Sam replied. He shifted the bags in his arms, seemingly oblivious to Zoe's skeptical tone.

Ben met Jenna's gaze, and she gave him a sweet smile.

"Come on in. Let's eat out on the back patio, so we don't wake Kate," Ben said, unfazed by his sister's words. He was walking on air. Jenna loved him, and she was going to stay. There was no amount of teasing that could deflate his mood. He was in love and wanted to shout it from the rooftop.

SAM MUST HAVE ORDERED one of everything off the menu. They sat around the patio table, small votive candles placed here and there illuminating the pulled pork, barbecue chicken, brisket, coleslaw, and fried pickles. A Kansas City feast. There was probably even more than that, but Jenna could barely focus on the delicious food. Her mind kept transporting her back to the kitchen pantry. Ben loved her, *loved her*, and she was going to start a life in Langley Park.

"Oh, no!" Kathy exclaimed, pulling Jenna from her daydream. "We should have invited Michael MacCarron to come for dinner. He was so sweet to come and help me. I'm sure he's starving, too."

"I don't think he'd come, Mom," Zoe replied. "He's probably at home. You know, he likes doing all that techno music mixing stuff."

Kathy nodded, her smile fading a fraction.

Zoe took a sip of her Boulevard Pale Ale and dropped her gaze to her plate.

There were a few beats of silence before Neil put an arm around Zoe protectively. "We're still planning on going up to my cousin's place in Maine next week. I think your mother should be healed up by then. That's as long as she stays off that ankle."

Neil paused, then looked at Ben. "I hadn't even thought about who's going to pick up Kate from camp while your mom's recuperating."

The conversation exploded as Ben, Zoe, Kathy, and Neil discussed their schedules, the light from their smartphones illuminating their faces.

"I could do it," Jenna said, popping a fried pickle into her mouth.

The four of them stopped their chatter.

Ben gave her a worried look. "I know you've got work to do. We can figure this out. I'm just up in Lawrence a lot this week getting this remodel squared away."

"It's no trouble. I'm just editing a textbook right now. It's not that time-consuming. I can get my work done easily while Kate's at camp."

She turned to Kathy. "I could keep Kate with me. That would give you more time to rest. We could go to the art gallery and the petting zoo. And isn't there a Legoland Discovery Center around here, too?"

"You're sure you've got the time?" Kathy asked.

"Jenna, I don't want you to feel like you have to do this," Ben said, placing his hand on top of hers.

"Ben, I want to do this." She was smiling ear to ear. She couldn't hide how much she wanted this time with Kate.

"A week with Jenna followed by a week in Maine with her grandparents," Sam said, a wide grin on his face. "I think you're going to make that girl the happiest kid in Langley Park!"

Zoe stood abruptly. "Well, that's settled. Jenna, help me grab some more beers from the kitchen."

Zoe walked over to where Jenna was sitting next to Ben and nearly dragged her from the table. Zoe stopped in the kitchen and opened the refrigerator door and pulled Jenna behind it, shielding them from the others on the patio.

Zoe crossed her arms. "You have totally, flipping fallen in love with my brother, haven't you, you naughty pantry girl?"

The cold air from the fridge felt good after sitting out in the humid night air, but it didn't stop the blush warming Jenna's cheeks. "And Kate, too. I think they're a package deal."

"I knew it," Zoe said, in a whisper-yell. "I mean, I've known that he was crazy in love with you since at least Sunday lunch at my parents' place. Jesus, probably before that. Does he know how you feel?"

"Yes, he does."

"And he's told you how he feels?" Zoe's voice was tentative.

"Yes, he did," Jenna answered with a smile as her gaze moved to the pantry.

"He told you he loved you in the kitchen pantry?" Zoe whisper-yelled again, reading her like a book.

Jenna put her hand over Zoe's mouth. "We were in the kitchen...organizing, and we didn't want Kate to walk in on anything. One thing led to another and..."

"And you ended up knocking boots in the pantry," Zoe added, finishing Jenna's sentence. "I may never eat in this kitchen again."

But the tears in Zoe's eyes betrayed her snarky comment. "I'm so happy for you guys. A little hanky-panky in the pantry, why not? I'm sure you guys aren't the first parents to do that."

Zoe grabbed a few beers out of the refrigerator and handed them to her. The word "parent" danced in her mind.

Other words followed—wife, family, roots, community.

Jenna was bursting with happiness. She was back in Langley Park. Her mother was getting better. Travis was out of the picture. Ben loved her, and there were no lies between them. She had never dreamed a life like this was possible.

"I think that's enough," Zoe said, closing the refrigerator door and snapping Jenna from her thoughts. "You good?"

Jenna looked out onto the patio and saw Ben, Neil, and Kathy laughing as they listened to one of Sam's stories. Ben must have sensed her watching him, and he turned in his chair to flash her the boyish smile that made the butterflies in her belly erupt into flight.

"I've never been better," she answered, unable to tear her gaze away from the smile she wanted to wake up to every day for the rest of her life.

25

"You can't tell me this was your first Kansas City barbecue experience," Sam said to Jenna, leaning back in his chair.

They had their fill of the barbecue feast, but no one, not even Kathy with her injured ankle, seemed keen on leaving.

Ben lit a few citronella candles, and a cool breeze swept in taking with it the mosquitoes and leaving only the fireflies to dance in the night air like tiny glowing sprites.

"I thought you were a Kansas girl?" Sam continued, his good-natured smile lighting his face.

All eyes were on Jenna, something that usually terrified her, but she wasn't anxious. Everyone at the table knew the secrets that brought her to Langley Park, and instead of the harsh judgment Jenna had always feared from others knowing her situation, these caring people had given her nothing but kindness and support.

"You're right. I lived all over Kansas when I was growing up, but my mom and I never stayed in any one place very long. I was born in a little farm town called Ballentine. You've probably never even heard of it. It's in the far southwest corner of the state, west of Liberal."

"When was the last time you went back?" Neil asked, cradling Kathy's injured ankle in his lap.

"I haven't been back. I left when I was five after my aunt passed away. But I was planning on going back on my way to..."

"On your way to where?" Kathy asked.

"To Albuquerque. Ballentine's on the way. That's where my Aunt Ginny is buried. I wanted to visit her and see if the farmhouse was still there. But now..."

Ben wrapped his arm around her, and she met his gaze.

"We'll go together," he said, dropping a kiss on the top of her head.

The table was quiet as Neil, Kathy, and Zoe all shared knowing glances. Sam, on the other hand, set his beer on the table and leaned forward in his chair.

"Those two are together?" he asked, motioning with his hands between Ben and Jenna. "When did this happen? Somebody could have told me."

"O.M.G, Sam," Zoe exclaimed. "You never see what's right in front of you, do you?" Her tone was playful, but there was a subtle edge to her words.

Kathy reached across the table and squeezed Jenna's hand. "I for one am delighted! What are your plans?"

"We haven't gotten that far," Ben answered.

"Maybe I'll teach at a school?" Jenna offered, excitement radiating off of her in waves.

Worry creased Ben's face. "Jenna, we don't have to decide anything now. I don't want you giving up everything you've worked for."

She looked around the table, taking in the smiling faces. "I don't feel like that at all. The thing I love most about my job is working with children, and, the last time I checked, there were plenty of them in Langley Park."

"I think you'll be fighting the job offers off with a stick," Kathy said, clapping her hands. "You should talk with Lynn Ramsay. She's the principal at Langley Park Elementary."

Jenna shared a knowing look with Ben.

"I met Lynn this morning," she replied.

"And Lynn nearly blew a gasket meeting Jenna. She already knew who Jenna was from her work with the Gwyer Reading Program."

"Look at that. Things always seem to work themselves out, don't they?" Neil said.

Jenna met Neil's gaze, and he tossed her a little wink.

"And your mother? How are things going with her? Have you told her you're staying?" Kathy asked.

"Not yet, but I will. She's doing well in treatment. I think we're working our way to a good place. I've told her I'm going to help her get settled. I'm hoping she'll want to stay in the area. We could start over, get to know each other again."

"That's fantastic news," Kathy said as everyone voiced their agreement.

Neil held up his bottle of beer. "To Jenna and Ben and what lies ahead."

They clinked bottles, and when Jenna moved to tap Ben's, he leaned in toward her. "To us," he said, cupping her cheek and pressing a tender kiss to her lips.

THE NEXT WEEK went by in a magical blur of days filled with picnics, trips to playgrounds, outings to museums, and bike rides. Jenna and Ben would walk Kate down to Kids Camp every morning. Then, instead of Ben heading straight to work as he usually did, they added in a quick morning run, followed by not-so-quick morning shower sex.

There were lots of trips to The Scoop for ice cream and strolls through the Langley Park Botanic Gardens. They also made sure to visit Kathy, who was recovering at record speed which she attributed to meditation and healing crystals much to Neil's chagrin.

Jenna couldn't remember a time when she'd been happier.

Eric had called late last week informing Jenna their Monday afternoon family therapy group was going to be postponed until Tuesday, giving her one last afternoon with Kate before she left for Maine with Kathy and Neil on Tuesday morning.

Jenna and Kate decided to stay close to home on their last afternoon together and planned to go geocaching in the botanic gardens. Mondays weren't as busy as most days at the gardens, and Jenna wasn't worried about bothering anyone as they searched for treasures. After about an hour of using the geocaching app on her phone, they managed to find two caches: a sparkly bouncy ball and a plastic butterfly ring.

"The ring looks like the butterfly I made for you," Kate said, admiring her find. Kate had presented Jenna with a small clay butterfly she'd created at Kids Camp. It was lumpy, lopsided, and absolutely perfect.

"It sure does. I love my butterfly. I hung it in my car, so I can have it with me everywhere I go."

Jenna laid out an old quilt near Lake Boley, and Kate pulled a few books out of Jenna's bag.

"I think I want to read *Henry and Mudge* today," Kate said, settling on the series about the adventures of a boy and his dog.

"Good choice! Do you want me to braid your hair while you read?"

"Yes," Kate answered in an excited whoop.

Jenna patted a spot on the quilt, and Kate plopped down.

"Jenna?" the little girl said. Her tone had softened.

"What is it, Kate?"

"I really, really like reading with you," Kate answered, opening the book to the first page.

A surge of warmth bloomed in Jenna's chest as she divided Kate's hair into sections. "I really, really like reading with you, too, Kate."

BACK IN HIS OFFICE, Ben massaged his temples while listening to the buzz of activity inside Fisher Designs. He had a headache from reviewing, and then redoing, the stair design plans Michael had drawn up himself.

"I'm going out for a bit, Mrs. G. If Michael stops in, tell him I'm about finished with his stairs and also tell him to stick to practicing law."

"Sweet, Michael! He never did like drawing, even as a child. He was always more into music."

Ben was almost out the door before Mrs. G called him back. "You should take a walk up to the gardens, Benjamin. I saw Kate and Jenna at Park Tavern when I was picking up lunch today. They were on their way to go geocaching there. I'm sure your girls would be thrilled to see you."

His girls. He loved the way that sounded.

As Ben entered the gardens, he saw Kate and Jenna sitting on a quilt by the water with their backs to him. Watching Jenna braid Kate's hair was a sight he would never get tired of seeing. He walked up, listening to Kate read but paused when he heard her stop.

"What's up, Kate?" Jenna asked, fastening the hair tie.

"I want to tell you something important. Super, major important."

"Of course. You can tell me anything, sweetheart."

Kate took a deep breath. "I really, really love you, Jenna."

Ben held his breath.

"Guess what?" Jenna said, voice cracking. "I really, really love you, too."

Jenna wrapped the little girl in her arms, and they sat there watching the ducks on the water until the sound of a twig breaking under Ben's foot made Jenna turn her head. Her eyes were shining, and when their gazes locked, she smiled up at him.

"Daddy!" Kate said, following Jenna's gaze. "Look what treasures we found today!" Kate handed her father the butterfly ring and the bouncy ball, but she lost all interest when a flurry of ducks waddled across the grass. "Can I go watch the ducks, Jenna?"

"You sure can. Just stay where I can see you, and don't get too close to the water."

Ben pocketed Kate's trinkets and sat down on the blanket next to Jenna. "Looks like you've got us both crazy about you," he said, watching Kate run down to the water's edge.

Jenna reached out, running her finger down the line of his jaw. He reached for her hand and kissed her palm.

"I never imagined..." she began, tears shining in her eyes.

"Me, neither," he replied.

He knew what she meant. He never expected to love like this, never expected someone could help heal the wounds he and his daughter carried in their hearts.

As Kate ran back to the blanket, he had an idea. "I've got some time before I need to get back to the office. I just thought of a playground nearby you both may like."

"Is it a new one?" Kate asked, sliding in comfortably between Jenna and her father.

"Not a new one, but it's a good one."

"I don't know, Kate. I think your dad may be trying to trick us," Jenna said, meeting his gaze.

"No tricks, I promise," he said, standing up and helping Jenna to her feet.

BEN INSISTED on driving to the playground, and Jenna felt an odd familiarity with the scenery. They had passed Village East High School, but many years and many schools had clouded her memories until they pulled up to the park.

The climbing wall.

The creek.

This was the playground from their night all those years ago.

Ben parked, and Kate bounced from the car. "I'll be on the swings," she said, running up the path leading from the parking lot to the play structure.

Jenna got out of the car then froze.

Ben walked over and took her hand in his. "Do you know where we are?"

She looked up at Ben's beautiful face, his eyes expectant and a little unsure. She couldn't speak, but the tear trailing down her cheek answered his question.

His hands went to her face, and he wiped the tear away with his thumb. "I've wanted to bring you here for a while. It seemed right to do it today."

Jenna couldn't stop looking at this man who had become so much to her in such a short time. A barely whispered, "Thank you," was all she could manage.

And then he kissed her, so gently and so sweetly, she thought she might be floating.

"Daddy?" Kate called out, skipping back to the parking lot. She narrowed her gaze. "I bet you love Jenna, too."

Ben picked up his daughter and wrapped his other arm around Jenna's shoulders. "I do, Jellybean. I think we both love Jenna. Like really, really, really love her."

Kate nodded sagely. "Daddy, where are my treasures?"

At first, Ben looked confused, but then he fished the bouncy ball and plastic butterfly ring from his pocket and handed them to Kate.

"You should give this to Jenna," Kate said, holding up the plastic butterfly ring. "Peter Simms gave Kayla Sanchez a ring he got out of a bubblegum machine, and then they were married for all of the first grade."

Ben turned to Jenna, and his boyish grin melted her heart. "I was hoping to do this with a real ring."

"I love plastic butterfly rings," she replied, the words rushing out and earning an approving nod from Kate.

Ben set his daughter down and whispered in her ear. Then Jenna heard the four most beautiful words that had ever been strung together as Kate and Ben asked in unison, "Will you marry us?"

Jenna sank to her knees, unable to hold back her tears. "Nothing in the world would make me happier."

Kate took the plastic ring and slid it onto her finger.

"This wasn't how I saw my proposal going," Ben said, glancing down at the plastic ring on her finger.

"It couldn't have been more perfect," she answered, brushing away tears of joy.

"Daddy," Kate said, little hands on her hips. "Aren't you forgetting something?"

"What do you mean, Jellybean?"

"You're supposed to kiss Jenna *now*."

Ben smiled at his daughter then gathered Jenna in his arms and kissed her.

A FEW HOURS LATER, the trio walked into Park Tavern, a tangle of excitement and smiling faces. Ben never made it back to Michael's stair design. Instead, they spent the rest of the afternoon playing with Kate on the playground, taking turns pushing her on the swings, and racing each other across the monkey bars.

The dinner rush at Park Tavern had started, and they were lucky to get one of the last outdoor tables, the gentle sounds of the town square fountain across the street filling in the spaces between the different conversations.

Jenna smiled down at her butterfly ring as she retrieved a notepad and pencil out of her purse and started playing a game of tic-tac-toe with Kate.

"If I win," Kate said, making the first X, "I get to plan your wedding."

Jenna bit back a laugh and shared a look with Ben. "What kind of wedding were you thinking?"

"Star Wars," the little girl said with a determined nod. "But your hair's the wrong color for Princess Leia."

A waitress set three glasses of water on the table, pulling Kate's attention from the game and the wedding planning.

"Where's Sam?" Kate asked.

"He should be back soon," the waitress answered, retrieving a pen from behind her ear. "He's picking up a friend from the airport."

They ordered their meals, and Kate went back into wedding planner mode.

"I think you should carry a lightsaber instead of a flower bouquet."

Ben chuckled. "What about you, Jellybean? What costume would you like to wear?"

Jenna glanced at Ben. He was smiling that easy, boyish smile she loved.

Kate chewed on her lip. "Ewok," she said, thoughtfully. "I'm just the right size, and I'd never get cold."

"I think we may need to talk to Michael," Jenna said, sharing another amused look with Ben. "Kate is one persuasive girl. We may have a budding attorney on our hands."

Before Ben could answer, Kate jumped up and waved her hands. "It's Sam!" she said and went skipping away from the table to greet him.

Jenna heard Kate's excited jabbering behind her. "And then we asked Jenna to marry us. And she said yes. So now I have to plan the wedding. I'm going to make it all Star Wars."

"I hear congratulations are in order," Sam said, extending his hand to Ben.

A man walked up and stood next to Sam.

"Nick?" Jenna gasped, not knowing if she could believe her eyes.

Sam's gaze flicked between Nick and Jenna. "You guys know each other? Small world!"

"Congratulations on your engagement, Jenna," Nick said. His expression momentarily flashed disbelief.

She rose to her feet, and Ben was at her side before she could blink. She glanced up at Ben. The easy smile was gone. It had been replaced with a stoic mask of indifference.

"How do you two know each other?" Ben asked. His tone carried a sharp edge.

"We're old friends," Jenna said, meeting Nick's gaze. "Ben Fisher, this is Nick Kincade."

The men shook hands, but Ben's expression remained neutral.

"How do you know Sam?" Jenna asked Nick, feeling Ben's arm wrap around her waist.

"We met in Central America."

Jenna's eyes went wide. For as much time as she had spent with Nick Kincade, she knew very little about him.

"Nick and I both spent the year after we graduated from high school helping to build schools in Honduras," Sam added. Sam glanced at his watch. "We should probably head inside, Nick. I need to get to work, and you've got to be starving."

Nick nodded to his friend.

"Wait," Jenna said, reaching out and touching Nick's arm. She felt Ben's eyes on her, but she needed to say this. "It's good to see you, Nick. I wish you well."

Nick held her gaze, and something passed between them. A mutual understanding that, what they had, whatever that was, it was over. His blue eyes warmed, and he gave her a genuine smile. "I wish you well, too, Jenna."

BACK AT THE TUDOR, Ben listened as Jenna helped Kate brush her teeth. Kate had asked Jenna to help her get ready for bed, and Ben was grateful for some time alone to pull his thoughts together.

They'd left the restaurant shortly after the encounter with Nick. He knew Jenna could feel the tension coming off him in waves, but he couldn't understand why he had such a foreboding feeling. Could it be the echoes of his years with Sara, always waiting for something to go wrong? Was it the fear that anytime anything good happened, it was always followed by heartbreak?

The stairs creaked as Jenna made her way into the kitchen. God, she smelled good, a mix of lavender and spring and home. Her scent alone made him want to take her right there on the kitchen table. But he needed to know who this Nick was to her.

"Was that guy an ex-boyfriend?" he asked, staring at the table.

"No," Jenna said, pulling one of the chairs closer to Ben and sitting down.

"You dated, at least?"

Now he knew why this hurt. He'd told Jenna everything about Sara, and she never mentioned having anyone serious in her life.

Jenna put her hand on top of his. His gaze went to the butterfly ring.

"We did, sort of date. For many years we used each other to..." She paused. "To temporarily fill the empty spaces. I think we both had demons in our past we weren't willing to acknowledge. Nick's not a bad person, Ben. He's kind. But I never loved him. I love you. You and Kate mean everything to me."

"I'm sorry," he said, leaning his forehead against hers.

"I love you, Ben Fisher. Don't you ever forget that."

He closed his eyes. "You're everything I've always wanted and never thought I could have."

Jenna tilted her head and pressed her lips against his. They stayed there for a long time telling each other the things only kisses can reveal. His hands found their way into her silky hair while her hands cupped his face.

Ben pulled back, eyes heavy and hooded. He brought her left hand to his lips and kissed each knuckle. He smiled before kissing the butterfly ring.

He'd never doubt her love again.

They walked upstairs and entered Ben's darkened bedroom. The only light came from the moon shining dimly through the window. Ben removed Jenna's clothes, letting the garments fall to the floor. Coming down to his knees, he dropped kisses on her stomach and wrapped his index fingers around the lace band of her panties. He kissed a trail down her inner thigh as he pulled the panties down, inch by inch.

"Ben," she moaned, twining her fingers into his hair, each tug making his cock jump in anticipation.

"I'm going to lick and suck every inch of your body," he growled into her thigh.

Jenna let out a raspy breath. He loved listening to her breath catch and paid extra attention to the skin below her navel. Nudging her toward the bed, Jenna reclined back on her elbows, her hair a golden tussled halo as he licked a slow line along her delicate folds.

"You taste so good," he said, draping her legs over his shoulders.

He brought his attention back to her center and tasted her sensitive bud. He could feel Jenna's need growing as her hips bucked, her body becoming impatient, wanting more. Ben increased his pace, licking and sucking harder and faster, finding a rhythm that made Jenna gasp for air. She was wet and hot under his tongue, making his cock want to plunge deep inside her. But he kept going, wanting to taste each drop of her pleasure.

Jenna's release came hard as she turned her head to the side, biting her fist to stifle the cries of pleasure. He held her hips as they rode out her orgasm, her soft gasps like a symphony to his cock.

His clothes were off in a few swift movements, and he was climbing over her, his hard length pressing against her thigh. He eased himself inside savoring the tight clench of her body, his gaze locked on her exquisite face. He wanted to memorize everything, the curve of her cheek, the way she parted her lips in a gasp of pleasure as he filled her completely.

"What is it?" Jenna whispered, searching his face.

His gaze locked with hers, and her eyes told him everything he needed to know.

She was his. But he needed to hear her say it. "Tell me you're mine. Now and forever." His words left him naked and raw.

Ben pulled out, then filled her again, the slow slide of friction causing her body to tremble beneath him. Their bodies continued this dance in perfect harmony, pleasure building, the quiet around them punctuated only by the sound of their breath and their bodies coming together in the darkness.

"I'm yours," Jenna answered as Ben worked her body. Every gasp, every touch, every moan, solidifying the promise that they belonged to each other.

26

Kathy and Neil's car pulled up the driveway, and Jenna walked down from the carriage house to greet them. It was Tuesday morning. Today, Kate would be leaving with her grandparents to visit Neil's relatives in Maine.

Kate ran from the house and waved to Jenna and her grandparents. She studiously checked Jenna's ring finger. "See," she said, gesturing to Jenna's hand. "Daddy and I asked Jenna to marry us, and she said yes."

Kathy's eyes sparkled with tears. "Welcome to the family. Neil and I couldn't be more thrilled."

"Thank you, Kathy. You and Neil have been so kind to me. I feel like I've found..."

"A home," Kathy offered, supplying the word Jenna was too scared to say.

Jenna teared up and could only nod in agreement.

Ben emerged from the house carrying Kate's suitcase and found Jenna and his mother in tears. "I hope you're not crying because you've done something else to your ankle."

"Benjamin! I'm all healed up," Kathy added, wiping a tear from her cheek. "And for the record, these are happy tears."

Neil shook Ben's hand, and then he kissed Jenna on the cheek. "You chose."

"I did. Thank you, Neil," Jenna whispered, brushing another tear away.

Neil checked his watch. "We better get a move on if we want to make our flight."

Ben and Jenna waved goodbye as the car made its way down Baneberry Drive.

"It feels so strange without her, doesn't it?" she said, gazing down the empty street.

Ben wrapped his arms around her waist. "It does."

"So, today," Jenna began, steadying her breath. The last twenty-four hours seemed almost surreal, and now with Kate leaving, it felt as if a piece of her heart had been broken off. Trying to ward off the lump in her throat, she started again. "Today, I have family therapy with my mom at one. Maybe we could meet for a late lunch after?"

Ben pressed a kiss to her neck. "I'd love that. My afternoon should be wide open unless Michael starts harping on me for his stair design."

"Speaking of Michael," Jenna said, turning around and wrapping her arms around Ben's neck. "He just sent me an email. It looks like he was able to take care of everything I'd asked him to do with the trust. How about I meet you at your office after family therapy? That would give me a chance to pop in next door and thank him."

"Sounds perfect. You know, I think what you're doing for your mom is very generous. I'm sure she'll be touched. Are you going to tell her today?"

Jenna smiled. "Yes, I'm going to tell her first thing."

Ben cupped her face in his hands and kissed her. Jenna melted into the kiss but tensed as the sound of voices got closer. A large group of retirees power walked past them, their conversations overlapping as they passed by the Tudor. But one distinct, cranky voice rose above the group.

"Harold never kissed *me* like that," a woman remarked to the walkers.

Ben and Jenna pulled apart and chuckled. But Ben's eyes darkened, making a chill run down her spine.

"I will always kiss you like this," he said, dipping his head as his lips met hers for one last kiss.

When he pulled back, Jenna saw a playful glint flash in his blue eyes.

"And Jenna," Ben continued.

"Hmm," she replied.

"I'll never be a Harold."

Jenna laughed and buried her head in the crook of his neck. She was going to marry this man. Her forever was about to begin.

JENNA PULLED into the parking lot of the Midwest Psychiatric Center. A giddy rush surged through her body. There were so many new beginnings happening. Her heart was bursting with pure joy. She slipped the plastic ring off her finger and into her purse. She wanted to share the news of her engagement with her mother but worried what Judith would think of a plastic ring.

"Look at you, all smiles," Nurse Sally said, greeting Jenna in the lobby.

Jenna couldn't help her enthusiasm. Dan and Elaine arrived, and she chatted easily. Eric met them in the lobby and walked them back to the group therapy room. The mood was festive as he showed them pictures of his new granddaughter on his cell phone.

Jenna entered the room and found her mother. "Mom, I have good news about the trust."

Judith's eyes lit up. "Go ahead, baby. I knew you'd come through for me."

Jenna took a breath. "You know how you went to the Rose Brooks Women's Shelter? It's the place that helped you get away from Travis and also the place that brought us together."

Judith's high wattage smile dialed down a notch.

"They do amazing work there," Jenna said, unable to contain her excitement. "Along with helping women escape abusive relationships, they also have programs to help abused children. I had my attorney check into the organization."

"I don't understand, JJ. Why would you need an attorney to look into Rose Brooks?"

Jenna held her mother's hand. "That's the exciting news! I've donated the entirety of my trust to Rose Brooks, and I've done it in your name."

Judith paled. "You gave your whole trust fund to the shelter? For me?"

"Yes!" Jenna said, squeezing her mother's limp hand.

"But, JJ, I told you I might need a little financial help gettin' back on my feet."

"Mom, I have enough money of my own to get you settled. It won't be anything fancy, but it will be someplace safe that will let you figure out what you want to do. You could even go to college if you wanted. There are so many possibilities."

Judith pulled her hand from Jenna's grip. "This is quite a bit to take in."

"I understand, Mom. I'm proud of you for leaving Travis and reaching out to me. We've got time to get to know each other now." And be like a real mother and daughter, Jenna thought. But she held back those words.

Judith opened her mouth to speak, but nothing came out.

Eric addressed the group. "All right, folks. I think the pictures have made the rounds. Let's all find a seat and begin."

Judith's posture went rigid, and she balled her hands into tiny fists.

Eric seemed to hone in on the change in Judith's disposition. "Is everything all right, Judith?"

Judith looked from Eric to Jenna. "You know, Eric, I think I may be comin' down with a migraine."

The group turned their attention to Judith which seemed to, at least momentarily, lift her spirits.

"Do you think you'll be able to make it through group?" Eric asked.

"I better not risk it. Without rest, it'll only get worse."

"Do you want me to walk you back to your room?" Jenna asked.

She knew she had shocked her mother with the news about the trust. She also knew the thought of starting a new life with so many unknowns had to be frightening for her mother.

"No, you know I just need a little rest, and then I'll be as right as rain."

"Mom, this is a new beginning for us. I have so much to tell you. We'll talk when you feel better."

Judith nodded to no one in particular and left the room.

AT A QUARTER PAST TWO, Jenna parked in front of Ben's office. She had stayed for the entire therapy session despite her mother leaving to tend to her headache.

She'd tried to focus on the group therapy conversation, but her thoughts kept going back to Judith. Had the news about her gift to the shelter been too overwhelming for her mother? Maybe all this change was too much for her to handle. In her excitement to start a life in Langley Park, perhaps she pushed her mother harder than she was able to go right now.

Jenna walked into Ben's office only to find Michael standing at Mrs. G's desk. She did a quick scan of the space. Ben wasn't there.

Mrs. G and Michael glanced up. They were reading something from the newspaper. The older woman met Jenna's gaze, but Mrs. G's usual wide grin was replaced with a wobbly smile. "Let me give you a hug. Ben shared the big engagement news with us."

Jenna returned the hug, but she could tell something was wrong. "Did something happen? Where's Ben? We were going to have a late lunch."

"Benjamin's fine. There was an issue with the contractor and some permits on the Lawrence remodel. He had to head up there last minute. He asked me to tell you he'll meet you at home. I think he texted you, too."

Jenna nodded. She'd silenced her phone for the therapy session.

Looking over Mrs. G's shoulder, she noticed Michael. He was still absorbed in the newspaper.

"I'm glad you're here, Michael. I wanted to thank you for all your help with the trust."

The attorney nodded, but he didn't stop reading.

"What's going on?" Jenna asked.

Mrs. G glanced over to where Michael was still engrossed in the paper. "Ben told us about the situation with Aidan Hadley—how he'd been bothering you since you got into town."

Jenna frowned. "We're not sure it was him, but he's the only person I've had any contact with in Langley Park that might be holding a grudge against me."

Michael handed her the newspaper. "It looks like Aidan Hadley was arrested in Denver a few days ago. It just made the Kansas City paper."

Jenna glanced down at the headline, 'Prominent KC Attorney's Son Arrested on Drug Charges in Denver.'

"At least we know that he's not a threat to anyone," Jenna said, still feeling as if she wasn't getting the whole story.

Michael crossed his arms. "That's the problem. The article says he's been in Denver since the nineteenth of May. It looks like the Denver Police Department's Narcotics Division had him under surveillance in order to catch his supplier. From the sound of it, this wasn't the first time he'd been involved in the drug scene there."

"That means Aidan Hadley left only a few days after I arrived," she paused, her mind connecting the dots. "He couldn't have slashed my tires, and he couldn't have been the man I saw watching me through the window."

"That's what I was thinking," Michael said grimly. "If you don't mind, I'd like to put in a call to a guy I trust at the Langley Park PD."

"We've been working with Officer Stevens, but he's on his honeymoon."

Michael jotted down Officer Steven's name on a piece of paper.

"Does Ben know about this?" Jenna asked, her mind racing through what Hadley's arrest meant for them.

Mrs. G shook her head. "No, I don't think so. He left about an hour ago, and that's when I finally got a chance to take a look at today's paper. Michael came in a few minutes before you did to say hello when I showed him the article."

Jenna nodded, trying to work out what to do next. "Thank you for letting me know about this. I think I'm going to head back to the house and wait for Ben. We'll figure it out from there."

"Do you want me to follow you home?" Michael asked, concern clouded his green eyes. "It wouldn't be any trouble."

"No, no, that won't be necessary, Michael. I'll be fine."

She didn't want to jump to any conclusions until she had more information. She needed some time to think. She'd go for a run. It would do her good to have a little time to herself to process things before Ben got home.

THE DRIVE back to the house felt off. Her mother's strange reaction to the shelter donation and then learning about Aidan Hadley's arrest had left Jenna feeling off balance.

Lost in her thoughts, she climbed the stairs to the carriage house apartment. She smelled something acrid. Cigarettes? After taking a few more steps, she heard something, a sort of tinny, buzzing sound.

As she entered the apartment, she saw a cell phone sitting in the middle of the large table. She picked up the phone and pressed the volume button. After a few taps, her stomach clenched.

Every Breath You Take.

Her breath caught in her throat, and she froze like a frightened rabbit cornered by a fox. The stink of tobacco and gaudy aftershave assaulted her sense of smell.

"JJ," his voice was gruff and oozed cruelty. "I knew you'd remember this song. It's my favorite. Even after all this time, it still makes me think of you."

27

Travis Mayer.

Jenna told herself to breathe. She was facing away from him, gripping the cell phone in her hand. She pivoted, bringing the phone up, trying to make contact with his face. She wanted to stun him long enough to give her a second, maybe two, to make it to the door and out of the carriage house.

She almost had him, but he was able to anticipate her movements. Travis grabbed her wrist and slammed the phone into the side of her head, knocking her off balance and causing the phone to fall to the floor.

"Little bitch," he growled, grabbing her by the hair.

He dragged her like a dog into the bedroom and pushed her onto the bed.

"Don't move unless you want me to punish you." A sadistic smirk spread across his face. "But we both know you do like a good whipping."

Jenna didn't move and kept her eyes pinched shut, trying to get her bearings.

"Now, Jenna Jo, I couldn't just leave without us getting to finish what you started all those years ago."

She remained silent. She knew Travis, in all his sick, twisted glory. He enjoyed watching her react, and she wasn't about to feed into his perverted fantasy.

"Why so quiet?" he asked, voice dripping of mock concern.

She opened her eyes and met his gaze. Same dark hair greased back. Same stubbled beard, except now it was threaded with gray. And the same disgusting smirk plastered on his smug lips like he had just kicked a puppy and enjoyed it.

But when she looked closer, she saw lines etched deep around his eyes and how his shoulders, once broad and strong, were now slightly hunched.

He looked like the worn-out version of the bastard she remembered.

"You want me to do all the talking? All right." Travis grabbed her hair, forcing her face inches from his. "I've been watching you play house with your new boyfriend and his runt of a daughter. You'll need to thank him for me for leaving a key to this place under the fucking flower pot."

Jenna's heart nearly stopped. In her daze, she hadn't realized the carriage house door was unlocked when she'd arrived home.

"It's been pretty damn entertaining watching you throw yourself at that architect. I wouldn't have picked you as the type to fuck in the woods. But don't get me wrong, I enjoyed the show."

Anger bloomed in her chest, and she blinked back angry tears.

"You always were a little whore, weren't you, JJ," he added, tightening his grip.

"It's been you. You slashed my tires. You were the one out there looking in my window."

A sick spark gleamed in Travis' eyes. "You should have seen your face when I threw those rocks at you. Sweet Jesus, you nearly pissed yourself. It took everything I had not to bust out laughing."

"What do you want?" she asked, scooting back on the bed. There was a coffee mug on the nightstand. If she could reach it, she could try and hit him with it.

"I think you know what I want. But that's all gone now, isn't it?" His words had lost the mocking tone and were now angry, agitated.

"Then why are you here? What do you want from me, you sick bastard?"

He struck her cheek. It was a sharp, quick jab that resonated and throbbed throughout her jaw. The blow sent her back, away from Travis and toward the coffee cup. It was almost within her reach.

"JJ, I wish I could take my time with you, but I'm sure your mama's been missing me. We've been apart for far too long."

Her mother. She had to warn her, had to tell someone at the hospital to be on the lookout for Travis.

He must have seen the fire ignite in her eyes. "No, no, no," he said, producing a switchblade. He held the blade to her neck and pushed her onto her stomach. "Look at you, all wanting to protect your mommy."

One of her legs hung off the bed as Travis shifted his weight, trying to take his belt off using only one hand. Even with a knife held to her throat, Jenna's anger overrode her fear. Travis lifted her skirt with his free hand, grabbed onto her hip, and pulled her another few inches to the side of the bed. The mug was only inches away.

"I can't decide if I'm gonna fuck this pretty ass now, or if I should give it a few licks with my belt first."

Her vision blurred as the blade sliced into her neck, but she ignored the pain and focused on the mug. Before she could reach for it, a chiming sound rang out from where Travis had shrugged his pants down.

His phone.

The noise gave Jenna the distraction she needed. Travis momentarily turned his whole body, including the hand holding the knife to look for the location of the sound.

Jenna slid forward, grabbed the mug, and hit him square in the temple. Travis stumbled back and dropped the knife. He recovered and grabbed the cup. In a fit of rage, he struck her with it on the back of her head. The sickening crack echoed through the room, and she dropped to the floor.

Jenna blinked once as she watched Travis retrieve his phone.

She blinked again and listened as he cursed under his breath, bringing the phone to his ear.

"I'm coming. Just a few loose ends to tie up," he said, running a hand through his hair.

His boots moved closer to where she was sprawled out on the floor.

One last blink, and then it all went black.

DISORIENTED, Jenna opened her eyes.

What was going on?

She was lying in the backseat of a car. Peering between the front seats, she saw Kate's ceramic butterfly hanging from the rearview mirror. She was inside *her* car. Her gaze veered from the clay insect, and she noticed the dashboard was lit up. The car was on, but it wasn't moving.

Then a rumble of chain and a sharp clatter echoed through the car.

In the space of a second, the gravity of her situation hit her like a wrecking ball. That noise was the sound of the garage door closing.

Travis had put her inside a closed garage inside a running car.

She shot up. She had to turn off the car, but the sudden movement sent shards of pain ricocheting through her head.

She closed her eyes as men's raised voices floated in the distance.

The light changed, and it was bright again. She tried to move, but all she could do was cover her head with her arms. If Travis were back, she would be powerless to stop him.

"Jenna!"

Not Travis.

Ben.

He lifted her out of the car and carried her outside. Her head was throbbing, but the fresh air helped her focus.

"Are you all right?" he asked, hands frantically checking over her body.

"I'm okay."

"Who was that guy, Jenna?"

She pushed herself up on her elbows as Ben scrambled to pull her into his arms. She held on to him, relief flooding her body until she remembered her mother. "Ben, we have to call the psychiatric center."

"No, I'm calling 911. You need an ambulance."

"No, Ben," she said, her hands grabbing his shirt. "There's no time to wait for an ambulance. That was Travis. He's been watching me, following me. It's been him, not Aidan Hadley, and he knows where my mother is. He told me he was going to get her. We have to get to the psychiatric center before he does."

"Jenna, you need to see a doctor."

She swallowed hard and met his gaze. "I'm going with or without you. Please understand, I need to get to my mother."

He nodded and helped her to stand. "You're not doing this alone. Let's go."

BEN HIT the gas as they sped toward the hospital. Jenna reached for her phone. Panic shot through her veins. She'd left her cellphone and purse back at the carriage house. She scanned the car's console and spied Ben's phone.

"Do you have the number for the psychiatric center in your phone," she asked, scrolling through his contacts.

"No, I just have the main line for the hospital."

Jenna called and asked to be transferred to the psychiatric center. The time on hold seemed like an eternity before a voice answered.

"This is Jenna Lewis. My mother, Judith Lewis, is a patient there. Eric Lucero is her counselor. It's very important for me to speak to him. A man, Travis Mayer, may be coming to try to see her."

"Jenna, this is Sally, one of your mother's nurses."

Jenna released a breath. "Sally, is my mother all right?"

"Your mother left treatment. Signed herself out not ten minutes ago. She told us she was going to be staying with you. She even signed herself up for outpatient treatment. Are you sure you didn't get your signals crossed?"

Jenna kept the phone pressed to her ear, but she couldn't reply. As they pulled into the psychiatric center's parking lot, Judith Lewis was walking out. She was dragging a suitcase toward a large white truck.

Jenna stared out the window as Ben parked the car.

"I know that truck, Jenna," Ben said. "Remember, it almost ran into that sedan."

Before he could say another word, Jenna opened the door and ran through the parking lot toward her mother.

"Mom! You don't have to go with him. I won't let him hurt you."

Judith handed her suitcase to Travis who hoisted it into the back of the truck. "What makes you think he's going to hurt me, JJ?"

"Mom, you had to go to a women's shelter to escape him."

"I wasn't escapin' anything, JJ."

"Then why? Why did you go to the shelter? Why did you threaten to kill yourself?"

"Look at you, always the drama queen and never that bright either," Judith said, glancing back at Travis. "JJ, we ran into a few financial snags and needed the money in your trust. But instead of helpin' me, you gave it all away."

Ben had caught up and stood by her side. He pressed a steadying hand to her back.

"This was all some big lie to try to get my money?" Jenna asked.

"Well, I didn't quite think that callin' you up after how many odd years and sayin', 'Hey, this is your mama, I need about three million in cash,' would go over very well."

"You did all this just to try to trick me, and you did it with him?" Jenna pointed at Travis.

Judith didn't answer. She looked down at her nails as if she was bored by the conversation.

"Mom, you know Travis was awful to me, beat me, tormented me. Do you know he's been watching me, following me? Mom, he tried to rape me!"

"Don't you dare," Judith said, her expression twisting with

contempt. "You'll say anything to try and hurt me, won't you? Ungrateful little bitch. You wouldn't even have that trust fund without me, and what did do you do with it? Piss it all away to some worthless shelter."

Ben stepped forward. "That's enough," he said, his tone low and deadly, first eyeing Judith, then moving his gaze to Travis.

Travis barked out a laugh. "What are you gonna do about it, pretty boy?"

In the space of a second, Ben had Travis by the throat, pressing him into the truck. "You are going to pay for what you did," he said, his words laced with fury. "I'm going to make sure of it."

Travis' cocksure façade fell from his face. He squirmed and struggled for breath, but Ben's grip was unrelenting.

"And you," Ben said, turning his wrath on Judith. "You don't deserve her love. You never did."

"Stop," Jenna said, her voice barely a whisper. She met Ben's gaze. "I know you're doing this because you care about me, but I need you to stop."

His eyes were wild but whatever he saw in her gaze brought him back to himself. He nodded and released his grip.

Travis scurried like a frightened rodent back into his truck and rubbed his neck. "Jude, we need to go."

Jenna looked at her mother. "I thought we were going to be a family."

Judith gave Ben a wary glance. She took a few steps back toward the truck and smoothed her shirt. She had grown a few shades paler after Ben's harsh rebuke, but the distance between them seemed to bolster her resolve. "You? My family? You, little girl, are my greatest disappointment. I have all the family I need in that truck."

"Jude, now," Travis said, craning his head out the window, a note of urgency in his voice.

Judith climbed into Travis' truck, and Jenna's vision blurred. She tried to call out but couldn't speak. She tried to count her breaths, but it was no use. Everything disappeared, and she spiraled away into an empty, black abyss.

28

"The doctors say she's going to be okay—no sign of carbon monoxide exposure. There's a contusion on the back of her head, but they think it was shock that caused her to pass out."

"Well, Christ, after the day she's had."

Jenna listened to the hushed voices. The last two were low, men's voices.

"But he didn't," a pause, then a sharp exhale of breath. "She wasn't raped?"

That was Zoe, she thought, feeling oddly proud of herself for identifying the speaker.

Jenna tried to open her eyes, blinking them slowly.

"No, at least she didn't have to endure that."

Ben's voice.

The room came into focus, and she was looking up at Sam.

"Hey," he said, surprise registering in his voice.

Sam looked different. He wasn't sporting the warm, relaxed smile she'd grown to love. He looked worried. She shifted her gaze and Ben and Zoe came into view.

Sam stepped out of the way, and Ben took his place. He looked tired, his dark hair a disheveled mess as if he'd been pulling at it in clumps. He held her hands. She looked down and saw an IV coming out of her arm.

"It's only some fluids. You were dehydrated and in shock."

It all came back to her like a blurry picture coming into focus. Travis' attack and Judith's deception.

"My mother," she whispered.

"I know," he answered, cupping her face in his hands. "I know. I'm so sorry."

Zoe was standing next to Sam with tears streaming down her cheeks. She wiped at her face with her sleeve. "We'll give you guys a minute, but we'll be right outside if you need anything."

"Ben, I don't want to be here," Jenna said, not knowing if she meant the hospital or Langley Park.

"I know, sweetheart. But listen, the police are here. They have a few questions, and then I'll work on having you released. We'll see if being the stepson of the Chief of Surgery at this place counts for anything around here."

He was trying to lighten the situation. Trying to do anything to help her. But her spirit was too broken to even fake a smile.

She spent the next hour with a Langley Park police detective recounting the events of the day. The detective showed her a picture of a recently filed bankruptcy document in her mother's name along with a copy of the marriage license of Judith Jo Lewis and Travis Scott Mayer from Las Vegas, Nevada, dating back fourteen years.

Her car had been towed to the LPPD lot to be processed and searched for evidence, and the carriage house was considered a crime scene. There was an APB out on Travis' truck, and the detective assured her the police were coordinating with other departments to locate Travis and her mother.

After the detective left, Jenna let out a shaky breath. "She married him the day after I left for Gwyer."

Ben nodded. His face was etched with concern.

Jenna trained her gaze on the wall. She could feel her heart breaking. "My mother never looked for me. I don't think she even cared that I'd left."

"There's no excuse for her behavior. She was a monster of a mother," Ben replied, but Jenna couldn't meet his gaze.

"A monster," she echoed and stared blankly at the wall.

It was close to midnight when she was released from the hospital. The Tudor was quiet as Ben held her hand and led her inside. Stopping at the foot of the stairs, he met her gaze.

"Do you want me to make you some tea, or do you just want to go to bed?"

Jenna looked down at their clasped hands. She loved his hands, loved the feel of her hand wrapped inside his.

"Bed," she whispered.

He let go of her hand, gathered her into his arms, and carried her up the stairs. Once inside the room, he set her down and took a hesitant step back.

She could tell he wasn't sure what she needed, so she decided to show him. She closed the distance between them and threaded her fingers through his hair.

"Make love to me, Ben."

"Are you sure? So much has happened, Jenna. I think you need to rest."

She saw the concern in his eyes, but biology was taking over. She arched into him, and his hard cock pressed against her belly.

She pushed up onto her toes and kissed him. His arms wrapped around her as he relented and deepened the kiss.

They undressed each other, clumsy fingers fumbling over buttons. Jenna eased back onto the bed and guided Ben on top of her.

His cock twitched at her entrance, but he stopped and lovingly smoothed a lock of hair behind her ear. "I need you to know we're going to get through this. I love you, Jenna. You're not alone."

She held her breath as if that could keep Ben's words from penetrating her heart. Then she lifted her hips, pushing the tip of him inside. Ben released a low growl.

She knew he loved her, knew he'd do anything to protect her. She almost cried, but she held back the tears, her heart already starting to harden. She didn't deserve a life with Ben. She loved him too much to stay. She would rather die than hurt him.

She was her mother's daughter. No matter how many lies she had told to the contrary, that was the ultimate truth. She couldn't risk becoming like her mother, couldn't risk what that would do to the two people she loved the most in this world.

The only way to protect Ben and Kate was to leave and go back to her old life. She thought about the pain Judith had caused her and swore she would never allow anyone, especially Ben or Kate, to know that kind of misery. They had been through enough already with Sara's death.

Jenna had always believed the lies she told were to protect her heart. She thought she was protecting herself from rejection, but the lies were there to keep others at a distance.

The lies were there to keep others safe from *her*.

Ben moved inside her while whispering sweet words of love. Too painful for her to hear, she kissed the words away and silenced his voice.

BEN WOKE up knowing something was wrong. The bed was cold, and the house was quiet, too quiet.

Pulling on a pair of pants, he walked downstairs. There was a note on the kitchen table and next to it, the plastic butterfly ring.

Ten minutes later, he was in his car with Zoe on speakerphone.

"It said that she was sorry, and she had to go back to where it all started. I've been driving all over town. She's not answering her phone. She's nowhere in sight."

"Okay, let's stop and think," Zoe said. "Pull over and stop driving in circles."

Ben pulled over near the fire station. He held the steering wheel with an iron grip, adrenaline and worry fueling his body. He had to find the woman he loved.

"We know she doesn't have her car. I'm sure the police are still processing it for evidence. She couldn't have gotten far," Zoe said as Ben listened to his sister typing frantically on her computer.

He was about to start driving around again when he heard the clicking stop.

"Bingo!" she said, a touch of relief in her voice. "Ben, there was a bus that left Langley Park this morning at 6:12 am."

He hadn't even thought of the bus.

"It's headed down to Wichita. From there, she could have gone..."

There were more typing and clicks.

"Wait, didn't Jenna tell us that she lived with her aunt in a little farm town near Liberal?" Zoe's voice was guarded but hopeful.

"Yes, it was a town called Ballentine."

"There's a bus from Wichita to Liberal. She could have made it based on the time her bus left Langley Park. She'd be getting into Liberal around one or so this afternoon. She's got a head start on you, but in a car, you'll probably make it there around the same time."

"Zoe, I can't thank you enough. I just need to make one stop first," he said, shifting the car into gear. He didn't have much time. He had to get to Jenna before he'd lost her to her demons for good.

JENNA WAVED goodbye to the farmer she'd met at the cozy diner in Liberal, Kansas. They'd made small talk over eggs and biscuits while sitting at the counter, and Jenna took it as a sign when he shared he was headed into Ballentine.

She turned away from the road and stared at the structure in front of her.

The windows were boarded up, and weeds had taken over the small side garden with only a few rogue sunflowers growing defiantly. The peeling white paint had turned a dishwater gray. Nobody had lived here for a very long time. But Aunt Ginny's farmhouse was still standing.

She walked up the old path, then up the two creaking steps, and onto the porch. As if on autopilot, she drifted over to where Aunt

Ginny used to have her rocking chair, the special spot where they'd sit and rock away lazy afternoons.

She stared at one of the posts with small notches cut into the wood then knelt down, running her index finger over the grooves. She paused near a spot caked with bits of earth and rubbed at it with her thumb. There was something etched into the wood. As she removed the dirt, gently carved letters appeared.

My Jenna Jo.

Her eyes filled with tears. Her aunt would tell her to stand tall like a soldier as she marked her height on the post with the old kitchen knife. Jenna leaned against the post, fingers still touching each carved notch as tears trailed down her cheeks. She released a sob, then let out a surprised gasp when the porch step squeaked.

It was Ben.

"How did you know I'd be here?" she asked, not meeting his gaze.

"Zoe figured it out." He knelt down next to her and ran his finger over the markings. "Your Aunt Ginny made these?"

Jenna nodded.

"She was good to you?"

Jenna swallowed back a sob. "Yes, I loved her very much."

He brushed the tears from her cheeks.

His touch was pure agony and sweet salvation. She wanted to sink into it, but she shook her head and stepped away. She needed to put distance between them.

Jenna let out a shaky breath. "You shouldn't have come."

"I couldn't let you go."

"Ben, I never want to hurt anyone the way my mother has hurt me, especially you or Kate."

Ben took a step toward her. "Jenna, that makes no sense. You'd never do that."

"Not intentionally, but I'm her daughter, her blood. I could become... I could turn out like her. I don't want it to happen, but it could, Ben. I couldn't live with knowing I brought you or Kate that kind of pain."

"You are not your mother. You are thoughtful and kind. And if there's anyone you take after in your family, I'd bet my life it's your Aunt Ginny."

Jenna bit down on her lip and blinked back hot tears.

He took a step toward her. "I love you. I can't imagine a life without you as my wife. You love Kate, and she loves you. Please, Jenna," he continued, tears streaking his cheeks. "We're a family, the three of us, and it doesn't work without you. Please, say you'll come home."

He reached into his pocket and took out a ring, but it wasn't the plastic butterfly. It was a beautiful, delicate ring with a sparkling round diamond glinting in the afternoon light.

"This is the ring my father gave to my mother, and now I'm asking you to wear it. Marry me, Jenna. Build a life with me. Please, come home."

Jenna closed her eyes and thought back to her days with Aunt Ginny. A gentle breeze lifted wisps of her hair, and her aunt was next to her, as real as when they used to stand together in the farmhouse kitchen, Jenna perched on a chair and Aunt Ginny by her side rolling out pie crusts.

"Don't run from love, my Jenna Jo."

Her aunt's words hung in the air surrounded by sunflowers. Then the winds shifted, and the voice floated away and faded into the big Kansas sky.

Jenna released a breath. A weight had been lifted, and she felt like she could fly. Judith Lewis and Travis Mayer no longer controlled the trajectory of her life. She alone would choose the way she lived and the way she loved.

She met Ben's gaze. A lifetime of love shined in his eyes. "Yes," she answered, smiling through her tears. "I'm ready to go home."

EPILOGUE

"How do we always end up in the pantry? Kate's not even home!" Jenna said, laughing as her husband removed her panties.

But her laughter was replaced with an audible gasp as Ben lifted her deftly against his body and thrust into her sweet center.

"You should thank the architect who designed a space so conducive to multiple functionalities," he said, tightening his grip on her ass.

"I think I'm doing just that," she breathed against his lips.

Ben let out a low growl. He claimed her mouth in a hot kiss and increased his pace, making intelligible speech impossible as their bodies found carnal release.

Jenna opened her eyes. Her body purred with a sated delight. She surveyed her husband and chuckled. He was covered in Cheerios and a Tootsie Roll. The breakfast cereal and sweet treat had gotten jostled off the shelf by their unconventional use of the pantry.

Ben released his grip, gently setting Jenna's feet on the floor. She reached up and plucked the Tootsie Roll off his shoulder. Jenna unwrapped the candy, popped it into her mouth, and released a satisfied sigh. "I love Halloween," she said, her words slurred by the chewy taffy-like candy.

"Are you sure you don't want me to pick up some Kit Kats?"

"Absolutely not," Jenna answered, running a finger across her husband's jawline. "I'd eat the entire bag before the first trick-or-treater knocked on the door."

BEN REACHED for Jenna's hand and brought it to his lips. He loved seeing her relaxed and happy. He kissed her ring finger and admired the diamond ring sitting atop the wedding band that matched his.

They belonged to each other now.

Ben thought back to their wedding day. Even though their lives had become a whirlwind after they returned from Ballentine, they didn't let the darkness overshadow their love. To everyone's happy surprise, they married the Saturday after Kate, Kathy, and Neil had returned from Maine.

They opted for a simple evening ceremony in his parents' back-yard with only his family and Sam and Michael in attendance. Ben could still picture Jenna walking toward him, hand in hand with Kate, down the makeshift aisle Zoe had created with flowers and candles.

Hanging lanterns had illuminated the yard, and his heart had skipped a beat watching Jenna coming toward him, grinning and radiant with love. Their ceremony was so much more than a wedding. It was not only a declaration of their love but a proclamation of their fortitude to weather any storm that came their way.

"I like that we have matching bands," Jenna said, gazing down at their matching wedding bands.

"Me, too," he replied, then pulled a Tootsie Roll from her disheveled hair. "We should think about reorganizing this pantry. Last week, Mrs. G pulled a Wheat Thin off the back of my sweater."

"Or, we could use the bed like normal people," she added half-heartedly.

"Beds are so overrated," Ben replied with a wicked grin.

He popped the candy into his mouth and kissed his wife. The

sweet, chocolate taste swirled between them before a buzzing sound made them pull apart.

It was his phone.

"Is it Kate?" Jenna asked, righting her outfit as they left the pantry.

Kate was spending the afternoon with Kathy and Neil at the Langley Park Senior Living Campus. Every year, the campus hosted an event for youngsters to come and trick-or-treat inside the facility. The residents and children alike dressed up, making it a wonderful celebration for all.

"No, it's a text from Clay. He wants to know if he can stop by?"

Officer Clayton Stevens, now Detective Stevens, had been promoted to detective, in part because of the work he'd done helping authorities find and arrest Judith and Travis Mayer.

"Of course. Let's call Michael and see if he can come over as well."

Michael MacCarron had been by their side at every police interview, helping them understand the chaos surrounding them when Travis and Judith were still on the run.

THIRTY MINUTES later came a knock at the door.

"Hello, Mrs. Fisher."

"Hi, Clay," Jenna replied, embracing the detective.

"Thanks for agreeing to meet with me. I'm sorry it had to be on Halloween," he said, giving his feet a few swipes on the doormat.

"It's not a problem at all," Jenna said, ushering him into the house. "I hope you don't mind, Michael's here."

"I don't mind a bit," Stevens said, extending his hand to the attorney.

"How are you, Clay?" Ben asked, motioning for everyone to have a seat at the kitchen table.

"I do not miss being a beat cop on Halloween," Stevens said, taking a seat and gesturing to a ceramic jack-o-lantern sitting on the kitchen counter.

"I can imagine. How many calls did you get for TP-ed houses?" Michael asked, reaching for his legal pad.

The detective shook his head. "Too many to count."

Everyone chuckled, but the room quickly quieted. A visit from Clay Stevens meant information about her mother and Travis.

Jenna turned to the detective. "What do you have for us, Clay?"

Nearly two months ago, Judith Lewis Mayer and Travis Mayer were arrested in Arizona, trying to cross the border into Mexico. They were currently being held without bail while awaiting trial.

Detective Stevens retrieved a file from his satchel and placed it on the table. "Everything I'm going to tell you must remain between us," he said. He met Michael's gaze. "We're off the record, counselor."

Michael nodded and pushed his legal pad aside.

Judith and Travis had been arrested, but they weren't extradited back to Langley Park. Federal agents had swooped in, and everything had become hush-hush. Federal warrants had been issued in their names due to their suspected business dealings with members of organized crime.

"It's my understanding," Stevens began, opening the file and glancing down at its contents, "that the plan was to gain access to your trust fund, Mrs. Fisher. Your mother checked into the Rose Brooks Women's Shelter, and then she made threats to take her life, hoping to lure you to Kansas City. She wanted to play on your emotions, knowing you'd never give her any financial support if she were associated with Mr. Mayer. She wanted you to think they had broken up."

Jenna nodded and squeezed her husband's hand. Even though she knew her mother and Travis couldn't hurt her, it still stung to hear about the deception.

"What Judith didn't plan on was the shelter sending her to Midwest Psychiatric Center. At that point, your mother and Mr. Mayer learned they were being pursued by members of a dangerous crime syndicate who had lent them money. They'd burned through your mother's trust, Travis' family had stopped supporting him financially, and time was running out for them to pay off their debts. Despite this setback, your mother and Mr. Mayer decided they'd follow the original plan of trying to convince you to give your mother access to your trust while Mr. Mayer stayed in hiding nearby."

"Can you tell us anything about the charges?" Michael asked.

"What I can tell you is that, between the federal charges they'll be facing as well as all the charges we intend to file, you're not going to have to worry about them ever trying to harm you or your family again."

An angry blush crept up Ben's neck. "What about what that monster tried to do to my wife? He needs to pay for that."

Jenna put a hand on her husband's shoulder. "Do you know if my mother knew Travis was stalking me? Does she know he tried to kill me?"

Stevens met her gaze. "In the interview tapes, your mother's gone on record stating she had no idea Travis was stalking you or had harmed you in any way. Travis was supposed to keep an eye on you, so he could feed her information that may have helped her persuade you to give her access to the trust."

"Do you believe her, Clay?"

Stevens frowned. "I can't answer that, Mrs. Fisher. I can tell you she was very adamant about wanting the interrogators to know that she didn't want you hurt, nor did she know Mr. Mayer was stalking you. She claims she was there to get your money, and then she planned to disappear with her husband with no physical harm coming to you."

Jenna stood, walked over to the kitchen sink, and peered out the window. She had started seeing a therapist in Langley Park shortly after her emotional visit to Aunt Ginny's farm. Jenna knew the demons haunting her wouldn't disappear just because the man she loved had put a ring on her finger. With Ben's full support, she began confronting her past with the guidance of a mental health professional and was learning how to live a life not dictated by lies or fear.

Her mind went to a quote her therapist kept framed on her desk by Daphne Rose Kingma.

Holding on is believing that there's a past; letting go is knowing that there's a future.

It was time to let it all go. It didn't matter if her mother's words were true or not.

"Thank you, Clay," she said, still staring out the window. "What you've told us today has helped me more than you'll ever know."

"Honey? Are you all right?" Ben asked, coming to his feet.

Jenna joined her husband. "I am," she said, meeting her husband's gaze. "My mother and Travis have no control over my life or my happiness."

"One more house?" Kate begged. Her eyelids were drooping, but she still maintained a firm grip on her pillowcase filled with Halloween candy.

"We can end with Michael's house," Zoe suggested to Ben and Jenna as the group walked up the path to his front door.

Kate rang the doorbell and danced around, her second wind kicking in. "Trick-or-treat," she sang out as Michael opened the door.

Michael waved to Zoe, Ben, and Jenna. "My goodness, Miss Kate, what are you for Halloween?"

Kate looked at Michael skeptically and repositioned the round glasses on her nose. She flung a burgundy and gold scarf dramatically around her neck. Then, in a British accent, replied, "Why sir, I'm Harry Potter."

Michael chuckled as Kate broke character upon hearing the pitter-patter sounds coming up behind him.

"Michael, can I pet Cody?" Kate asked, peeking inside the house.

"Sure thing," Michael answered.

The old Golden Retriever sauntered out into the yard with Kate trailing behind him. Michael followed close behind and greeted Ben, Jenna, and Zoe.

"No more Star Wars?" Michael asked with a wry grin.

"That would be my fault," Jenna said, linking her arm with Ben's.

"She's moved on to Harry Potter. It's a travesty. But I'm surviving," Ben added. He gestured to Michael's house. "The house looks like it's holding up."

"I've been here almost five years," Michael replied, wry grin vanishing.

"My parents saw your dad today, Michael," Zoe said. "They brought Kate to the Langley Park Senior Living Campus for the Halloween party. My mom said your dad seems to be doing a little better."

"Yeah. I was there today for a bit," Michael answered stiffly.

"It's a top-notch facility," Ben said, putting a hand on Michael's shoulder. "I'm sure he's in good hands."

Jenna was about to agree with her husband when she noticed Michael's dog sitting alone on the porch. She looked around the yard for Kate but didn't see her. "Kate?" she called out.

"She couldn't have gone far," Ben replied.

"I see her," Zoe said, pointing to the darkened house next door.

"Kate, nobody's— " Michael began, but before he could finish, a light flicked on, and the door to the darkened house opened.

"You are my first trick-or-treater," came a young woman's voice.

"Your light's off. Nobody will knock on your door if your house is dark," Kate said, cocking her head to the side.

"You knocked," the voice answered back.

A stumped Kate scratched her head. The woman laughed and produced a large bowl of candy, and Kate made quick work of snagging several chocolate bars.

"Em? Is that you?" Ben asked, surprise lacing his words.

The woman stepped off the porch. "It is."

"It's Ben Fisher."

Jenna walked to her husband's side and gazed up at the young woman. Her striking auburn hair was styled in an inverted fishtail braid that looked like a waterfall cascading down over her shoulder. Her eyes were smoky with makeup and heavily lined with black eyeliner. For being a petite woman, she looked quite formidable.

"This is my wife, Jenna, and our daughter, Kate."

"Em," Kate said, looking back at her Aunt Zoe. "Is this one of your favorite gingers, Auntie?"

Everyone's gaze went to Zoe, who opened her mouth, but no words came out.

Sensing something strained, Jenna stepped forward and shook Em's hand. "I love your hair. Maybe sometime you could show me how to do that. Kate's obsessed with braids, and I'm sure she'll be asking me to do her hair like yours when we get home tonight."

Em kicked at a few stones on the ground. "Yeah, sure."

"I don't think she'll be asking for braids tonight, honey. Looks like she's all trick-or-treated out," Ben said, picking up a wobbly and weary-looking Kate, her second wind expired.

A cool breeze carried a few fallen leaves across the lawn, and Em pulled her sleeves down, allowing only the tips of her fingers to remain visible. It was quiet a beat. Something strained loomed in the darkness.

"I didn't know you were home," Michael stuttered, breaking the silence. "You're—you're back."

Without speaking a word, Em turned around, walked back inside her house, and slammed the door.

SNEAK PEEK--THE SOUND OF HOME: LANGLEY PARK SERIES BOOK 2

Not ready to leave Langley Park? You're in luck! Keep reading for a sneak peek of the second book in the Langley Park series: The Sound of Home.

THE SOUND OF HOME: CHAPTER 1

12 YEARS AGO

"Come on, Em. You're eighteen now. You've got to learn to live a little."

Mary Michelle MacCaslin, known to her friends and family as Em, exited the car and met the gaze of Zoe Stein, one of her oldest friends and her only real link to normal teenage life.

"I mean, seriously, Em. Have you ever even been to a field party at Sadie's Hollow?"

Zoe knew she hadn't. "It's not really a field," Em shot back.

"You have to walk *through* a field to get there," Zoe countered, removing a small flask from her backpack and taking a long pull. She held it out, but Em waved her off. "Come on, one little taste. I promise you'll find Mr. Daniels to be quite the social lubricant."

"Mr. Who?"

Zoe pulled two sleeping bags from the car. "Christ on a cracker, Em! Jack Daniels. It's whiskey. Come on, Virgin Mary. Take a swig."

"You know I hate it when people call me that."

"Can I call you *Wunderkind*? That's what the paper calls you, and I don't see you getting all pissed off with them."

Em rolled her eyes. Zoe could really be a pain in the butt sometimes.

A beat passed, and Zoe let out an audible breath. "Okay, okay. I take it back. But that outfit, Em..."

"What about my outfit?" she asked, fingering her pearl necklace while throwing a quick glance at her plaid skirt.

"It's way more Great Aunt Ethel than it is naughty schoolgirl, Britney Spears, circa 'Hit Me Baby One More Time.' "

"Zoe, you know I had a performance tonight. I'm lucky my dad let me go out at all."

"I know. I know," Zoe replied and placed the flask in Em's hand. "That's why you need to drink this. We've only got a few more weeks before everyone starts leaving for college. Tonight is about being stupid, having fun, and being stupid."

"You said *being stupid* twice."

"Yes, because we need to be double-double stupid tonight. And no writing in your little datebook. I don't want to see *drank alcohol in excess* written in your quasi-obsessive-compulsive log."

Em gave her a sideways glance. Zoe had always teased her about her many journals and datebooks.

She wasn't going to acknowledge her friend's little dig, so she changed the subject. "I know I've only done online high school, but I'm pretty sure the word you're looking for is *doubly*."

Em MacCaslin didn't live the life of a typical teenager. Scratch that. Em MacCaslin's entire existence had been quite different from most people's. When she was four years old, her parents enrolled her in piano lessons. She was playing complicated pieces by Chopin, Rachmaninoff, and Beethoven before she turned five. At six, she had taken up the violin, and the results were the same. Newspaper articles from her hometown of Langley Park, Kansas, proclaimed her a "Wunderkind" and a "Child Musical Prodigy." By twelve, she'd focused solely on playing the violin and was living out of a suitcase, traveling to study with master teachers all over the world and taking part in elite competitions.

Zoe put on her puppy dog eyes. "Please, Em. We get the whole night. Your dad thinks you're spending the night at my place, right?"

Em never lied to her father, but Zoe had been begging her to go to Sadie's Hollow all summer. She grabbed her backpack and met Zoe's gaze. Her friend had added an exaggerated pouty lip to her puppy dog eyes.

Em glanced at the ground. "Do you think Michael's going to be there?"

Zoe's lips curved into a wry smile. She knew she had won. "I'll answer that question after you take three pulls off my pretty little flask of Jackie D."

Em glanced at the flask. "I mean, it doesn't matter if he's here. I just thought it would be nice to see him."

"That's it? You just thought it would be *nice* to see him? He is your next door neighbor, isn't he? Are you telling me you haven't seen him since you've been back?"

Zoe was right. Michael MacCarron was her next door neighbor. Just about every childhood memory she had included him. Born on the same day at the same hospital, Midwest Medical in Langley Park, Kansas, Michael Edward MacCarron and Mary Michelle MacCaslin came into this world looking like twins with their small tufts of auburn hair and fair complexions.

Em twisted her pearls. "I haven't been around that much. You know that, Z."

She had been traveling nonstop for the last three years. Two stints in Vienna and then zigzagging back and forth between London, New York, and Tokyo. It had been thrilling, but it didn't leave any time to visit Langley Park.

She had been back a few weeks to perform at several fundraisers for the Kansas City Symphony and had only caught glimpses of Michael. But from her brief glances, it was safe to say, he was no longer the lanky boy, all knobby knees and sharp elbows, shooting hoops while listening to Nine Inch Nails. Earlier that morning, she had peeked out her window and watched him mow the grass. She couldn't take her eyes off the boy she used to share a plastic kiddie pool with when she was a toddler.

During her time away, he had transformed into an Adonis of a man with sculpted shoulders, long, strong legs, and a back that rippled with muscles.

Not that it mattered.

She had no time to worry about boys. Soon, life on the road was going to end. She had received a full-ride scholarship to attend The Juilliard School in New York City. In less than two weeks, she was going to be something she hadn't been since grade school: an ordinary student.

Maybe ordinary wasn't the right word to describe her.

She was as ordinary as someone who had played a private audience for the Queen of England. Em knew her reputation might intimidate some of the students; but she hoped as they studied and played together, they'd come to see her as a real person. A person who needed music to survive just as one needs air to breathe. A person who couldn't imagine a day without Beethoven, Mendelssohn, or Tchaikovsky. Her life was always going to revolve around music, and now she was going to be surrounded by people her age with the same passion and drive.

Zoe gestured to the flask, her cocky smile still in place. "You give me something. I'll give you something."

Em brought the flask to her lips and swallowed the burning, bitter liquid. "This stuff tastes even worse than it smells."

"Come on, *Wunderkind*. You've got two more sips to go."

The alcohol from the last two pulls settled in her belly. "This stuff is terrible."

"Aw, quit your complaining and take a sleeping bag. We need to get a move on."

Em took the sleeping bag and looked around. "Where the heck are we?"

They had driven at least an hour south of Langley Park and were now squarely in what looked like the middle of nowhere.

"The tiny little town of Lyleville," Zoe replied, leading Em into the darkness. "We just have to pass through this field and hang a left at the cemetery."

"Cemetery?"

"I didn't tell you?" Zoe asked, taking another long pull from the flask before handing it to Em. "That's what's so great about this place. Sadie's Hollow is this little crater near the Lyleville Cemetery. Cops can't see us if they drive past, and the townspeople—what's left of them—don't come here because of the legend."

"Zoe, stop messing with me."

"I'm not messing with you, Wunderkind. The legend goes, a long ass time ago, a girl named Sadie Wilson was supposed to meet her true love here. Her father, some wealthy merchant back when this place was a real city, had forbidden them to marry. So they decided to elope. Except, he never came. Sadie's so-called true love ended up running off with another woman. The next morning, Sadie was found hanging dead in a tree. They never knew if she was murdered or if it was suicide."

Em glanced over at the old headstones. A chill crept up her spine. Sadie Wilson's headstone glowed eerily in the moonlight like a warning beacon. She swallowed hard and started down a set of limestone steps leading down into the hollow when she heard Zoe let out a shriek.

"Hey," Zoe said, grabbing onto her backpack and pulling her off the steps. Her friend's wry grin was replaced with a stern glare. "Don't go on those steps. I'm serious."

"Why not?"

"People say those are The Steps to Hell. They also say that when it's a full moon, you can see Sadie sitting on them, calling out for the man who betrayed her."

Em shook her head. This was crazy talk, but that didn't stop another shiver from running down her spine.

"The whole 'Sadie's ghost thing' is probably just some stupid campfire tale, but why tempt fate?" Zoe added, softening her tone.

Em nodded and followed her friend down the steep incline. The Jack Daniels was making her limbs feel lighter and her head a blissful kind of fuzzy as the overlapping sounds of various conversations permeated the humid night air.

They emerged from the trees and passed into a clearing. Em saw at least forty, maybe fifty kids standing in clusters. Small tents dotted the hollow while flashlights bobbed back and forth like fireflies, and teenagers moved from group to group, laughing and horsing around.

"I can see why you guys come here," Em said, surveying the large oak and willow trees that enclosed the area. But Zoe wasn't paying attention to her.

Zoe increased her pace. "I see Gabe. Let's go say hi."

"Do you have a thing for Gabe Sinclair?"

"No way, nothing like that," Zoe said and took a long pull from the flask.

But before Em could ask another question, Zoe was hauling it down into the hollow.

"Hey! Look who's back in town."

He handed Em and Zoe cups containing a blue liquid.

Em sniffed the cup. "What is this?"

Gabe took a sip from his own cup. "It's called Blue Dinosaur. It's Everclear and Blue Raspberry Kool-Aid."

"Just drink it, Em," Zoe said, scanning the crowd, then focused on Gabe. "Is your brother going to stop by?"

"Yeah, Sam will be by. He said he would drop off some beer."

"How is Sam?" Em asked, surprised at how easily the blue dinosaur punch went down compared to the burn of Zoe's whiskey.

Gabe smiled. "He's good. He still thinks he can tell me what to do, classic older brother complex, but he's been a lot more chill since he met Kara."

"Who?" Zoe asked, the dyed pink tips of her bob flying across her face as she turned her attention to Gabe.

"Kara's his new girlfriend," Gabe answered, looking over Zoe's shoulder. "I think that's them now."

Em and Zoe turned to see the outline of two people walking hand in hand, the larger of the two carrying a case of beer.

Zoe stiffened and turned her attention to a tall guy walking by wearing a Portishead t-shirt.

"Ladies and gentlemen, the psychedelic pharmacy is open. If you want it, I've got everything you need to forget about your troubles. Anybody want to take a trip to Mary Jane Land?" he asked, shaking a baggie. "Flights are departing."

"Me!" Zoe said. She dropped her sleeping bag and backpack on the ground then turned to Em. "Can you just drop our stuff in front of an empty tent? Michael always sets one up for me. I'll find you in a little bit, okay?"

Before Em could even respond, Zoe was halfway inside a tent surrounded by clouds of hazy smoke.

Gabe gestured toward Zoe's pack and sleeping bag. "Do you want any help with that?"

"No thanks, Gabe. I'm good," Em answered.

She drank the last few sips of the dinosaur punch and blinked her eyes. The light from the electric lanterns hanging from the tent posts blurred into the night. She blinked again, trying to focus her gaze.

"Zoe's tent is the blue one at the end of the row." Gabe put a steadying hand on her elbow. "And, Em, go easy on the punch. When that Everclear kicks in, it hits like a motherfucker."

That made her laugh. She giggled as she set off for their tent and threw the packs and sleeping bags inside. Someone handed her another cup of punch, and she downed the tasty liquid in seconds.

She surveyed the hollow and smiled. These were ordinary kids partying at Sadie's Hollow before they went off to college—and tonight, she was too.

She walked the perimeter of the hollow and searched the teenagers' faces as they passed by in fuzzy blurs of shrieks and laughter. Even though she had left Langley Park when she was twelve to study abroad, she recognized many of the kids from grade school. Their once rounded, rosy cheeks were leaner now, but she could see reminders of the children she remembered.

It was as if she had hopped into a time machine and fast-forwarded into the future.

"I'm Dr. Who, time traveler extraordinaire," she giggled.

She stretched her arms toward the sky, tried to focus on the full moon, and twirled with her head thrown back, watching the moonlight dance on her fingertips.

Magic fingers.

That's what her first violin teacher, Tom Lancaster, had called them. She smiled and made a mental note to stop by and see him before she left for New York. But just as she was about to tuck the thought of Mr. Lancaster away, her foot hit a rock, and she pitched forward. Just as she was about to fall flat on her face, two strong hands gripped her around her waist.

"I didn't think you would be able to stay upright for much longer, Miss Time Traveler Extraordinaire."

A solid body pressed into her back. She turned, wanting to learn the identity of her rescuer, but drew a blank when she gazed into the eyes of a young man with sandy blond hair.

"You don't remember me, do you?"

Em shook her head and tried to clear the alcohol buzz. "Wait. I do. You're Kyle, Kyle Benson. I'm Em MacCaslin."

"I know who you are, Em. Everybody knows who you are."

"You took violin lessons with me when we were little, right? See I do remember!" Em added. Her tongue tingled and felt heavier than usual when she spoke.

Kyle let out a laugh, his hands still wrapped around her slim waist. "That's right, but you were always the best."

"You were pretty good," Em replied. "Do you still play?"

"Nah, I quit a few years ago. I was good enough to compete in some state and local competitions, but nothing close to your level."

"Now it's photography, right, Benson?" came a voice from the darkness.

Em's heart skipped a beat. She would have recognized that voice anywhere.

THE SOUND OF HOME: CHAPTER 2

"Michael," Em said and took his hand.

His grip was every joyful childhood memory translated into touch.

"I can take it from here, Benson."

Kyle deflated a notch and stepped back.

"Here," Michael said, pressing a camera into Kyle's chest. "You must have set this on the ground. I'm sure you don't want anything to happen to it."

"Thanks, MacCarron," Kyle replied, his tone void of even a shred of gratitude. "I was just making sure Em was okay."

"She'll be fine. I'm here."

Michael met Kyle's gaze, and a testosterone charge rippled between them. An age-old game of chicken. The only question was who would duck out first?

Kyle broke the standoff. "It was good to see you, Em." Conceding defeat, he turned and walked toward a clump of teens standing around a keg.

"What are you doing, Em?" Michael asked. His first impulse was to continue holding her hand, but he let go when an uneasiness settled in the pit of his stomach.

Em smiled up at him. "I was spinning. Zoe's gone to Mary Jane Land, and I've mostly been walking around with blue dinosaurs."

His lips quirked into an amused smirk.

"What I mean is, I've been walking around *drinking* Blue Dinosaurs."

Michael chuckled. "I see you've tried the punch. How much have you had?"

Em held out her hand. She raised her index finger, then slowly added her middle finger. Her eyes narrowed as if muscle control required a supernatural level of concentration.

Michael shook his head. "Em, you can't even weigh a hundred pounds. I think you've had enough."

"I've missed you, Michael," she said, her gaze abandoning her fingers and meeting his.

He felt the urge to touch her. He wanted to brush his fingers over each tiny freckle that dusted her cheeks.

Knock that shit off, MacCarron. This isn't one of your groupie cheer-leaders vying for attention. This is Em.

"Let's sit down on the rocks," he said.

He stuffed his hands into his pockets and led her over to a cluster of large boulders. They settled on one, and Em leaned into him. The alcohol was loosening her inhibitions, and he liked it—he liked it more than he wanted to admit.

He couldn't stop throwing glances her way. Had she always been this pretty? The last time he saw her was three years ago when she had returned to Langley Park to spend Christmas with her father. Em's parents divorced when she was young, and she used to split her time between Langley Park with her father and Sydney, Australia, with her mother. But once she began traveling to study violin all over the world, he had seen her less and less.

Em smoothed out the pleats of her skirt, and he chuckled. While most of the girls at the party were wearing cut-off jean shorts and tank tops, leaving very little to the imagination, Em had on a plaid skirt, a short-sleeved cardigan, and a string of pearls.

Fucking pearls.

"Why are you looking at me like that?" Em asked, attempting to look incredulous.

"You wore pearls to a Sadie's Hollow party," he answered. He'd never thought pearls and plaid were sexy before tonight.

"I'll have you know," she raised her index finger, "that tonight I helped raise quite a bit of money for the Kansas City Symphony. Like big time dollars."

Jesus, she was an adorable drunk. "You did, did you?"

"I most certainly did," Em replied, coming to her feet and pretending to play an air violin.

"What did you play?" Michael asked, unable to hold back an ear to ear grin.

She closed her eyes and began to bow with her right hand. "Just Paganini. *Nel cor piu non mi sento.*"

"Oh, yeah, *just* Niccolo Paganini's most difficult composition, and arguably one of the most technically challenging pieces ever written?"

She opened her eyes and met his gaze. "Just that."

Holy shit, she was stunning.

"Could you lose the air-violin for a minute and sit back down. I'd hate to see you fall on your ass again."

"I *almost* fell on my bottom. Thankfully, Kyle Benson was there to catch me," Em replied and settled herself on the rock.

"You can say *ass*, Em. Nobody will hear you."

"I know."

"Then say it. Your dad's not here."

She twisted her pearls.

"You can't do it, can you? Once a good girl, always a good girl."

"Hey," Em said, grabbing his hand. Her touch sent a rush of electricity surging from the point of contact. "Do you remember when we played "Heart and Soul" on the piano back when we were in kindergarten?"

"How could I forget? Your dad let us stay up late and watch *Big*. You lost your mind watching Tom Hanks and that old dude jump around on the giant keyboard."

"Do you remember your part?" she asked, her face hopeful and glowing creamy white in the moonlight.

Sweet Christ, she was beautiful. When the hell did that happen?

Michael tried to push any sexual thoughts from his mind. He had to remind his twitching cock that nothing could happen between them. "I could knock out my part if I had to."

"Let's do it," she said, then turned toward the long, smooth rock.

Em positioned her hands on the rock as if it were a piano, then gestured with her chin for him to do the same. "Ready, and..." she said, and began to play. She watched as he pretend-played alongside her, then furrowed her brow. "You're doing it wrong. The notes are more staccato."

"Em, we're playing on a fucking rock. How can you even tell?"

"I just know, Michael. It's like the music talks to me, like it lives inside of me. It's always been with me."

He nodded. Fuck, he could get lost in her eyes. Did she still wear those little cotton panties, the ones with tiny flowers, like she did when she was just a girl?

Enough, MacCarron!

He mentally punched himself in the mouth. Of course, she didn't. She wasn't eight. She was eighteen, a woman. The little girl he used to play piano duets and flashlight tag with had grown up.

Em nudged him with her shoulder. "Put your hand on top of mine. Then you'll be able to feel how the notes were meant to be played."

He draped his large hand over hers. For a second, he thought Em trembled, but then she began to play. As her fingers danced across the imaginary piano keys, Michael felt each note and could hear the music almost as if he was inside her, connected to her.

"See, if you played each note with a bit more—"

He silenced her with a kiss. Her body tensed. He pulled back a fraction, allowing his teeth to nip at her bottom lip. The contact made his head swim. Her lips parted, and he deepened the kiss. She sighed into his mouth, her breaths becoming shallow. If kissing Em was the last thing he would ever do, he'd die a happy man. But he wanted more. He slipped his tongue into her mouth and caressed her in a hot, desperate rhythm, begging her to match his intensity.

Em was sweet. So fucking sweet. He tasted the raspberry punch on her tongue, but it had an edge to it. She must have been drinking something before the punch, something spicy like whiskey or rum. The two flavors assaulted his senses and teased his cock. He knew Em MacCaslin was innocent, everyone did. But the intensity of this kiss told him there was something deeper, something darker inside her even she didn't know existed.

Then it hit him. He was kissing Mary Michelle MacCaslin.

Jesus, what was he doing?

His second-guessing ended when she whispered his name, her voice hungry with need.

"Oh, Michael."

Em spoke not only to his cock, which was begging for release like a bull in a bucking chute, but to his soul. When she guided his hand across the pretend piano keys, an almost spiritual awakening burst inside him, like standing at the crossroads of a tornado and a tidal wave.

He lifted his hand from where it rested on top of hers, dragged his fingertips up her arm, trailed them across her shoulder, and found the string of pearls resting around her neck. He wrapped the delicate pearls around his fingers and pulled her in closer. Each time he twisted another segment of the necklace around his fingers, Em gasped as if she was moving closer and closer toward something her body never knew it needed and could no longer deny.

His breath grew ragged, and he nearly came in his pants when her hand moved to rest on his thigh. "Em, you taste like every color of the rainbow," he whispered. He pulled on the necklace, forcing her to turn her head and allow him to kiss and lick the delicate skin of her neck and the sensitive area behind her ear.

"Michael," she breathed again.

When she said his name, it sounded so new, an enduring melody locked in his heart.

He released the necklace and cupped her face in his hands. "What is it, Em?"

She smiled up at him. "That was my first kiss."

The admission was so honest, so real, so raw. He could only answer it by pressing his lips against hers.

"Um, Michael?"

Dammit. That wasn't Em's voice. It was Tiffany Shelton's.

Tiffany's tone was like the screech of an emergency brake on a speeding train. He released his grip on Em's pearls. "Hey, Tiff."

Tiffany kept her gaze locked on him, her snub nose, which he once considered cute, now looked childish. "Gabe says all the equipment is ready to go. This party is fucking L, A, M, E, *lame* without decent tunes."

Michael turned to Em. "I deejay most parties. I'm getting pretty good."

"Pretty good?" Tiffany barked. "You are the fucking boss."

Michael didn't even acknowledge Tiffany's praise. "Let me get the music going. Do you want me to get you another drink first?"

"Got that covered," Tiffany said, holding out a red Solo cup of the blue punch.

Em took the cup. She smiled up at him, and her swollen lips made his cock strain against his shorts. "I'll be fine. I'll go find my tent. I want to change into more comfortable clothes."

Tiffany snorted. "I guess nobody told you it's a strictly no plaid zone at Sadie's Hollow."

He threw an irritated glance at Tiffany, then took Em's hand. "Let me get the music going. I'll come find you in a little while."

Em nodded, then took a sip of the punch.

He rose to his feet and followed Tiffany. They weren't fifty feet away before she pulled him behind a tent. "Do you think "Miss Grandma Pearls" over there would know what to do with this." She palmed his hard cock through his cargo shorts.

Michael couldn't help his response. He was already worked up from that kiss with Em. Tiffany wasn't his girlfriend, not even close. They had hooked up at every Sadie's Hollow party, and she was hot, a cheerleader with killer legs. With Tiff, it was fucking, pure and simple.

What would it be with Em?

Nothing.

It wouldn't be anything because he wasn't going to fuck her—not at a high school Sadie's Hollow party. That's not what Em deserved. And she wasn't just *some girl*. She was literally one of the foremost violinists on the planet.

The fucking planet.

Em was going to go on to a glowing career, playing all over the world. And what would he be doing? He wanted to study music. He wanted to mix and produce tracks. He wanted to feel the thump of the base as he layered sounds one on top of the other, creating something that was powerful, emotive, and real. But what would he be doing instead? Following his father's plan. The law school plan. The plan to carry on his father's legacy.

"You know where I'll be after you finish rocking the shit out of this party," Tiffany purred. Still facing him, she took several steps back. She was trying to come off as alluring but only succeeded at looking cheap.

"Damn noisy birds," Michael moaned, rubbing the sleep out of his eyes.

He untangled himself from the long leg draped over his thigh. He was a fucking idiot. He'd let Tiff bring him beer after beer while he was playing his set. And just like every other damn night at the hollow, he ended up fucking her doggie-style in a drunken haze.

He climbed out of the tent and surveyed Sadie's Hollow. Other teenagers were emerging from their tents, shielding their eyes from the morning sun like zombie-vampire hybrids. He saw Zoe walking around in a crumpled Portishead t-shirt.

She smiled at him, but her face fell when Tiffany crawled out of the tent.

"Michael!" Zoe called out, eyeing Tiffany Shelton. "Where's Em?"

Michael scratched his head. "I figured she found you. I haven't seen her since—"

"Since you had your tongue down her throat then dropped her ass for this twat waffle."

"Oh, screw you, Zoe," Tiffany tossed back, then tried to pull him in for a kiss.

"Give it a rest, Tiff," he said, turning away and walking over to Zoe.

He crossed his arms. "What do you mean, you don't know where she is? This isn't her scene, Zoe. Somebody could have taken advantage of her. She was pretty drunk when I left her."

"I know this isn't her scene, but I saw her with you! I figured she'd be safe with you of all people. I didn't think you'd ditch her for Tiffany "easy fuck" Shelton. Aren't you over that shit yet?"

Michael shook his head and rolled his neck from side to side. "Let's search the hollow. She couldn't have gone far. She probably just passed out somewhere."

A layer of sticky sweat coated his skin, but it wasn't from the muggy Kansas humidity. "Do you see her?" he yelled out to Zoe who was searching the opposite side of the hollow.

She didn't answer back, but her pace became frantic as she shook tents, waking the sleeping inhabitants, none of whom were Em.

"Let's check the trees," he called out. "You don't think she would wander into the cemetery, do you?"

Zoe's face drained of all its color. "How would I know? Jesus, Michael, where is she?"

"Shit!" His gaze was drawn to the ground, and he scooped up a broken string of pearls.

"Oh, shit," Zoe said, taking the pearls out of his hand.

"The steps," Michael called out and ran toward The Steps to Hell.

Long auburn hair fanned out over the limestone stairs. Em was still wearing the same plaid skirt and cardigan, but her clothes were crumpled and dirty with dustings of grayish powder like she had bumped into a blackboard covered with chalk. Her knees were scraped and bloodied.

"Em! Em! Are you okay?" He scanned her face, her torso, her legs, and then he saw her hand. Her left hand. The hand that was responsible for playing some of the most beautiful pieces of music ever composed.

Zoe fell to her knees. "Fuck! What happened to her hand, Michael?"

He ignored Zoe's words and gathered Em into his arms. "Em! Wake up!"

She was breathing, the rise and fall of her chest gave him some hope until she opened her eyes and panic spread across her face. "You never came back, Michael. You never came back! And then there were the tall men! The tall men came after the bridge! And Paganini! He was there, too!"

Zoe fell to her knees and cupped Em's cheek in her hand. "Michael, she's burning up. And, dammit, look at her eyes. Somebody gave her something, maybe Ecstasy? Shit, I don't know."

Beads of sweat glistened on Em's upper lip, and her dilated eyes flooded with fear. Michael clenched his jaw. Fuck, he was an idiot. "I think she's on LSD or some shit like that. She's not making any sense. She must be coming down from a bad trip."

Michael gunned the engine of his old Range Rover and merged onto the highway. "What about your dad, Zoe? We can take her to your house, and your dad can fix her hand."

Zoe sat in the backseat holding Em in her lap, a towel wrapped around her left hand. "Jesus, Michael! I think she's got at least two broken fingers and that gash on her ring finger. I can see right down to the bone. What are we going to do? She's supposed to leave for Juilliard in a few days."

"Zoe, focus! Your dad is a surgeon. Can't we just take her to your house?"

"My parents are in Phoenix this weekend meeting my brother's fiancé's mother. They don't get back until late tonight. Should we just take her home?"

"Fuck, no, Z. We have to get her to a hospital. It's her left hand that's all mangled. Do you know what that could mean?"

Zoe stared down at Em. "Just get us to the hospital, Michael. It has to be my dad's hospital. It has to be Midwest Medical in Langley Park. It's the closest level one trauma center. They'll be able to get a hand surgeon there faster than any place else."

He pressed his foot on the gas pedal, pushing the car well over the speed limit. He glanced back at Zoe in the rearview mirror and watched her face crumple as tears streamed down her cheeks.

ACKNOWLEDGMENTS

This book wouldn't have come to light if it wasn't for the kindness and support of friends and family dear to my heart.

Michelle Dare, my friend, mentor, and gifted author, whose gentle guidance gave me the courage to breathe new life into *The Road Home*.

Corinne, Stacey, Laura, and Chris, who went line by line and edited *The Road Home* with their eagle eyes.

Kendra and Loni, my book club crew, who read through each rough draft and provided spot-on suggestions.

Heather, who was with me from the beginning.

Dawn, who introduced me to the world of happily ever afters.

My father, Joe, who, in a million years, never imagined he'd be reading a romance novel written by his daughter.

My husband, David. My true love. My best friend. My home.

And to you, the reader. It's the greatest honor and the most humbling gift to have you read my book. Thank you for visiting Langley Park. I hope you come back soon.

ABOUT THE AUTHOR

 If there's one thing Krista Sandor knows for sure, it's that romance saved her. After she was diagnosed with Multiple Sclerosis in 2015, her world turned upside down. During those difficult first days, her dear friend sent her a romance novel. That kind gesture provided the escape she needed and ignited her love of the genre. Inspired by the strong heroines and happily ever afters, Krista decided to write her own romance series. Today, she is an MS Warrior and living life to the fullest. When she's not writing, you can find her running 5Ks and chasing after her growing boys in her adopted home of Denver, Colorado.

Don't miss a release, contest, or author event! Visit Krista's website and sign up to receive her exclusive newsletter.

https://kristasandor.com

facebook.com/krista.sandor

twitter.com/Krista_Sandor_

instagram.com/kristasandor

bookbub.com/authors/krista-sandor

ALSO BY KRISTA SANDOR

The Langley Park Series

A steamy, suspenseful second-chance at love series set in the quaint town of Langley Park.

Book One: The Road Home

Book Two: The Sound of Home

Book Three: The Beginning of Home

Book Four: The Measure of Home

Book Five: The Story of Home

～

The Bergen Brothers Series

A sassy and sexy series about three brothers who are heirs to a billion-dollar mountain sports empire.

Book One: Man Fast

Book Two: Man Feast

Book Three: Man Find

Sign up for my newsletter to stay in the loop.

https://kristasandor.com/newsletter-sign-up/

Made in the USA
Coppell, TX
26 September 2020